CHRIS BRADFORD

YOUNG SAMURAI
THE WAY OF THE WARRIOR

Disney • HYPERION BOOKS / NEW YORK

Young Samurai: *The Way of the Warrior* is a work of fiction, and while based on real historical figures, events, and locations, the book does not profess to be accurate in this regard. Young Samurai is more an echo of the times than a reenactment of history.

First published in the U. K. by Puffin Books in 2008
First U.S. edition, 2009

Text copyright © 2008 by Chris Bradford

Printed in the United States of America

First U.S. Edition

10 9 8 7 6 5 4 3 2 1

Library of Congress Cataloging-in-Publication Data on file.

ISBN 978-1-4231-1871-8

Reinforced binding

Visit www.hyperionbooksforchildren.com

For my father

CONTENTS

PROLOGUE—MASAMOTO TENNO

Kyoto, Japan, August 1609

THE BOY snapped awake. He seized his sword.

Tenno hardly dared to breathe. He sensed someone else in the room. Moonlight seeped through the lucent paper walls, and as his eyes grew accustomed to the dark, he searched for signs of movement. But he could see only shadows within shadows. Perhaps he had been wrong. . . . His samurai training, though, warned him otherwise.

Tenno listened intently for any indication there might be an intruder, but he heard nothing unusual. The cherry blossom trees in the garden rustled like silk as a light breeze passed through. There was the familiar trickle of water as it flowed from the small fountain into the fishpond, and nearby a cricket chirped. The rest of the house lay silent.

He was overreacting. . . . It was probably just some bad *kami* spirit disturbing his dreams.

This past month the rumor of war had set the whole Masamoto household on edge. There was talk of a rebellion, and Tenno's father had been called into service to help quell any potential uprising. The peace Japan had enjoyed for the past twelve years was suddenly under threat, and the people were afraid. No wonder he was so tense.

Tenno lowered his guard and settled back on his futon. The moment he did, the night cricket chirped a little louder, and his hand tightened around the hilt of his sword. His father had once said, "A samurai should always obey his instincts." Now his instincts told him something was wrong.

He rose from his bed to investigate.

Suddenly a silver star spun out of the darkness.

Tenno threw himself out of the way a second too late.

The *shuriken* sliced through his cheek before burying itself deep into the futon, where his head had just been. He felt a rush of hot blood stream down his face. Then he heard a second *shuriken* thud into the *tatami*-matted floor, and in one fluid movement he sprang to his feet, bringing his sword up to protect himself.

Dressed head to toe in black, a figure drifted ghost-like out of the shadows.

It was a ninja: one of the Japanese assassins of the night.

With measured slowness, the ninja unsheathed a vicious-looking blade from his *saya*. Unlike Tenno's large curved *katana* sword, the *tantō* was short, straight, and ideal for stabbing.

The ninja took a silent step closer and raised the *tantō*: a human cobra preparing to strike.

Tenno, anticipating the attack, cut down with his sword, slicing across the body of the approaching assassin. But the ninja deftly evaded the boy's sword, spinning around to kick him squarely in the chest.

Thrown backward, Tenno crashed through the paper-thin *shoji* door of his room and out into the night. He landed heavily in the middle of the inner garden, disoriented and fighting for breath.

The ninja leaped through the torn opening and landed catlike in front of him.

Tenno attempted to stand and defend himself, but his legs gave way. They had become numb and useless. He tried to call for help, but his throat had swollen shut. It burned like fire, and his cries became suffocating stabs for breath.

The ninja shifted in and out of focus before vanishing in a swirl of black smoke.

The boy's vision folded in on itself, and he realized that the ninja's *shuriken* had been dipped in poison, which was paralyzing him limb by limb. His body quickly succumbed to the poison's lethal powers, and he lay there at the mercy of his assassin.

Blinded, Tenno listened for the ninja's approach, but could only hear the *chirp-chirp* of the cricket. He recalled his father once telling him that ninja used the insect's calls to mask the noise of their own movements. That must be how his assassin had slipped by the guards undetected.

Briefly his eyesight returned, and under the pale light of a waning moon, a shrouded face floated toward him. He drew so close that Tenno could smell the assassin's breath, sour and stale as cheap *saké*. He could see a single emerald green eye blazing with hatred through the slit in the hood of the assassin's *shinobi shozoku*.

"This is a message for your father," hissed the ninja.

Tenno felt the deadly cold tip of the *tantō* on the flesh above his heart.

A single sharp thrust and his whole body flared white-hot with pain. . . .

Then nothing . . .

Masamoto Tenno had passed into the Great Void.

CHAPTER 1

FIREBALL

Pacific Ocean, August 1611

T
HE BOY snapped awake.

"*All hands on deck!*" bellowed the bosun. "That means you too, Jack!"

The bosun's weather-beaten face loomed out of the darkness at the boy, who hastily dropped from his swaying hammock to the wooden floor of the ship's middle deck.

Jack Fletcher, only twelve, was nonetheless tall for his age, and slim and muscular from two years at sea. His eyes—hidden behind the straggly mess of straw-blond hair he had inherited from his mother—were an azure blue, and glinted with a determination and fire far beyond his years. He pushed his hair aside and groaned, his limbs aching from the relentless work the crew had been forced to do while battling a tirade of storms.

Men, weary from the long voyage on board the *Alexandria*, slid from their bunks and pushed past Jack, hastening to the upper deck.

Suddenly there was an almighty crash, followed by a shrieking of the timbers. Jack was thrown to the floor. The small oil lantern suspended from the central beam of the dingy hold swung wildly, its flame spluttering.

Jack landed heavily among a pile of empty casks, sending them spinning across the bucking floorboards. He struggled to find his footing as several grime-ridden, half-starved crewmen stumbled past in the flickering darkness. A hand grabbed the back of his shirt and dragged him to his feet.

It was Ginsel.

The stocky Dutchman grinned at Jack, revealing a set of jagged teeth that made him look like a great white shark. Despite his severe appearance, the sailor had always treated Jack with kindness.

"When will these storms stop hounding us? It sounds as if hell itself has opened up its gates!" growled Ginsel. "Best get yourself up on the foredeck before the bosun has your hide."

Jack hastily followed Ginsel and the rest of the crew as they scrambled up the companionway and emerged into the heart of the storm.

Menacing black clouds thundered across the heavens, and the complaints of the sailors were immediately drowned by the relentless wind that ripped through the rigging. The smell of sea salt was sharp in Jack's nostrils, and ice-cold rain slashed at his face, stinging him like a thousand tiny needles. But before he could take it all in, the ship was rolled by a mountainous wave.

The deck flooded and foamed with seawater, and Jack was instantly drenched to the skin. The water had barely cascaded away through the scuppers when another tumultuous wave roared across the deck. This one, stronger than the first, swept Jack off his feet. He barely managed to grab hold of the ship's rail to stop himself being washed overboard.

Jack recovered his footing as a jagged line of lightning scorched its way across the night sky and struck the main mast. For a brief moment, the entire ship was illuminated in a ghostly light. The three-masted ocean trader was in turmoil. Her crew was scattered across the decks like pieces of driftwood. High up on the yardarm, a group of sailors battled against the wind, attempting to furl the mainsail before the storm ripped it away, or worse, capsized the ship entirely.

On the quarterdeck, the third mate, a seven-foot giant of a man with a fiery red beard, was wrestling with the wheel. Beside him was Captain Wallace, a stern figure who shouted commands at his crew, but all in vain: the wind whipped his words away before anyone could hear them.

The only other man on the quarterdeck was a tall, powerful sailor with dark brown hair tied back with a thin piece of cord. This man was Jack's father, John Fletcher, the pilot of the *Alexandria*, and his eyes were fixed on the horizon as if he hoped to pierce the storm and seek out the safety of land beyond.

"You lot!" ordered the bosun, pointing at Jack, Ginsel, and two other crew members. "Get yourselves aloft and unfurl that topsail. Now!"

They immediately headed for the bow of the ship, but as they crossed the main deck to the foremast, a fireball plummeted out of nowhere—straight toward Jack.

"*Watch out!*" cried one of the sailors.

Jack, having already experienced several full-on attacks from enemy Portuguese warships during the voyage, instinctively ducked. He felt a rush of hot air and heard a deep howl as the fireball flew past and plunged into the deck. The impact, however, lacked the fearsome crack of iron against wood that a cannonball caused. This sounded as dull and lifeless as a dropped bale of broadcloth.

With sickening horror, Jack's eyes fell upon the object now at his feet.

It was no fireball.

It was the burning body of a crewman, struck dead by the lightning.

Jack stood transfixed. The dead man's face was etched in agony and so disfigured by fire that he was unrecognizable.

"Holy Mary, mother of God," exclaimed Ginsel. "Even the heavens are against us!"

But before he could utter another word, a wave crested the rail and swept the body out to sea.

"Jack, stay with me!" said Ginsel, seeing the shock rise in the boy's face. He grabbed Jack's arm and tried to pull him toward the foremast.

But Jack remained rooted to the spot, a sickness rising from the pit of his stomach. He could still picture the burned-out eyes of the dead sailor. This was by no means the first death he'd witnessed on the voyage, and he knew it would not be the last. His father had warned him that crossing both the Atlantic and the Pacific would be fraught with danger. Jack had seen men die from frostbite, scurvy, tropical fever, knife wounds, and cannon shot. Still, such familiarity with death did not make Jack numb to its horror.

"Where're you going?" yelled Ginsel, as Jack ran for the quarterdeck. "We need you aloft!"

Jack, though, was lost to the storm, struggling toward his father in a chaotic battle against the elements as the ship pitched and rolled from one side to the other. He knew he should go with Ginsel, but the need to help his father outweighed any duty to the ship.

He had barely managed to reach the mizzenmast when another colossal wave plowed into the *Alexandria*. This one was so powerful that Jack was whipped off his feet and washed across the deck. The wave bore him in the direction of an open gangway, and he slid inextricably toward the dark seething ocean.

CHAPTER 2

RIGGING MONKEY

J ACK HUNG ON to the gunnel and braced himself against the rails, hoping he could withstand the impact of the next wave, but he lost his grip. Then his body was unexpectedly jerked upright, and he found himself hanging over the edge of the ship, the ocean rushing violently beneath him.

Jack looked up at a tattooed hand clamped firmly around his wrist.

"Don't worry, boy, I've got you!" grunted the bosun, who hoisted him back on board. Jack collapsed in a pile at the man's feet, heaving up mouthfuls of seawater.

"You'll live. Natural sailor like your father you are, though a little more drowned," said the bosun with a humorless smile. "Now get yourself up the foremast and unsnag the top gallant sail, or else you'll get a taste of the *cat*!"

"God bless you, Bosun," muttered Jack, and quickly made his way back to the foredeck, aware that a lashing from the cat-o'-nine-tails was no empty threat.

Still, Jack hesitated when he reached the bow. The foremast was taller than a church steeple, and pitching wildly in the storm. Jack's fingers, already numb with cold, couldn't even feel the rigging, and his sodden clothes had become cumbersome and heavy. But he knew the longer he stalled, the colder he would get, and soon his limbs would be too stiff to save himself from falling.

Come on, he willed himself. You're braver than this.

Deep down, though, he knew he wasn't. In fact, he was truly terrified. During the lengthy voyage from England to the Spice Islands, he had acquired a reputation for being one of the best rigging monkeys on the ship. But his ability to climb the mast, repair the sails, and untangle fouled ropes at great heights hadn't come from confidence or skill—it was born out of pure fear.

Jack looked up into the storm. The sky had been whipped into a frenzy, and dark thunderous clouds streaked across a colorless moon. In the gloom he could just make out Ginsel and the rest of the crew among the shrouds. The mast swayed so violently that the men swung like apples being shaken from a tree.

"Don't be afraid of storms in life," his father had

said on the day Jack had been tasked with climbing to the crow's nest for the first time. "We must all learn how to sail our own ship, in any weather."

Jack remembered how he had watched the new recruits attempt the terrifying ascent. Every one of them had either frozen with fear or puked their guts out onto the sailors below. By the time it was Jack's turn, the wind had got up so much that the rigging was rattling almost as fretfully as his own legs. Back in England he had scaled trees just like any other boy, but never one as impossibly high as this.

Jack had looked to his father, whose face conveyed utter faith in him.

Not wishing to disappoint him, Jack turned and launched himself at the rigging and didn't look down until he had hauled himself over the lip and into the safety of the crow's nest. Exhausted but elated, Jack had let out a yell of delight. Fear had driven Jack all the way to the top. Getting down had proved another matter. . . .

An icy blast of sea spray brought Jack back to the present. Shaking off his memories, he grabbed hold of the rigging and pulled himself aloft. He quickly fell into his usual rhythm, the comfort of habit providing some reassurance. Hand over hand, he gained height and could soon see the white crests of the waves that charged at the ship. But they were no longer the only threat. Fearsome gusts of wind did their utmost to drag Jack off into the night, but he clung to the ropes and continued upward. Before long he was standing next to Ginsel on the yardarm.

"Jack!" yelled Ginsel, who looked worn out, his eyes bloodshot and sunken. "One of the halyards got fouled up. The jib sail won't drop. You're going to have to go out there and unsnag it."

Jack looked up and saw a thick sail rope tangled in the rigging of the gallant, its block and tackle flailing dangerously.

"Has no one else tried?" asked Jack, nodding toward the two petrified sailors hanging on for grim life on the other side of the yardarm.

"I would've asked your friend Christiaan," replied Ginsel, glancing over at a small, terrified-looking Dutch lad, "but he's no Jack Fletcher. You're the best rigging monkey we've got."

"All right," said Jack, though he realized his task was nearly suicidal. "You'd better be ready to catch me!"

"Trust me, little brother, I wouldn't want to lose you now," said Ginsel. He attempted a reassuring smile, but his sharklike teeth only made him appear maniacal. "Tie this rope around your waist. I'll keep hold of the other end. Best take my knife, too. You'll need to cut the halyard free."

Jack secured the rope and clamped the roughly hewn blade between his teeth. He then clambered up the mast to the topgallant. Using the little rigging available, Jack edged along the spar toward the tangled halyard. He hung on tight. If he failed to cut the topsail loose, it wasn't just his own life that hung in the balance, but those of the entire crew. Without that sail, there would be no way the captain could control the ship and steer her clear of danger.

The going was treacherously slow, and the wind was pulling at him with a thousand unseen hands. Glancing down, Jack could barely make out his father on the quarterdeck below. For a moment he swore he saw his father wave at him.

Then out of the corner of his eye, Jack saw the loose block and tackle come flying straight at his head. He threw himself to one side, dodging it, but lost his grip and slipped from the spar in the process.

Jack snatched for the rigging, grabbing hold of a loose halyard as he fell. His hands ripped down the rope, the rough hemp cutting deep into his palms. Somehow he kept his grip, despite the searing pain.

He hung there, flying in the wind.

The sea. The ship. The sail. The sky. All of them swirled around him.

"Don't worry. I've got you!" shouted Ginsel above the storm.

Ginsel pulled on the tie rope strung over the topgallant and hauled Jack toward it. Jack reached up and flipped his legs over the spar, swinging himself upright. It took several moments for him to regain his breath, sucking in air between teeth still clamped around Ginsel's knife.

Once the burning pain in his hands had subsided, Jack resumed his painstaking crawl along the spar. Eventually the tangled halyard was only inches from his face. Jack took the knife from his mouth and began to hack at the sodden rope. But the knife proved too blunt, and it took him several attempts before the threads started to cleave apart. Jack's fingers were icy to the core, and his bloodied palms made his grip slippery and awkward. A blast of wind shunted him sideways, and he let go of the blade while attempting to steady himself. It spun away with the storm.

"Noooo!" cried Jack, futilely reaching after it.

Shattered from his efforts, he turned to Ginsel. "I've only cut half the rope! What now?"

Ginsel, lifeline in hand, gestured for him to come back, but another gust slammed into Jack so hard he could have sworn the ship had run aground. The entire mast shuddered in its bed, and the topsail yanked hard at the halyard. Weakened by Jack's cutting, the rope snapped as if it were a breaking bone, the canvas unfurled and, with an almighty crack, caught the wind.

The ship surged forward.

Ginsel and the other sailors gave a cheer as the

Alexandria turned in the wind and the breaking waves stopped battering her decks. Jack's spirits were lifted by their unexpected turn of fortune, but his joy was short-lived.

The sail, in dropping, had jerked the block and tackle tight against the mast, where it had promptly snapped away and now plummeted like a stone toward Jack, leaving him nowhere to go.

CHAPTER 3

DEVIL AND THE DEEP BLUE SEA

J ACK'S ONLY option was to jump.

He let go of the spar and dived out of the block and tackle's path.

Ginsel strained to hold him on the other end of the tie rope as he arced across the sky and crashed into the rigging on the far side of the foremast. Jack looped his arm through the ropes and clung on desperately.

The block and tackle now dropped straight toward the deck, where it struck an unfortunate sailor who was sent spinning into the sea.

Jack could only watch helplessly as the sailor struggled against the mountainous waves, disappearing and reappearing until, with a pitiful scream, he was finally dragged under.

* * *

"You did well up there, boy," commended the bosun when Jack returned to the foredeck. "Now go see your father—he's in his cabin with the captain."

Jack bolted for the companionway, thankful to escape the raging tempest. Within the belly of the ship, the storm felt less of a threat, its unrestrained fury above becoming a muffled howl below. Jack weaved his way through the bunks to his father's berth in the stern, quietly entering the small, low-beamed room.

His father was bent over a desk, studying a set of sea charts with the captain. His wet hair dripped onto the map, and he wiped it away to reveal a broad handsome face with eyes as blue as the ocean, just like Jack's.

"You said you knew these waters!" barked the captain, pounding the desk with his fist. "You said we'd make landfall two weeks ago! Two weeks ago! By the hand of God, I can sail this ship in any storm, but I've got to know where to go! Perhaps there are no Japans, eh? It could *all* be legend. A cursed Portuguese deception designed to ruin us."

Jack, like every other sailor on board, knew about the fabled islands of Japan. Since the islands were full of unfathomable riches and exotic spices, a trading mission would make wealthy men of them all; but so far only the Portuguese had ever set foot on the Japans, and they were determined to keep the route secret.

"The Japans exist, Captain," said John Fletcher,

calmly opening a large leatherbound notebook to a crude map. "My rutter says they exist between latitudes thirty and forty north. By my calculations, we're only a few leagues off the coast. Look here."

John pointed to the roughly drawn map within the rutter.

"We're in striking distance of the Japanese port of Toba—here. That's several hundred leagues off our trading destination, Nagasaki. So you can see, Captain, the storm has blown us way off course. But that's not our only problem; I'm told this whole coastline's rife with pirates. Toba's not a friendly port, so they'll probably think we're pirates, too. And worse, another pilot in Bantam informed me that Portuguese Jesuits have set up a Catholic church there. We won't know friends from enemies. They'll have poisoned the minds of many of the locals. Even if we make it ashore, we risk being slaughtered as Protestant heretics."

There was a deep boom from within the bowels of the ship, followed by the groaning of timbers as a vast wave peeled along the side of the *Alexandria.*

"In a storm such as this, Pilot, we've little choice but to make for land, whatever the cost. It may be a choice between the devil and the deep blue sea, John, but I'd prefer to take our chances with a Jesuit devil!"

"Captain, I've another suggestion. According to my rutter, there are some sheltered bays two miles south of

Toba. They'll be safer, but getting there won't be easy. The bays are lined with reefs."

Jack watched as his father pointed to a small series of jagged lines etched onto the map.

The captain's fierce eyes bored into John's. "You think you can get us through?"

John put his hand on the rutter. "If God be on our side, yes."

As the captain turned to leave, he caught sight of Jack. "You'd better hope your father's right, boy. The life of this ship and its crew are in his hands."

He swept past, leaving Jack and his father alone.

John carefully wrapped a protective oilskin around his rutter and walked over to a small bunk in the corner of the cabin. He lifted the thin mattress and slid back a hidden compartment into which he placed the rutter before clicking it shut. He gave Jack a conspiratorial wink as he patted the mattress back flat.

John studied his son with concern. "How are you holding up?"

Jack understood that his father's confidence in the rutter was unshakeable. For everyone else, though, it was a leap of faith. "Are we going to make it?" Jack asked bluntly.

"Of course we are, son," John replied, drawing Jack to him. "You got the foresail down. With sailors like you, we cannot fail."

Jack tried to return his father's smile, but he was

genuinely scared. The *Alexandria* had met with storm after storm, and even though his father claimed they were close to their destination, it seemed like they'd never feel land under their feet again. This was a darker fear than that which he had felt in the rigging, or at any other point on the grueling journey so far.

His father bent down to look him in the eye. "Don't despair, Jack. The sea is a tempestuous mistress, but I've been through storms far worse than this and survived. And we will survive this one."

Jack kept close to his father as they made their way back to the quarterdeck. Somehow he felt protected in his presence; his father's unwavering confidence gave him hope.

"Nothing like a good storm to swab the decks, eh?" jested his father to the third mate, who was still wrestling valiantly with the wheel, the exertion sending his face as red as his beard. "Set a course for north by northwest. But let it be known there are reefs ahead. Warn the lookouts to stay sharp."

Despite Jack's father's faith in the direction they were heading, the ocean stretched on and on, wave after wave pounding the *Alexandria*. Jack's own confidence began to ebb away with the sand in the binnacle hourglass.

It was not until the sand had run dry a second time that the cry of "Land, ho!" came forth. A wave of elation and relief ran through the entire crew. They had been battling the tempest half the night. Now they could ride out the storm, tucked behind a headland or within the shelter of some bay.

But almost as quickly as their hopes had been raised, they were dashed by a second cry from the lookout.

"Reefs to starboard bow!"

Then shortly after . . .

"Reefs to larboard bow!"

Jack's father began to shout bearings at the third mate.

"Hard to starboard! . . . Now hold your course. Hold . . . Hold . . . Hold . . ."

The *Alexandria* rose and fell over the churning waves, skirting reefs as it ran headlong for the dark mass of land in the distance.

"HARD-O'-LARBOARD!" screamed his father as he threw his own weight behind the wheel.

The rudder bit into the churning sea. The deck heeled sickeningly. The ship swung the other way . . . but too late. The *Alexandria* collided with the reef. A halyard snapped, and the weakened foremast cracked, crumpled, and fell away.

"CUT THE RIGGING!" ordered the captain. The ship was lurching dangerously under the drag of the foremast.

The men on deck fell upon the ropes with axes. They hacked away, freeing the mast, but the ship still failed to respond. It was apparent her hull had been breached.

The *Alexandria* was sinking!

CHAPTER 4

LAND OF THE RISING SUN

THE WHOLE CREW had battled all night to keep the ship afloat, though it had seemed a futile attempt. Seawater had flooded the bilge, and Jack had worked alongside the men, frantically attempting to pump it out, but the waters rapidly rose past the level of his chest. He had desperately fought to control his panic. Drowning was a sailor's worst nightmare: a watery grave where crabs crawled over your bloated body and picked at your cold, lifeless eyes.

Jack retched over the *Alexandria*'s side for the fourth time that morning, remembering the way the dark brackish water had lapped at his chin. Holding his breath, he had still kept pumping. But what other choice had there been? It was either save the ship or drown trying.

Then fortune returned to their side. They reached the safety of a cove. The ocean had suddenly calmed, the *Alexandria* eased down, and the water level quickly fell away. Jack recalled sucking in the rancid air of the bilge like it was the sweetest mountain breeze as his head cleared the surface and he heard the heavy *whomp* of the anchor being dropped.

Recovering now on the quarterdeck, the pure sea air cleared his head, and his stomach began to settle.

Jack stared out to sea, its waves now gently lapping around the hull. The roar of the tempest had been replaced by the early morning call of seabirds and the occasional creak of the rigging.

He let his mind drift with the peace of it all. Within minutes a glorious crimson sun peeked above the ocean, revealing a spectacular sight.

The *Alexandria* was anchored in the center of a picturesque cove with a towering headland that jutted out into the ocean. The bluff was swathed in lush green cedar trees and red pines, and a glorious golden beach rimmed its inner bay. The cove's emerald green waters were alive with an ever-shifting rainbow of colorful fish.

Jack's attention was drawn by something catching the morning light on the peninsula. He lifted his father's spyglass to his eye to get a better look. Among the trees stood an exquisite building that appeared to have grown out of the rock itself. Jack had never seen anything quite like it.

Perched upon a massive stone pedestal were a series of pillars made of deep-red wood. Each pillar had been painstakingly gilded in gold leaf with images of what appeared to be dragons and exotic swirling symbols. Resting upon these pillars were intricately tiled roofs that curled up toward the heavens. At the very peak of the highest roof was a tall thin spire of concentric golden circles that pierced the forest canopy. In front of the building and dominating the bay, a huge standing stone thrust up from the ground. This, too, was engraved with the same ornate symbols.

Jack was trying to figure out what the symbols were, when he glimpsed movement.

A glorious white stallion emerged from behind the standing stone, and in its shadow, barely reaching the height of the saddle, was a slim dark-haired girl. She appeared as ephemeral as a spirit. Her skin was as white as snow, while her jet-black hair cascaded down past her waist. She wore a bloodred dress that shimmered in the haze of the early morning light.

Jack was transfixed. Even at this distance he could feel her gaze upon the ship. He raised his hand hesitantly in greeting. The girl remained motionless. Jack waved again. This time the girl bowed ever so slightly.

"Oh, glorious day!" exclaimed a voice from behind. "One so much sweeter for the passing of the storm."

Jack turned around to see his father admiring

the ruby red disk of the sun as it rose over the ocean.

"Father, look!" cried Jack, pointing to the girl on the peninsula.

His father glanced up and searched the headland. "I told you, son! This land is gilded with gold," he said jubilantly, pulling Jack to him. "They even build their temples with the very stuff. . . ."

"No, not the building, Father, the girl and . . ." But the girl and the horse had disappeared. Only the standing stone remained. It was as if she had been carried away on a breeze.

"What girl? You've been at sea too long !" teased his father, a knowing smile on his lips, which quickly faded as if stolen by a forgotten memory. "Far too long . . ."

He trailed off, gazing mournfully at the headland.

"I should never have brought you, Jack. It was foolhardy of me. Your mother—God rest her soul—would never have allowed you on this journey. She would have wanted you to stay home with Jess."

"I wanted to come," insisted Jack. "Like you said, to be the first Englishman to set foot in Japan."

"Well now, here you are in the Japans," replied his father, his mood lightening. Jack suddenly found himself enveloped within one of his father's massive bear hugs. "And by my life, son, you proved your mettle last night. How proud your mother would have been. You'll grow up to be a fine pilot."

Jack felt his father's pride seep into his very bones. He buried his head in his father's chest, wanting never to be let go.

"Jack, if you've already spied someone on the headland, then we had best remain on our guard," continued his father, taking the spyglass from Jack. "*Wakou* ply these waters and one can never be too vigilant."

"What are *wakou*?" asked Jack, pulling his head away.

"They're Japanese pirates," explained his father, scanning the horizon. "They're disciplined, they're ruthless, and they're feared in all places. They have no qualms about killing Spanish, Dutch, Portuguese, and Englishmen alike. They're the very devil of these seas."

"And they are the reason, young man," interrupted the captain from behind, "why we must make haste to repair the *Alexandria*. Now, Pilot, did you get the damage report from the first mate?"

"Yes, Captain," replied Jack's father as he and the captain made their way to the helm. "It's as bad as we feared."

Jack remained close by. He wanted to hear more about these *wakou*. How could they be any worse than the Spanish or Portuguese pirates they'd already encountered? Yet his father was not one to exaggerate. With a dread fascination, Jack caught snatches of their conversation as he continued to search the headland for signs of the mysterious girl.

"The *Alexandria*'s taken quite a beating. . . ." said his father.

"At least two weeks to get her into proper ship-shape . . ."

". . . I want the *Alexandria* seaworthy by the turn of the new moon."

"That's barely a week away. . . ." protested his father.

"Double shifts, Pilot, if we are to be spared the fate of the *Clove*. . . ."

". . . dead to the last man. Beheaded—each and every one."

The news of double shifts did not go down well with the men, but they were too afraid of the bosun and his cat-o'-nine-tails to complain. For the next seven days, Jack, along with the rest of the crew, labored like galley slaves, the sweat pouring off them in rivulets under the hot Japanese sun.

While repairing the foresail, Jack often found himself gazing up at the temple. Shimmering in the heat haze, it appeared to be floating above the headland. Every day he had been on the lookout for the girl—but was beginning to think he'd imagined her.

Perhaps his father was right. Maybe he *had* been at sea too long.

"I don't like this. I don't like this at all," complained Ginsel, rousing Jack from his daydream. "We're a trader ship with no sail. We've got a cargo of cloth, sappan-wood, and guns. Any pirate worth his salt is going to know we're a prize for the taking!"

"But there's over a hundred of us, sir, and we have a cannon," Christiaan pointed out. "How could they possibly beat us?"

"Don't you know nothing, you little sea urchin?" spat Piper, a bony man with skin that hung off his scrawny frame like dry parchment paper. "This here is the Japans. The Japanese ain't no defenseless bare-breasted natives. They're fighters. Killers! You ever heard of the samurai?"

Christiaan shook his head in mute reply.

"The samurai are said to be the most deadly, evil warriors to walk this earth. They'll kill you as soon as look at you!"

Christiaan's eyes widened in horror. Even Jack was taken aback by the terrifying description, though he was well aware of Piper's reputation as a teller of tall tales.

Piper paused to light his small clay pipe and suck lazily on it. The sailors all huddled closer.

"Samurai work for the devil himself. I've heard they'll chop your head off if you don't bow to them like serfs!"

Christian gasped . . . a few men laughed.

"So if you ever meet a samurai, lads, bow low. Bow very, very low!"

"That's quite enough, Piper! Less of your scaremon-gering!" interjected the bosun, who had been watching them from the quarterdeck. "Now get this boat ship-shape—we must be ready to sail by sunrise tomorrow!"

"Aye, aye, Bosun," the men roared, hastily returning to their duties.

During the night, there was a growing uneasiness among the crew. Rumors of samurai and *wakou* had spread like wildfire, and the day watch had sighted black shadows moving through the forest.

The next morning, all eyes were fixed on the shore. Even though the coastline remained deserted, there was a feverish anxiety in the way the men worked.

It was close to dusk by the time the *Alexandria* was fit to sail. The bosun called all hands on deck, and Jack waited with the rest of the crew to hear the captain's orders.

"Gentlemen, you have done a fine job," announced Captain Wallace. "If the wind is fair, we sail in the morning to Nagasaki and our fortune. You've all earned yourselves an extra ration of beer!"

The crew cheered. It was rare for the captain to demonstrate such generosity. As the cheering died down, though, the watchman from the crow's nest could be heard shouting.

"Ship ahoy! Ship ahoy!"

They all turned as one and looked out to sea.

There, in the distance, was the ominous outline of a ship . . . bearing the red flag of the *wakou*.

CHAPTER 5

SHADOWS IN THE NIGHT

THE OLD MOON had waned, leaving the night as black as pitch, and the *wakou* ship was soon swallowed up by the darkness.

Up on deck, the captain had doubled the watch in case of an attack, while below, those off duty whispered their fears to one another. Exhausted, Jack lay silent in his bunk, staring blankly at the flickering oil lamp, which made the men's faces appear gaunt and ghostly as they talked.

Jack must have drifted off, because when he opened his eyes again, the oil lamp had gone out. The night was soundless, apart from the heavy snoring of his fellow crew members.

Jack dropped from his bunk and padded up the

companionway. It was no lighter up on deck. Not a single star could be seen, and Jack found the absolute darkness unsettling. He made his way across the deck, feeling his way as he went. The fact that there appeared to be no one around only increased his sense of unease.

Then, without warning, he collided straight into a watchman.

"Bleeding idiot!" snarled the sailor. "You scared the living daylights out of me."

"Sorry, Piper," said Jack, glimpsing the white clay pipe between the man's lips. "Why are all the lamps out?"

"So the *wakou* can't find us, stupid," whispered Piper harshly, sucking on his unlit pipe. "What are you doing up on deck anyway? I've the mind to clip you one."

"Er . . . I couldn't sleep."

"Right. Well, this ain't the place for a midnight stroll. We've been issued with guns and swords in case the *wakou* attack, so you get below. Wouldn't want to spoil that pretty little face of yours now, would I?"

Piper gave Jack a wide toothless grin and raised a rusty-looking blade in front of Jack's face. Jack wasn't sure whether Piper was serious or not, but he wasn't going to wait to find out.

Jack retreated to the companionway.

He was about to go below, when he took a final backward glance at Piper, who was now over by the rail, lighting his pipe. The tobacco glowed red, a single ember in the darkness.

The tiny fire suddenly disappeared as though a shadow had engulfed it. Jack heard a soft exhalation of air, the clatter of the pipe landing upon the deck, and then he saw Piper's body slump noiselessly to the floor. The shadow flew through the air and into the rigging.

Jack was too shocked to cry out. What had he just seen? His eyes had become more accustomed to the dark, and he could just make out shadows crawling all over the ship. Two other watchmen on the foredeck were swallowed up by these shadows, then collapsed. The unnatural thing about it all was the absolute silence of the attack. And that, Jack realized, was what it was—an *attack*!

Jack flew down the stairs and dashed straight to his father's cabin.

"Father!" he cried. "We're under attack!"

John Fletcher bolted from his bunk and snatched the sword, knife, and two pistols that were lying on his desk. He was fully dressed, as if he had been anticipating trouble, and hurriedly buckled the sword around his waist, ramming the pistols and knife into his belt.

"Why wasn't there a call from the watch?" his father demanded.

"There is no watch, Father. They're all dead!"

John stopped in his tracks. He spun around in disbelief, but one look at Jack's ashen face convinced him otherwise. He removed the knife from his belt and handed it to Jack, along with the key to the room.

"You are *not* to leave this cabin. Do you understand? Whatever happens, do not leave," commanded his father.

Jack nodded obediently, too stunned by the unfolding of events to argue. He had never seen his father so serious. Together they had survived full-on enemy attacks from Portuguese warships while navigating South America and its infamous Magellan's Pass. But never had Jack been told to stay in the cabin. He had always fought side by side with his father, helping to reload his pistols.

"Lock it and wait for my return," ordered his father, closing the door behind him.

Jack heard him disappear down the corridor, gathering the men.

"ALL HANDS ON DECK! MAN THE GUNS! PREPARE TO REPEL BOARDERS!"

Jack locked the cabin door.

Not knowing what else to do, he sat on the bunk, still holding his father's knife. He could hear the pounding of feet as the men rallied to his father's call. There were shouts and cries as they flooded up the companionway and onto the deck.

Then there was silence.

* * *

Jack listened intently. All he could hear was the creak of the boards as the men cautiously moved about. There appeared to be some confusion.

"Where's the enemy?" called one of the crew.

"There ain't any attack. . . ." said another.

"Quiet, men!" ordered his father, and the men were hushed.

The utter silence was unnerving.

"Over here." It was Ginsel's voice. "Piper's dead."

Suddenly it sounded as if all hell had broken loose. There was the crack of a pistol, followed by more shots. Men screamed.

"THEY'RE IN THE RIGGING!" came a cry.

"My arm! My arm! My—" screamed someone, until his anguished cries were ominously cut short.

Swords clashed. Feet thundered across the decks. Jack could hear the grunts and oaths of hand-to-hand fighting. He didn't know what to do.

The sounds of battle were joined by the groans of the dying, but Jack could still hear his father rallying the men to the quarterdeck. At least his father was alive!

Then something crashed against the cabin door. Jack jumped up from the bed. The handle was frantically jerked back and forth, but the lock held.

"Help me! Please help! Let me in!" came a thin desperate voice from the other side. It was Christiaan, his hands hammering on the locked door. Torn between his friend's need and his father's order, Jack struggled with his conscience and his own fear of what lay on the other side.

"No! No! I beg you—" There was a frantic scrabbling. A soft fleshy thump followed by a pitiful moan.

Jack ran to the door. Fumbling with the key, he dropped it before he could get it in the lock. Panicking, he picked it up again, turned the lock, and flung open the door, his father's knife in his hand, ready to defend himself.

Christiaan fell into the room, a small throwing knife sticking out of his stomach. Blood gushed onto the floorboards, and Jack felt it run warm and sticky beneath his feet.

Christiaan's eyes stared right up at him, terrified and pleading.

Jack dragged his friend into the cabin, ripping bedsheets from his father's bunk to stem the bleeding. Then he heard his father cry out in pain. Forced to leave Christiaan where he lay, Jack stepped out to confront the shadows in the darkness.

CHAPTER 6

FEVER

JACK SCREAMED in agony.

It was still night, but a glaring white light broke the darkness.

Strange voices encircled him, alien and confusing.

Jack could make out a man's face hovering over him. One side was pitted and horribly scarred as though melted away. Curiously, the man's eyes showed great concern.

The man reached out to him.

Jack's whole arm suddenly flared white-hot, and beads of sweat broke from his fevered brow. Gasping and writhing, he tried to pull away from the excruciating pain, but felt himself slipping away, weightless, as if floating on a bed of soft straw. . . .

He drifted in and out of consciousness . . . and dark memories took hold. . . .

Jack was on the quarterdeck.

He could hear his father shouting. Men lay dead or dying, their bodies piled one upon another. His father, still standing but covered in blood, was surrounded by five shadows. John Fletcher spun the ship's grappling hook in circles around his head, fighting with the ferocity of a lion. The shadows, clad head to toe in black, a single slit for the eyes, couldn't get near.

One lunged at him.

His father brought the hook down sharply, catching his assailant in the side of the head with a sickening crunch. . . . The shadow crumpled to the deck.

"Come on!" his father roared. "You may be phantoms, but you still die like men!"

Two of the shadow warriors attacked. One was armed with a vicious-looking blade attached to a chain, while the other rapidly twirled two small scythes. Neither could get close. The group circled Jack's father, waiting for him to tire.

Jack couldn't bring himself to move; his feet were nailed to the deck with fear. He'd never used a knife in battle before. He raised his father's blade with a shaking hand, steeling himself to attack.

One of the shadows threw a glimmering star. . . .

* * *

Everything was dazzlingly bright. Jack squinted into the daylight. His body was on fire and his head pounded. A dull ache pulsed in his left arm. He lay there unable to move, staring at a ceiling of polished cedar. This wasn't the ship. . . .

His father didn't see it coming, but Jack did.

The shuriken *struck his father on the bicep. John Fletcher grunted with pain, then ripped the metal star out with disgust. A thin stream of blood seeped from the wound. His father laughed at the pathetic little weapon.*

But the shuriken *was not meant to kill; it had merely been a distraction. A shadow dropped silently from the rigging behind his father: a spider pouncing on its prey.*

Jack yelled a warning, but it was too late.

The shadow slipped a garrotte around his father's throat and yanked back hard.

Jack felt utterly helpless. How could he possibly save his father? There were too many, and he was just a boy.

In despair, Jack screamed and made a wild charge with his father's knife. . . .

Disoriented, he turned his head, the muscles in his neck stiff and sore.

A woman was kneeling quietly beside him. She

looked familiar, but he couldn't be sure; everything was out of focus.

"Mother?" asked Jack. The woman edged closer. His mother had always nursed him when he was sick, but how could she be *here*?

"*Yasunde, gaijinsan,*" came the gentle reply, as soft as the trickle of a stream.

The woman was wrapped entirely in white. Her long black hair brushed his cheek as she pressed a cool cloth against his forehead. Its feathery touch reminded Jack of his little sister . . . Jess's hair was just as soft . . . but Jess was in England . . . This woman . . . no, she was a girl . . . looked like . . . an angel all in white . . . Is this Heaven? . . . A veil of darkness enveloped him once again. . . .

The shadow warrior stared directly at Jack.

A single emerald green eye baited him with vindictive pleasure. The shadow had Jack by the throat and was slowly squeezing the life out of him.

Jack dropped the knife, which went clattering to the deck.

"Rutter?" hissed the green-eyed shadow, turning to Jack's father.

John Fletcher, now restrained by one of the other shadows, stopped struggling against his garrotte, the unexpected demand momentarily bewildering him.

"Rutter?" repeated the green-eyed shadow, unsheathing the sword strapped to his back and aiming its sharpened tip at Jack's heart.

"Leave him . . . He's just a boy!" spluttered his father, rising to attack.

John Fletcher's eyes flared with anger. He writhed against the garrotte, reaching out to his son, but it was futile. The shadow yanked back hard. John gagged, and gradually all the fight in him ebbed away. Defeated, he went limp as a rag doll.

"Cabin . . . in my desk . . ." he wheezed, pulling out a small key from his pocket and throwing it on the deck.

The green-eyed shadow didn't appear to understand.

"My cabin. In my desk," repeated John Fletcher, pointing first to the key and then in the direction of his cabin.

The shadow warrior nodded to one of his men, who picked up the key and disappeared below.

"Now let my son go," pleaded Jack's father.

The green-eyed shadow gave a throaty laugh, drawing back his sword to deliver the killing strike. . . .

Jack screamed, his eyes flying open, his heart pounding.

He looked frantically around the room. A single candle flickered in the corner. A door slid open, and the girl came and knelt beside him.

"Aku rei. Yasunde, gaijinsan," said the girl, with

that same gentle voice he had heard previously.

She placed the cool cloth to his forehead once again and settled him back down.

"What? I . . . I . . . I don't understand," stuttered Jack. "Who are you? Where's my father?"

The laughter echoed on.

John Fletcher exploded with rage as he realized the shadow was intent on killing Jack.

He flung back his head, striking his captor in the face and breaking his nose. The garrotte loosened and fell away. John threw himself at his knife lying on the deck and, in one last desperate attempt to save his son, seized the blade and slammed it into the green-eyed shadow's leg.

The shadow warrior grunted with pain before he could deliver the killing blow, and Jack, released from the shadow's choking grip, collapsed in a barely conscious pile. Whipping his sword around, the shadow flew at his attacker.

With a battle cry of "KIAI," the green-eyed shadow drove his weapon downward into John's chest. . . .

CHAPTER 7

SAMURAI

SPOTLESSLY CLEAN, the floor of the small, unadorned room was covered in a geometric pattern of soft straw mats. The walls were squares of translucent paper that softened the daylight, lending the air an unearthly glow.

Jack lay on a thick futon, covered by a quilt made of silk. He'd never slept under silk before, and its touch on his skin felt like a thousand butterfly wings.

After so long at sea, the nauseating motionlessness of the floor made his head spin when he tried to sit up. He moved to steady himself, but a sharp jolt of pain shot through his arm.

On examination, he discovered that his left arm was swollen and discolored and appeared to be broken, but someone had set it, securing it with a wooden splint.

Now that his fever had broken, the disjointed images that had flashed through his mind became lucid and painfully real. Christiaan dying. Shadows in the darkness. The crew of the *Alexandria* slaughtered. His father fighting, a garrotte around his throat. The shadow warrior thrusting his sword into his father. . . .

Jack could then remember lying on the bloodied deck for what seemed an age. The shadows, thinking he was dead, had left the quarterdeck to ransack the ship. Then, as if surfacing from a deep dive, he had heard his father.

"Jack . . . my son . . ." he cried feebly.

Jack dragged himself out of his paralysis and crawled over to his dying father.

"You're alive . . ." he said, a thin smile appearing on his bloodied lips. "The rutter . . . it will get you home. . . ."

Then the light faded from his father's eyes, and he exhaled his final breath.

Jack buried his head in his father's chest, trying to stifle his sobbing. He clung to his father like a drowning sailor seizing a lifeline.

When his crying finally subsided, Jack realized he was utterly alone, stranded in a foreign land. His only hope now for getting home was the rutter.

He ran for the lower decks. The *wakou*, occupied

with loading the guns, gold, and sappanwood into their own ship, failed to notice him. Belowdeck, Jack stepped over body after dead body until he entered his father's cabin, where he found the now-lifeless corpse of Christiaan.

The room had been ransacked, his father's desk turned over, charts scattered everywhere. Jack flew to his father's bunk, pulling away the bedding. He pressed on the concealed catch beneath, and, to his relief, there was the rutter, safe in its oilskin.

He shoved the book inside his shirt and ran out of the cabin. He had almost reached the companionway when a hand shot out of the darkness, grabbing him by his shirt.

A blackened face loomed into sight.

It grinned manically, revealing a set of sharklike teeth.

"A plague on 'em! They ain't beaten us yet," whispered a wild-eyed Ginsel. "I've set fire to the magazine. BOOM!"

Ginsel's arms exploded outward in a gesture of destruction. He laughed briefly, then grunted, a look of surprise registering on his face. He collapsed to the deck, a large knife attached to a chain sticking out of his back.

Jack looked up to see a sinister figure emerge from the shadows. A single green eye glared at him and then at the rutter stuffed inside his shirt. The shadow jerked on the chain, whipping the knife back into his grasp. Jack spun on his heels and fled up the companionway, praying he could reach the ship's rail in time. . . .

Jack was flung as high as the yardarm by the massive explosion before dropping with the rest of the wreckage into the ocean. . . .

He had little memory of anything after that. There was only flaring pain, darkness, then a blinding light and a man's scarred face, followed by strange voices.

Jack was suddenly aware he could hear those same voices now, talking outside the room. For a moment he didn't breathe.

Were they *wakou*? Why then was he alive?

Jack spotted his shirt and breeches neatly folded in the corner of the room, though there was no sign of the rutter. He staggered to his feet and hastily pulled on his clothes. He crossed the room and searched for the door, but was met with an unbroken grid of panels.

He was at a loss. There wasn't even a door handle.

Jack grabbed hold of the wooden slats to pull, but still unsure on his feet, he reeled slightly, and his hand shot straight through the wafer-thin paper wall. The conversation on the other side of the *shoji* door abruptly ceased.

The panel slid sharply open, and Jack stumbled back, embarrassed by his clumsiness.

A middle-aged woman with a round face, and a stocky young man with dark, almond-shaped eyes, glared at him. The man's expression was fierce. Two swords—one daggerlike, the other long and slightly curved—were thrust into his bloodred waistband. He stepped forward, his hand firmly gripping the hilt of the larger blade.

"Naniwoshiteru, gaijin?" challenged the man.

"Sorry. I . . . I don't understand," said Jack, retreating in fear.

The woman spoke firmly to the man, but his hand didn't leave his sword.

Jack was afraid the man was about to use it on him. Terrified, he scanned the room for a means of escape. But the man barred his way, partly withdrawing his sword. Jack's eyes fell upon the gleaming blade, its razor-sharp edge primed to cut off his head.

Then he remembered Piper's words. "If you ever meet a samurai, lads, bow low. Bow very, very low!"

Although Jack had never seen, let alone met one, the fearsome man looked like he should be a samurai. He wore a T-shaped robe in crisp white silk over wide black leggings spotted with golden dots. He had shaved the crown of his head, pulling the back and sides of his remaining black hair into a tight knot on the top. His face was severe and impenetrable—a warrior's face. The man had the look of someone who could kill Jack as easily as stepping on an ant.

Jack's body was battered and bruised, and every muscle ached, but he forced himself to bow. As he did so, the man stepped back in amazement.

Then the samurai began to laugh, an amused chuckle that grew into a deep roar.

CHAPTER 8

OFURO

JACK MUST HAVE cried himself to sleep after they'd put him back to bed, for when he rolled over, his pillow was damp with tears.

The round-faced woman was kneeling by his side, a look of motherly concern etched upon her face. Like the samurai the day before, she wore a silk robe, but hers was a deep blue, decorated with images of white and pink flowers. She smiled sweetly and offered him water. Jack took the small bowl and gulped the liquid down. It was cool and fresh.

"Thank you. May I beg you for a little more?"

She frowned.

"Can I have some more water?" said Jack, pointing to the small bowl in his hand and making slurping noises.

She smiled and bowed. Disappearing through the sliding door, which had already been repaired, she returned with a scarlet lacquered tray bearing three small bowls. One contained water, one a thin steaming soup that smelled of fish, and the third a small pile of white rice with a serving of pickles.

Jack drained the water, and the fish soup warmed him, although he didn't like the peppery taste. He then greedily shoveled the rice into his mouth, eating with his fingers. Jack had seen rice once before, when his father had brought some back from a trading trip for his mother to cook. To Jack it was a bit tasteless, but he didn't care since he hadn't eaten for days. Licking his fingers clean, he gave the woman a broad smile to show that he appreciated the food.

The woman looked utterly shocked.

"Err . . . thank you. Thank you very much." Jack didn't know what else to say.

Obviously upset, the woman collected the empty dishes and scurried out of the room.

What had he done? Perhaps he should have offered her some, too?

A few moments later, the wall panel slid open again, and she entered with a white robe, which she laid by his bed.

"*Kimono wo kite choudai,*" she said, gesturing for him to put it on.

Jack, aware he was naked under the quilt, refused.

The woman appeared perplexed. She pointed to the robe once again.

Frustrated at their inability to communicate, Jack signed for her to go through the sliding panel. Clearly bewildered by his need for her to leave, she still bowed and departed the room. Jack stood up as quickly as his aching body would allow, and taking care with his splinted arm, put on the silk robe.

He moved over to the door and slid it open, being careful not to damage it this time. The woman was waiting outside on a wooden veranda that circled the house. A set of steps led to a large garden surrounded by a high wall. The garden was unlike anything he had ever seen.

A little bridge spanned a pond filled with pink water lilies. Pebbled paths weaved their way through colorful flowers, green shrubs, and large ornate stones. A tiny waterfall ran into a stream that wound around a glorious cherry blossom tree, then flowed back into the pond.

Everything about the garden was so perfect, so peaceful, thought Jack. How his mother would have loved the colorful flowers. It was another world to the muddy patches of herbs, vegetables, and hedges that were strewn across England.

"It's like the Garden of Eden," Jack murmured.

The woman indicated for Jack to put on a pair of wooden sandals, then shuffled along the path in tiny steps, beckoning him to follow.

On the other side of the pond a bony old man, evidently the gardener, tended an already perfect plot with a rake. He bowed low as they passed by. The woman gave a slight bow in return, and Jack followed suit. It appeared bowing was the thing to do, at all times.

They entered a small wooden building on the other side of the garden. The room was pleasantly warm, and inside was a long stone bench and a square wooden tub filled with steaming water. To Jack's horror, the woman signed for him to get in.

"What? You don't expect me to get in *there*, do you?" exclaimed Jack, backing away from the bath.

Smiling, she held her nose, pointed at Jack, then at the bath. *"Ofuro."*

"I don't stink!" said Jack. "I washed barely a month ago." Didn't they know that baths were disease pits? His mother had warned him that he could catch the flux—or worse.

"Ofuro haitte!" she said again, slapping her hand on the bath. *"Anata ni nomiga tsuite iru wa yo!"*

Jack didn't understand and didn't care. There was no way he was going to get in that bath.

"Uekiya! Chiro! Kocchi ni kite!" shouted the woman, making a grab for Jack.

He ran around the tub and headed for the door, but the gardener appeared and blocked his path. A young maid then dashed in and caught hold of him. The woman pulled off his robe and began to sluice him down with cold water.

"Stop that! It's freezing!" cried Jack. "Leave me alone!"

"Dame, ofuro no jikan yo, ohkina akachan ne," the woman said, making the maid laugh.

Jack struggled and kicked so much that the gardener had to help hold him down, too, though the old man took great care to avoid Jack's broken arm.

Jack felt like a baby as they scrubbed him down and then lowered him, still protesting, into the steaming bath. The heat was almost unbearable, but every time he tried to get out, the woman gently pushed him back in.

Eventually they let him out, but only to wash him down again, this time with warm soapy water. By now, though, he was too tired to resist, and resigned himself to the indignity of it all. The worst thing was that the water was scented. He smelled like a girl!

They dunked him back in the bathtub, his skin now bright pink from the heat. After a while they let him out, only to subject him to a final dousing of cold water before drying and dressing him in a new robe.

Exhausted, he was led back to his room, where he collapsed on his quilt and immediately fell into a deep sleep.

CHAPTER 9

KIMONOS AND CHOPSTICKS

"O<small>FURO</small>," said the woman.

"I had one yesterday. . . ." complained Jack.

"*Ofuro!*" she scolded.

Jack, realizing it was futile to resist, put on the fresh gown and wound his way through the garden to the bathhouse. This time he almost enjoyed the experience.

Apart from the throbbing pain in his arm and a dull ache in his head, he had to admit that the bath had done him some good. He felt rested, and his scalp didn't itch with lice or sea salt anymore.

When Jack returned to his room, garments similar to those that the samurai had worn were laid out upon his bed. What did these people want with him? They fed and bathed him and now clothed him, but otherwise kept their distance.

The round-faced woman entered.

"Chiro!" she called, and the girl came scurrying in, bowing low.

The girl was petite, maybe eighteen years old, but it was difficult for Jack to judge: her skin was so smooth and unblemished. She had small dark eyes and a short bob of black hair, and, though pretty, the maid didn't compare to the girl who had nursed him through his fever.

So where was she? And, for that matter, where was the man with the scarred face? He had only seen two other men in the house so far—the old gardener, whom the woman called Uekiya, and the fierce-looking samurai—and neither of them bore scars. Perhaps the girl and the scarred man were both figments of his imagination, like the girl he'd seen on the headland.

"*Goshujin kimono,*" said the woman, pointing at the clothes.

Jack realized the woman meant him to put the garments on, but, looking at the puzzling array of items, he wondered where to start. He picked up a pair of funny-looking socks with split toes. At least it was obvious where these went, but his feet were too big to fit into them. The maid saw his predicament and giggled softly behind her hand.

"Well, how should I know how to put all this on!" mumbled Jack, tetchy at being ridiculed.

The maid ceased laughing, dropped to her knees, and bowed apologetically. The woman stepped forward.

Jack put the socks down and submitted to the woman and young maid helping him dress. First they pulled on the white *tabi* socks, which, thankfully, stretched a little. Then they gave him some undergarments, a white cotton top and skirt they called *juban*. Next a silk robe was wrapped around him, the women carefully ensuring that the left side of the robe overlapped with the right side. All of this was tied off from behind with a wide red belt called an *obi*.

Jack stepped out onto the veranda. He felt awkward in his new clothes—he was used to trousers and shirts, not dresses and skirts. As he moved, the kimono proved disconcertingly drafty, but he had to admit the smooth silk was far more pleasant than stiff breeches and the rough hemp of his sailor's shirt.

The maid disappeared into another room while the woman led him along the veranda to a *shoji*. They entered a small room similar to his own, except this had a low oblong table and four flat cushions arranged on either side. On the far wall, hung from a ceiling beam, were two magnificent swords with dark red woven handles and gleaming black scabbards inlaid with mother-of-pearl. A small shrine was inset into the wall beneath these weapons. Two candles and a stick of incense burned within it, filling the air with the light scent of jasmine.

A little Japanese boy sat cross-legged upon one of the cushions, staring in wide-eyed amazement at the foreigner with golden hair and blue eyes.

The woman gestured for Jack to sit next to the boy, while she made herself comfortable on the opposite side.

There was an awkward silence.

Jack noted that the fourth cushion remained unoccupied, and presumed they were waiting for someone. The little boy continued to stare at Jack.

"I'm Jack Fletcher," he said to the little boy, attempting to break the silence. "What's your name?"

The little boy convulsed in giggles at hearing Jack speak.

The woman spoke sharply to him, and he went quiet. Jack looked at the woman.

"I'm Jack Fletcher," he said, pointing at his chest and then pointing at the woman. "You are?"

Jack repeated the gesture several times. She still didn't appear to understand, maintaining the same infuriatingly enigmatic smile. He was just about to give up trying to make himself understood, when the little boy piped up.

"Jaku Furecha"—then pointing at his nose—"*Jiro.*"

"Jiro. Yes, yes, my name is Jack."

"Jaku! Jiro! Jaku! Jiro!" cried the boy in delight, alternately pointing at Jack and then at himself.

With a flood of understanding, the woman bowed. *"Watashi wa Dōte Hiroko. Hi-ro-ko."*

"Hi-ro-ko," repeated Jack slowly, returning the bow. At least he knew their names now.

A side *shoji* slid open, and Chiro entered, bearing six small lacquered bowls on a tray. As she laid each one upon the table, Jack became aware of how hungry he was. There was fish soup, rice, strips of odd-looking vegetables, what appeared to be a thick wheat porridge, and small pieces of fish. The maid bowed and left.

Jack wondered where the rest of the meal was. The small table was dotted with the little bowls of food, but surely there wasn't enough for all of them? Where was the meat? The gravy? A bit of buttered bread? He noticed the fish wasn't even cooked! Fearful of offending his host again, Jack waited to be served. There was a long moment of uncomfortable silence, then Hiroko picked up two little sticks by her bowl.

Jiro did the same.

Then, holding them in one hand, they began to pick up small amounts of food, delicately putting the morsels into their mouths. All the time they eyed Jack warily.

Jack hadn't even seen the sticks by his bowl. He examined the pencil-thin bits of wood. How on earth was he supposed to eat with these?

Jiro smiled at Jack through a mouthful of food.

"*Hashi,*" said the little boy, pointing to them.

Jiro opened his own hand to show Jack how to hold the *hashi* correctly. But even though he managed to mimic Jiro's scissor-like action, he couldn't keep a grip on the fish or the vegetables long enough to lift them from their bowls.

The more he dropped the food, the more frustrated he became. Never one to admit defeat, Jack decided to attempt some rice. This had to be easier, since there was more of it. But half the rice immediately slid straight back into the bowl, the other half dropped all over the table. By the time it reached Jack's mouth, all that remained was one grain.

Nonetheless pleased by his accomplishment, Jack chewed on the solitary grain. He pretended to rub his belly in satisfaction.

Jiro laughed.

The little boy may have enjoyed the joke, thought Jack, but if he didn't learn how to use these *hashi* soon, he was going to starve.

CHAPTER 10

ABUNAI!

$\mathbf{J}$ACK FELL INTO a routine of bathing, eating, and sleeping.

His body gradually recovered from the fever, his arm began to mend, and he was able to take regular walks around the garden. Most days he sat beneath the cherry blossom tree and watched Uekiya weed the flower bed or prune back some shrub with infinite care. He would acknowledge Jack's presence with a brief bow of the head, but little passed between them since Jack couldn't make head or tail of their strange language.

Jack soon got restless, his world now confined to a monotony of indistinguishable rooms, daily bathing, and flawless gardening. He felt trapped, like a canary in a gilded cage. What did they want from him? He was constantly watched, but no one tried to speak with him. He was allowed to wander the garden and house, but was always stopped from exploring farther. Were they deciding his fate? Or were they waiting for someone who would?

Jack was desperate to know what lay beyond the garden walls. Surely there had to be someone out there who could understand English and help get him home, or maybe he would find a ship bound for a foreign port. He could then smuggle aboard with the hope the next port of call would have passage back to England, back to his sister—the last fragment of his family. It had to be better than sitting under a tree doing nothing.

Jack resolved to run away.

Each day he had seen the young samurai Taka-san, who appeared to be Hiroko's house guard, enter and leave through a small gate in the garden wall. That was his way out. It was pointless asking if he could leave—he was a prisoner both of language and circumstance. They simply bowed and responded, *"Gomennasai, wakarimasen,"* to everything he said, which, by their expression and tone, he presumed meant, "Sorry, I don't understand."

On the tenth day of his captivity, after the now-familiar breakfast of rice, a few pickled vegetables, and wheat gruel, he went for his daily walk around the garden. When Uekiya bent over to tend an already immaculately pruned bush, Jack made for the gate. He made sure that Jiro and Hiroko were inside the house before pulling on the latch and silently slipping through. The gate closed with the tiniest of clicks, but Uekiya heard it and shouted after him.

"Iye! Abunai! Abunai!"

Jack ran.

Not caring about the cries of alarm or where he was headed, he darted down a dirt road and weaved between buildings until he was out of sight.

Quickly taking his bearings, Jack saw that the village sat in the bowl of a large natural harbor with mountains rising up in the distance. Surrounding the village were countless terraced fields dotted with farmers tending rice beds. There were perhaps two hundred wooden dwellings tucked around the harbor's edge, most with thatched roofs, a few tiled with red shingles. Despite the pain in his arm, Jack dashed downhill toward the sea. Stunned villagers stared in disbelief at the fleeing boy with blond hair.

Jack turned a corner and unexpectedly found himself in the middle of the village square. Ahead was a large cobblestone jetty, where men and women were gutting fish and repairing nets. In the harbor, myriad fishing boats dotted the waters. Women dressed in thin white slips dived from the boats, disappearing and reappearing with bags full of seaweed and oysters. A small sandy island lay in the center of the bay, a red wooden gateway dominating its beach.

A hushed silence descended upon the square, and Jack became aware of hundreds of eyes studying him. The whole village appeared frozen in time. Women in vibrantly colored kimonos knelt motionless by sellers in mid-purchase; half-gutted fish in the hands of fishermen glinted in the bright sunshine; and a samurai warrior, statuelike, glared stonily at him.

After a moment's hesitation, Jack tentatively bowed. The samurai barely acknowledged his greeting, but moved on, ignoring him. A few women returned Jack's bow, bemusement shining in their eyes, and the villagers resumed their daily activities. Only too aware that all were still eyeing him with suspicion, Jack crossed the square to the jetty and made his way down to a small beach.

He scanned the boats, seeking a foreign ship. But every vessel was Japanese and crewed by Japanese. Despairing, Jack huddled down next to a small fishing boat and stared blankly out to sea.

England was two years and four thousand leagues away. The only home he knew, and Jess, the only family he had left, were on the other side of the world. What hope did he have of ever reaching her? What had been the point in running? He had no money. No rutter. Not even his own clothes!

Jack watched the little boats in the harbor bob up

and down, at a loss for what to do next. Then a girl appeared, rising up out of the water like a mermaid. She had the same snowy white skin and jet black hair as the girl he had seen at the temple with the white stallion.

Jack watched her slip into one of the boats closest to shore. A fisherman pulled in a bag loaded with oysters, and while she stood and dried herself, he pried the oysters open to search for pearls, in the same way Jack had seen the Java fisherman do in Bantam. The girl ran her hands through her ebony hair, the seawater cascading off and reflecting the morning sunlight like a thousand tiny stars.

Even as the fisherman rowed across the harbor, the girl remained completely at ease with the swaying motion of the boat, her slender body moving with the grace of a willow tree. It was almost as if she were floating across the water. As the girl neared a little wooden jetty, Jack could see her features more clearly. She wasn't much older than he was. Blessed with soft, unblemished skin, her half-moon eyes were the color of ebony, and beneath a small rounded nose was the blossom of a mouth, with lips like the petals of a red rose. If Jack had ever imagined a fairy-tale princess, she would have looked like this.

"*GAIJIN!*"

Jack, snapping out of his daydream, looked up. Blinking into the bright sunlight, he saw two Japanese men standing over him, dressed in plain kimonos and thong sandals. One was squat with a round, bulbous head and a flattened nose, while the other had tightly slit eyes and was as skinny as a rake.

"*Nani wo shiteru, gaijin?*" challenged Flat Nose.

The thin man peered over his friend's shoulder and prodded Jack sharply in the chest with a wooden staff.

"*Eh, gaijin?*" he chimed, in a thin reedy voice.

Jack tried to back away, but he had nowhere to go.

"*Onushi ittai doko kara kitanoda, gaijin?*" demanded Flat Nose, who then tugged Jack's blond hair in cruel amazement.

"*Eh, gaijin?*" the thin man taunted, purposefully planting his staff on Jack's fingers.

Jack snatched his hand away.

"I don't understand. . . ." he stammered and began desperately to search for a means of escape.

Flat Nose grabbed Jack by the scruff of his kimono and jerked him up to eye level.

"*Nani?*" he spat into Jack's face.

"*YAME!*"

Jack barely registered the booming command before Flat Nose's eyes almost popped out of their sockets, a hand knifing into the back of the man's neck. Flat Nose collapsed face-first into the sand. He lay there motionless, even as the waves washed over him.

Taka-san, the young samurai from Jack's house,

having appeared from nowhere, now spun on Jack's other assailant, withdrawing his sword in one fluid motion. The thin man threw himself to the ground and apologized feverishly.

The sword cut through the air and arced down toward the prostrate man.

"*Iye! Taka-san. Dōzo,*" instructed another voice, and Taka-san stopped the sword barely an inch from the man's exposed neck.

Jack immediately recognized the gentle voice.

"*Konnichiwa,*" she said, walking up to Jack and bowing gently to him. "*Watashi wa Dāte Akiko.*"

The girl on the headland, the same girl from his fevered dreams, was Akiko.

CHAPTER 11

SENCHA

THAT EVENING, when Jack was summoned to dinner, Hiroko and her son, Jiro, sat in their usual places, but the fourth cushion was now occupied by Akiko. Above her hung the two gleaming samurai swords.

Akiko's presence made Jack feel elated and awkward at the same time. She had the finesse of a lady of class, yet possessed an aura of authority that Jack had never encountered in a girl before. The samurai Taka-san obeyed her every word, and the household bowed very low when in her company.

Jack had been somewhat surprised that he was not punished for his escape. In fact, the household appeared more concerned than angry—Uekiya the gardener especially, and Jack felt a twinge of guilt for worrying the old man.

After dinner, Akiko led Jack out to the veranda, where they sat on plump cushions in the fading evening sunlight. A silence had settled over the village like a soft blanket, and Jack could hear the tentative chirps of crickets and the trickle of the stream as it wound itself through Ueyika's garden.

Akiko sat absorbing the peace, and for the first time in days, Jack allowed his guard to drop.

Then he noticed Taka-san standing silently in the shadows, his hand resting upon his sword. Jack instantly tensed. They were taking no chances: he was being watched now.

A *shoji* slid open, and Chiro brought out a tray with a beautifully embellished pot and two small cups. She laid the tray on the floor and carefully measured out some hot, green water. The liquid reminded Jack of "tea," a new drink Dutch traders had begun importing into Holland from China.

With both hands, Chiro passed a cup to Akiko, who then offered it to Jack.

Jack took the cup and waited for Akiko to pick up hers, but she signed for him to drink first. He hesitantly sipped the steaming brew. It tasted like bitter boiled grass, and he had to force back a grimace. Akiko drank from her own cup. A look of quiet contentment spread across her face.

After several moments of silence, Jack plucked up the courage to speak.

He pointed to the green liquid she evidently enjoyed so much. "What is this drink called?"

There was a brief pause as Akiko attempted to understand his question before replying. "*Sencha.*"

"*Sen-cha,*" repeated Jack, feeling the word in his mouth and working it into his memory. He realized he would have to acquire a taste for *sencha* in the future. "And this?" he said, indicating the cup.

"*Chawan,*" she replied.

"*Chawan,*" copied Jack.

Akiko quietly applauded and then began pointing at other objects, giving Jack their Japanese names. She seemed pleased to teach him her language, and Jack was relieved, since this was the first time that anyone had attempted to communicate properly with him. Jack continued to press for new words until his head was overflowing with them and it was time to go to bed.

Taka-san led him back to his room, closing the *shoji* door behind Jack.

Jack settled down on his futon, but couldn't sleep. His head whirled with Japanese words and turbulent emotions. As he lay there in the darkness, looking at the soft glow of the night lanterns through the walls, he allowed a sliver of hope to enter his heart. If he could learn the language, then perhaps he could survive in this strange land. Maybe gain work with a Japanese crew, get to a port where his fellow countrymen were, and from there work his way back to England. Perhaps Akiko was the key. Maybe she could help him get home.

A shadow shifted on the other side of the paper wall, and Jack realized Taka-san still stood outside, guarding him.

Jack was completing his early morning walk in the garden the following day, when Jiro came flying around the corner of the veranda.

"*Kinasai!*" he shouted, dragging Jack to the front entrance of the house.

Jack could barely keep up.

Outside, Akiko and Taka-san were waiting. Akiko wore a shimmering ivory kimono that was embroidered with the image of a crane in flight. She held a crimson-colored parasol over her head to keep off the sun.

"*Ohayō gozaimasu*, Jack," she said, bowing.

"*Ohayō gozaimasu*, Akiko," echoed Jack, wishing her a good morning.

She seemed pleased at his response, and they set off down the dirt track toward the harbor.

At the jetty, they climbed into the boat of Akiko's pearl fisherman, who rowed them across to the island in the middle of the harbor. As they drew closer, Jack was astonished to see that a huge crowd had gathered along a wide stretch of the beach in front of the red wooden gateway.

"Ise Jingu Torii," Akiko said, pointing at the structure.

Jack nodded his understanding. The *torii* was the color of evening fire and the height of a double-story house. It was constructed from two upright pillars cut across by two large horizontal beams, the uppermost of which had a narrow roof of jade green tiles.

Their small craft landed on the southern tip of the island, and they joined the thronging mass of villagers—women in brightly-colored kimonos and sword-bearing samurai. The crowd had formed an orderly semicircle, but the villagers all bowed and gave way as Akiko and her entourage moved toward the front, joining a large group of samurai.

The warriors immediately acknowledged Akiko's arrival with a low bow. Akiko returned their greeting, then began to converse with a samurai who seemed to be Jack's age. He had chestnut brown eyes and spiky black hair. The boy threw Jack a disdainful look before turning his head away.

The villagers, however, remained astonished by Jack's presence. They gave him a wide berth, whispering to one another behind their hands, but Jack didn't mind, since this allowed him a clear view of the makeshift arena.

A lone samurai stood like an ancient god under the *torii*.

The warrior was dressed in a black-and-gold kimono decorated on the chest, sleeves, and back with a circular symbol of four crossed bolts of lightning. His hairstyle was fashioned with a topknot of black hair pulled forward over a shaved pate. This samurai, though, had tied a thick band of white cloth around his head. Stocky and powerful, with menacing eyes, the samurai warrior reminded Jack of a large bulldog bred for fighting.

In his hands was the largest sword Jack had ever seen. The blade itself stretched over four feet in length, and together with the hilt, was as long as Jack was tall. The warrior, his eyes fixed on the distant shoreline of the harbor, shifted impatiently, and his sword caught the bright sunlight. For a brief moment it flashed like a bolt of lightning. Seeing the amazement in Jack's eyes, Akiko whispered the sword's name: *"Nodachi."*

The warrior stood alone in the arena, and Jack wondered where the man's opponent could be. No one else appeared to be preparing for combat. As Jack looked around the crowd, he noticed that a group of samurai on his opposite side were emblazoned with the same lightning emblem as the warrior, while those samurai surrounding him bore the round crest of a phoenix.

So where was *their* champion?

Jack gauged that an hour must have passed, for the sun had traversed some fifteen degrees across the cloudless sky. The heat had intensified and the villagers were now growing restless. The samurai under the *torii* had begun to pace the beach like a caged tiger.

Another hour went by.

The mutterings of the crowd grew louder as the heat became unbearable. Jack dreaded what he would have felt like in his old shirt and breeches, instead of the silken kimono he now wore.

Then, just as the sun reached its zenith, a small boat cast off from the jetty.

The listless crowd instantly became animated. Jack could see a little fisherman rowing unhurriedly across the harbor, while a larger man sat Buddha-like at its prow.

The boat drew closer. The crowd let out a huge cheer and began to chant, "Masamoto! Masamoto! Masamoto!"

Akiko, Taka-san, and Jiro joined in the thundering refrain of the samurai's name.

The group of samurai bearing the lightning crest challenged the call with a rallying cry of their own champion, "Godai! Godai! Godai!" and the warrior stepped forward, thrusting his *nodachi* high in the air. His followers roared even louder.

The boat came to rest on the shoreline. The little fisherman shipped his oars and waited patiently for his occupant to disembark. Another huge cheer went up from the crowd as the man stood up and stepped barefoot onto the beach.

Jack let out an involuntary gasp of surprise. Their champion, Masamoto, was the man with the scarred face.

CHAPTER 12

THE DUEL

THE MASS of rough skin and reddened welts fanned out like molten lava from above Masamoto's left eye, across his cheek, and down the line of his jaw. Jack wondered what had happened to disfigure him so badly, for his remaining features were otherwise even and well defined. He had the solid and muscular build of an ox, and his eyes were the color of honeyed amber. He wore a dark-brown-and-cream kimono that bore the circular emblem of a phoenix, and like Godai, he had a headband, but his was crimson red.

Unlike Godai, Masamoto had a completely shaved head, though he maintained a small trimmed beard that encircled his mouth. To Jack, Masamoto appeared more monk than warrior.

Masamoto surveyed the scene before turning to retrieve his swords from the boat. He slipped them, along with their protective *sayas*, into the *obi* of his kimono. First the shorter *wakizashi* sword, followed by the longer *katana*. Taking his time, he walked up the beach toward the *torii*.

Furious at his opponent's late and disrespectful arrival, Godai screamed insults as he approached.

Unperturbed, Masamoto maintained his stoic pace, even pausing to acknowledge his samurai following. At last he came face-to-face with Godai and bowed ceremoniously. This infuriated Godai even more. Blinded with rage, he charged at Masamoto in an attempt to take him off guard before the contest officially commenced.

Masamoto, however, was prepared for just such an offensive. He sidestepped Godai, the massive *nodachi* narrowly missing him. In a single motion, Masamoto unsheathed both his swords from their *sayas*, his right hand raising the *katana* to the sky and his left drawing the *wakizashi* across his chest to protect himself from any counterattack.

Godai brought his *nodachi* around for a second assault, the sword arcing at lightning speed toward Masamoto's head. Masamoto shifted his weight, angling his *katana* to deflect the strike off to the left. Their swords clashed and the *nodachi* scraped along the back of Masamoto's blade.

Masamoto pressed forward under the crushing blow, cutting his *wakizashi* across Godai's midriff. The sword sliced through Godai's kimono, but failed to meet flesh. Godai spun away to prevent Masamoto from extending his strike and drawing blood.

Masamoto pursued the retreating Godai into the sea, his two swords a furious blur, but he was immediately cut short by the returning *nodachi* and barely had time to leap beyond its reach.

Jack was astounded at the skill and agility of these two warriors. They fought with the grace of dancers, pirouetting in an exquisite yet deadly ritual. Each strike was executed with the utmost accuracy and commitment. Masamoto wielded his two swords as if they were natural extensions of his own arms. It was no wonder that Jack's fellow crewmen had been slaughtered so effortlessly by the *wakou*. They stood little chance against an enemy proficient enough in fighting to make it an art.

Godai drove Masamoto back up the beach while his samurai cheered him on.

Godai was devastatingly adept with the *nodachi*, despite its massive size. He wielded it as if it were no heavier than a shaft of bamboo. Godai continued to force Masamato backward and into the throng of spectators, right to where Jack was standing.

Godai bluffed a strike to the right then switched his attack and sliced at Masamoto's exposed arm. Masamoto managed to avoid the strike, but Godai's immense effort to connect drove his weighty sword on into the crowd.

In panic, the villagers scattered, but Jack remained rooted to the spot, paralyzed with fear at the man's unwavering determination.

At the very last second, Taka-san wrenched Jack out of the way, but the villager behind Jack was not so fortunate. The little man tried to protect himself, but the sword sliced straight through his outstretched fingers.

Godai, ignoring the screaming villager, flicked the blood from his blade and began another onslaught on the retreating Masamoto.

It was only then that Jack realized he was watching a fight to the death.

Two of Masamoto's samurai dragged the wounded villager away as the crowd surged forward, anxious not to miss the action, the amputated fingers trampled under a sea of feet.

Akiko, seeing Jack's ashen face, looked at him with concern. Jack forced a smile, though in truth he was sickened to the pit of his stomach. He swallowed down the bitter shock of what he had just witnessed. How could a people who invested their time in cultivating idyllic gardens and decorating kimonos with images of butterflies be so barbaric? It made no sense.

Jack turned his attention back to the combat in order to avoid Akiko's anxious gaze. The two samurai had broken apart, breathing heavily from their exertions. They circled one another, waiting for the next move. Godai feigned an advance, and the crowd surged backward, desperate to avoid being injured.

Masamoto, now familiar with Godai's tactics, slipped to his blindside, parrying the *nodachi* with his short sword and countering with his *katana*. The *katana* scythed toward Godai's head. Godai ducked, and the *katana* sliced over the top of his head.

The two warriors spun around on one another and froze. The crowd became silent. Then Godai's topknot slipped from his head and fell limply onto the beach. Masamoto smirked at Godai's public disgrace, and his phoenix samurai began chanting "Masamoto! Masamoto! Masamoto!"

Incensed at the humiliation of losing his topknot, Godai screamed a *kiai,* then attacked. His *nodachi* struck downward, and then, like an eagle snatching up it's prey, flicked skyward at an angle that defeated Masamoto's *katana.*

Masamoto, bending back to avoid the blow, brought his sword up to deflect the blade from his neck, but his *katana* was knocked out of his hand, and the tip of the *nodachi* cut deep into his right shoulder. Masamoto grunted in pain, dropping backward and rolling away in an attempt to distance himself from Godai. After several controlled rolls, he flipped himself back onto his feet.

It was now the turn of Godai's samurai to cheer.

Godai was certain to win now that Masamoto had forfeited his *katana*. The shorter *wakizashi* was no match for a mighty *nodachi*. Masamoto's samurai realized their champion had little chance of overcoming such a disadvantage. For the first time in his life, Masamoto's legendary handling of two swords had not withstood the onslaught of a *nodachi*.

Masamoto retreated down the beach, edging toward the fishing boat he had arrived in. Godai gloated, sensing that victory was close at hand. He quickly maneuvered himself between Masamoto and the wooden vessel, preventing his escape.

Masamoto appeared defeated. Blood seeped from the gash on his shoulder. He weakly lowered his *wakizashi*. The crowd gave a despondent groan. Godai grinned from ear to ear, and he slowly raised his weapon for the final blow.

That was the moment of overconfidence Masamoto had been waiting for. With a sharp flick of his wrist he sent his *wakizashi* spinning through the air. Taken by surprise, Godai stumbled back to avoid the flying blade and lost his footing in the sand.

Little more than a blur, Masamoto shot past Godai and headed for the boat. Godai, getting back to his feet, screamed at his fleeing opponent.

But Masamoto didn't intend to escape. Instead he

grabbed the long wooden oar from the boat and spun around to face Godai. Now Masamoto possessed a weapon of equal length to the *nodachi*.

Immediately Godai charged at Masamoto, who parried his blows with the oar. Chunks of wood flew through the air. Godai then struck low, attempting to chop off Masamoto's legs.

Masamoto jumped over the blade and brought his oar straight down on Godai's exposed head. The oar connected, and Godai's legs crumpled under the force of the blow. He collapsed like a felled tree.

Masamoto's samurai cheered, and the crowd took up a chant urging him to kill Godai. But Masamoto stepped away from the prone body of Godai. His victory clear and decisive, he had no reason to kill.

As he approached the crowd, they fell silent, and all dropped to their knees, bowing their heads to the sand. Even Akiko, Jiro, and Taka-san followed suit.

Jack alone remained standing, unsure of what he should do. He was not one of them, but the man emanated such absolute authority and power that Jack found himself bowing anyway. As he eyed the sand, Jack sensed Masamoto approaching him.

The bare feet of the scarred man planted themselves directly in front of him.

CHAPTER 13

FATHER LUCIUS

"*VOCÊ FALA PORTUGUÊS?*" the priest asked Jack.

The priest knelt on the floor in front of Masamoto, who now sat on a raised platform in the main room of the house.

"*Parlez vous Français?*"

The priest, who had hard glassy eyes and greasy thinning hair, wore the distinctive buttonless cassock and cape of a Portuguese Jesuit. He had been summoned to translate for Masamoto. He studied Jack suspiciously.

"*¿Hablas español?* Do you speak English?" he finally asked in frustration.

"*Falo um pouco. Oui, un petit peu. Sí, un poco,*" Jack replied fluently. "But I prefer my own tongue, English. My mother was a teacher, always getting me to learn different languages. Even yours . . ."

"Cursed child! You'd be wise not to make more of an enemy of me than you already have. You're the offspring of an English heretic and not welcome on these shores—"

He gave a sharp rasping cough and wiped dark yellow spittle from his lips with a handkerchief.

Jack shrank back from the man's illness. His father had cautioned him against men like the Jesuit priest. The Portuguese, like the Spanish, had been at war with England for nearly twenty years, and while the conflict was now officially over, the two nations still harbored great animosity toward one another. Since the Jesuit Catholics remained the worst of England's enemies, Jack, being an English Protestant, was in serious trouble.

"The only reason you're still alive," he continued, "is because you're a child."

Jack had already thought he was as good as dead when Masamoto had stood over him on the beach. But he had merely ordered Jack to accompany him and his samurai back to the mainland, where Hiroko was waiting to escort them up to the house.

"*Doushita? Kare wa doko kara kitanoda?*" asked Masamoto.

His shoulder wound having been dressed, the samurai

had changed into a crisp sky-blue kimono patterned with white maple leaves. He placidly sipped a cup of *sencha*. Jack could not believe this was the same man who had been fighting for his life just two hours earlier.

Masamoto was flanked on his right by two armed samurai. Akiko knelt at his left, and the spiky-haired boy she had been talking to earlier was beside her. From the moment Jack entered the room, the boy had glowered at him: threatening as a thundercloud.

"*Sumimasen, Masamoto-sama,*" apologized the priest.

The priest, who knelt on the floor close to Jack, bowed with considerable deference to Masamoto, making the dark wooden cross that hung from his neck graze the *tatami*-covered floor.

"His lordship Masamoto Takeshi wants to know who you are, where you are from, and how you came to be here," he said, turning to Jack.

"My name is Jack Fletcher. I'm from England. I arrived on board a trader ship. . . ."

"Inconceivable. There are no Englanders in these waters. You're a pirate, so don't waste my time, or his lordship's, with lies. I've not been brought here to translate your deceit."

"*Douka shimashita ka?*" interjected Masamoto.

"*Nani no nai, Masamoto-sama . . .*" replied the priest, but Masamoto immediately cut him off with what sounded to Jack like an order.

"*Moushiwake arimasen, Masamoto-sama,*" the priest said emphatically, and bowed, coughing harshly into his handkerchief. He turned back to Jack and continued. "Boy, I ask you again, how did you come to be here? And by the blood of Christ, you had better speak true!"

"I've just told you. I came on the *Alexandria*, part of a trading fleet for the Dutch East India Company. My father was the pilot. We'd been sailing for nearly two years to get to the Japans. . . ."

The priest translated as Jack spoke, before interjecting "By what route did you sail?"

"South, through Magellan's Pass—"

"Impossible. Magellan's Pass is secret."

"My father knew."

"Only we, the Portuguese, the righteous, possess safe passage," countered the priest indignantly. "It's well-protected against Protestant heretics like your father."

"My father outran those warships in a day," said Jack, a fiery sense of pride filling him as the priest begrudgingly informed Masamoto of this Portuguese humiliation.

Jack studied the priest distrustfully. "Who are you?"

"I am Father Lucius, a brother of the Society of Jesus, the protectorate of the Catholic Church and their sole missionary here in the port of Toba." The priest made the sign of the cross upon his chest, then kissed the wooden talisman that hung from his neck. "I report to

God and my superior, Father Diego Bobadilla, in Osaka. I am his eyes and ears here."

"What position does this samurai hold?" asked Jack, glancing at Masamoto. "And if you're so important, why do you bow to him?"

"Boy, I'd be more prudent with your words in the future—if you want to live. Samurai demand respect."

Bowing low again, the priest continued. "This is Masamoto Takeshi, Lord of Shima and right-hand man to Takatomi Hideaki, *daimyo* of Kyoto province—"

"What's a *daimyo*?" interrupted Jack.

"A feudal lord. He rules this whole province on behalf of the Emperor. The samurai, including Masamoto here, are his vassals."

"Vassals? . . . Do you mean slaves?"

"No, the peasants, the villagers you've seen, are more like slaves. The samurai are members of the warrior caste, much like your knights of old, but considerably more skilled. Masamoto is an expert sword master—undefeated. He is also the man responsible for plucking you, half-drowned, from the ocean and fixing your broken arm, so show him due deference!"

Jack was astonished. He knew such medical skill was unheard of in England. A broken limb at sea meant a slow, agonizing death from gangrene, or a painful and risky amputation. He was extremely fortunate to have met Masamoto.

"Please, can you thank him for saving my life?"

"You can do it yourself. *'Arigatō'* means 'thank you' in Japanese."

"Arigatō," repeated Jack, pointing at his broken arm, then bowing as low as his arm would allow. This appeared to please Masamoto, who acknowledged the courtesy with a slight nod of his head.

"So is this Masamoto's house?"

"No, this is his sister Hiroko's house. She lives here with her daughter, Akiko." The priest started coughing violently again, and it took a moment for him to recover. "Enough of your questions, boy! Where's the rest of your crew?"

"Dead," said Jack, the word coming cold and lifeless to his lips.

"Dead? All of them?"

"A storm drove us off course. We were forced to shelter in a cove, but a reef hulled the *Alexandria*. We had to make repairs but were attacked by . . . I'm not sure . . . shadows."

Masamoto's interest piqued as the priest translated Jack's story.

"Describe these shadows," Father Lucius asked for Masamoto.

"They were men, I think . . . dressed in black. I could only see their eyes. They had swords, chains, throwing knives. . . . My father thought they were *wakou.*"

"Ninja," breathed Masamoto.

"Whatever they were, one of them killed my father," said Jack, his voice taut with emotion, the memory of the night rising up like fire in his chest. "It was a ninja with a green eye!"

Masamoto leaned forward, tense and clearly disturbed by Father Lucius's translation of Jack's outburst.

"Repeat exactly what you just said," demanded Father Lucius on behalf of Masamoto.

The image of the ninja's hooded face and his father's death replayed in Jack's head. He swallowed hard before continuing. "The ninja who murdered my father had one eye. Green like snakeskin. I'll *never* forget it."

"Dokugan Ryu," spat Masamoto, as if he had swallowed poison.

The samurai guards visibly stiffened at his words. The black-haired boy's face flashed with fear, and Akiko turned to Jack, her eyes full of pity.

"Doku-what?" asked Jack, taken aback by everyone's reaction to Masamoto's words.

"Dokugan Ryu. It means 'Dragon Eye,'" explained Father Lucius. "Dokugan Ryu was the ninja responsible for murdering Masamoto's first son, Tenno, two years ago. Masamoto-sama had foiled an assassination attempt on his *daimyo* and was hunting down those responsible. Dokugan Ryu was sent to kill his son as a warning to stop the search. The ninja has not been sighted since."

Masamoto spoke gravely to Father Lucius.

"Masamoto wants to know the whereabouts of the rest of your family. What of your mother? Was she on board?"

"No, she died when I was ten. Pneumonia." Jack looked meaningfully at Father Lucius, recognizing the priest's symptoms for what they were. "My father left my little sister with a neighbor, but she was old and didn't have enough room to look after both of us. That's why I was on the ship. I was old enough to work, so my father got me a job on the *Alexandria* as a rigging monkey."

"I am truly sorry for the death of your mother. And of your father," said Father Lucius, with apparent sincerity.

He then recounted Jack's history to Masamoto, who listened solemnly. Masamoto poured himself some more *sencha*. He studied the cup before sipping its contents.

No one broke the silence.

Masamoto put down the cup and addressed the room. As he spoke, the color drained from the priest's face, and Akiko's eyes widened in astonishment. Jack saw that the black-haired boy had turned rigid as stone, his thunderous expression darkening with barely contained malice.

With a slight tremor in his voice, Father Lucius translated.

"Masamoto-sama has deemed that you, Jack Fletcher, are to be taken under his care until you are 'of age.' This being the second anniversary of his son's death, he believes you to be a 'gift from the gods.' You have suffered under the same hand of Dokugan Ryu. You are therefore to take Tenno's place by Masamoto's side and shall henceforth be treated as one of his own."

Jack was stunned. He didn't know whether to laugh or cry at the idea of being adopted by a samurai lord. But before he had a chance to respond, Masamoto had summoned Taka-san into the room. Taka-san was carrying a package bound in a hessian cloth, which he laid at Jack's feet.

Masamoto addressed Jack, Father Lucius translating as he spoke.

"Masamoto-sama found you clutching this to your person when he pulled you from the sea. Now that you are recovered, he is returning your rightful possessions."

Masamoto signed for Jack to unwrap the rectangular object. Jack tugged at the binding, and the cloth fell away to reveal a dark oilskinned parcel. The entire room watched with mounting interest. Father Lucius edged closer.

Jack knew exactly what it was without removing the oilskin. It was his father's rutter.

The room swirled around him, and out of nowhere Jack could see his father's face. He lay dying on the deck, blood bubbling from his lips.

"Jack? Are you all right?" asked Father Lucius, bringing Jack back to his senses.

"Yes," said Jack, quickly gathering his wits. "I'm

just upset. This was my father's."

"I understand. These are your father's charts, perhaps?" said Father Lucius nonchalantly, but all the while his glassy eyes coveted the oilskin-covered object.

"No . . . no . . . It's my father's diary," said Jack, thinking quickly and snatching up the rutter.

Father Lucius narrowed his eyes, apparently unconvinced, but let it pass.

With the presentation of the book finished, Masamoto had clearly decided the meeting was over, and stood. Everyone bowed as he spoke.

"Masamoto-sama has ordered that you rest," translated the priest. "He will meet with you again tomorrow."

Everyone bowed again, and Masamoto swept from the room, swiftly followed by his two guards and the moody black-haired boy.

Father Lucius got up to leave too, but broke into a coughing fit that rattled his lungs. As the fit subsided, he turned and wiped the sweat from his brow.

"A pox on your heretic ship! It's brought an ill wind— I've been struck down ever since you landed upon these shores," he croaked, holding on to the *shoji* for support.

He looked Jack in the eye.

"A word of warning, Jack Fletcher. Never forget your savior is a samurai. The samurai are a gifted but utterly ruthless people. Step out of line and he'll cut you into eight pieces."

CHAPTER 14

THE SUMMONS

JACK SPENT that afternoon in the garden.

He still couldn't quite believe that he'd been adopted by a samurai. He supposed he should be grateful. He had food and shelter, and the household no longer treated him like some stray dog they had taken in. Jack felt more like an honored guest. Taka-san had even bowed to him.

Yet he did not belong here. He was a stranger in a land of warriors, kimonos, and *sencha*. The question, though, was where did he belong?

With his father and mother both dead, he had no home to speak of. His sister was living with their neighbor Mrs. Winters, but what would happen when the money his father gave the woman to look after her ran out? Or if the old woman died? Jack needed to find a way home so he could be there for Jess. But with England on the far side of the world, there was no conceivable way a boy of twelve could sail across two oceans, even with his father's rutter.

Despite the heat of the day, Jack shuddered with the helplessness of his situation. He was stuck in Japan until he discovered a ship bound for England, or was old enough to strike out on his own.

Staying was a matter of survival, not choice.

He sat down under the shade of a cherry blossom tree and contemplated the fragile hope the rutter held for him.

Jack could distinctly recall the intense excitement he had felt when his father had first handed him the leather-bound book. The rutter had seemed heavy with knowledge and secrets. When he had opened it, Jack swore he could smell the ocean in its pages.

Inside were intricate hand-drawn maps, compass bearings between ports and headlands, observations of the depth and nature of the seabed; there were detailed reports of his father's voyages; places where there were friends, and the ports where there were foes; reefs were pinpointed, tides marked, havens circled, and on every page secret ciphers that protected the knowledge of safe passage from enemy eyes.

"A rutter for a pilot," his father had told him, "is the

equivalent of a Bible for a priest."

Jack had listened, rapt, while his father explained how it was easy enough to work out latitude by the position of the stars, but it was still impossible to fix longitude to any degree of certainty. This meant that once a ship was out of sight of land, it was for all intents and purposes lost. Any sea voyage was consequently fraught with danger. Unless . . .

"Unless," his father had said, "you have a rutter. This book, my son, contains all the knowledge you will ever need to guide a ship safely across the seas. These notes were obtained at great cost to life and limb. Now, every time I complete a sailing, I add my own observations. This rutter is invaluable. There are only a few truly accurate ones in existence. Possess this book and you rule the seas! And that is why our enemies, the Portuguese, would dearly love to get their hands on a rutter such as this . . . at any cost. . . ."

Now it was Jack's.

The rutter was his sole link to his previous life. To his father. Indeed it contained his only real hope of getting home, a tenuous thread of directions that circumnavigated the world.

As Jack flicked through its pages, a loose piece of parchment fell to the ground. Jack picked it up. The parchment, brittle with sea salt, its edges tattered and worn from repeated handling, revealed a childish drawing of four figures in a little garden with a square house. Jack immediately recognized it.

There was his father, tall with a black scribble of windswept hair, himself with an unfeasibly large head and a mop of chalky hair, his little sister in a smock, one hand waving, the other holding Jack's hand, and above them all in the center of the picture was his mother, complete with angel wings.

Jess had drawn the picture and given it to their father the day they had left England for the Japans. Jack choked back tears, trying not to cry. How would Jess cope when she knew her father was dead too?

Jack looked up from the hand-drawn picture of his family, suddenly aware he was being watched. The black-haired boy was staring at him from the house. *How long had he been there?*

Jack wiped his eyes, then acknowledged the boy with a brief bow. That was the polite thing to do. The boy ignored him.

What grudge does he hold against me? thought Jack. The boy was clearly of some standing, having arrived with Masamoto, but he had not yet introduced himself, and he had been hostile toward Jack from the start.

Then Akiko rounded the house with Jiro, who was excitedly brandishing a slip of paper, and the black-haired boy slid the *shoji* shut. Jack folded up his sister's picture and placed it carefully back inside the rutter.

Akiko bowed to Jack before taking the paper from Jiro and respectfully handing it to Jack with both hands.

"*Arigatō*," said Jack, thanking her.

"*Dōmo*," she replied.

Jack was frustrated that he could not communicate with her any further. He now had so much he wanted to say, questions he needed answered. He was surrounded by gracious strangers, yet utterly isolated by language. His impromptu lesson with Akiko the previous evening had been the closest he'd come to a proper conversation with these people since his fever had broken some two weeks ago.

Jack opened the note and read the message inside.

Your presence is required. Please come to my quarters directly following breakfast tomorrow. I reside at the fourth house to the left of the jetty.

Father Lucius

Jack leaned back against the tree. What could Father Lucius possibly want with him?

CHAPTER 15

YAMATO

FATHER LUCIUS'S HOUSE was a small affair, set back from the main road. Taka-san, the samurai from Jack's house, rang the bell hanging by the gate and waited for a response.

Jack heard shuffling footsteps, then the gate swung back. Father Lucius appeared, bleary-eyed and wheezing.

"Welcome to my humble home, heretic. Do enter," he said, eyeing Jack distastefully and beckoning him in with a half-hearted wave of the hand.

Jack stepped through the gateway and into a small garden that bore little resemblance to Uekiya's paradise. This was a muddy patch of root vegetables and herbs. There were no ornamental features or pretty little streams, just a solitary apple tree bearing the beginnings of a few fruit. The garden was clearly for growing, not contemplation.

Taka-san, having delivered Jack, bowed and left.

Father Lucius led Jack into a small room, simply furnished with a table, two chairs, and a makeshift altar. A large wooden crucifix adorned the back wall.

"Take a seat," instructed Father Lucius, who settled himself into the chair on the opposite side of the table. He coughed sporadically into his handkerchief.

"How is the young samurai today?" asked Father Lucius dryly.

"Why have you summoned me?" Jack said, ignoring the priest's jibe.

"I am to teach you Japanese."

"Why?" asked Jack, incredulous. "You didn't seem too willing to help me yesterday."

"It is wise to do what Masamoto asks of you." He looked Jack in the eye. "We shall begin at this time every morning. You will do as I say, when I say. Perhaps you can even be saved."

"I don't need saving."

Father Lucius slammed the flat of his hand on the table. "God protect you from your ignorance. We shall start. The sooner you know their language, the sooner you can hang yourself with your own tongue!"

He wiped his mouth of spittle, then continued. "The key to the Japanese is their language. It has a vocabulary and sentence structure all of its own. In a word, it is unique. It reflects their whole way of thinking. Understand Japanese, and you understand them. Do you follow so far?"

"Yes. I have to think like a Japanese person to speak it."

"Excellent. I see your mother taught you to listen, at least."

Father Lucius reached behind and slid back a small panel in the wall to reveal a cupboard, from which he removed a thick book, paper, a quill, and ink. He laid them upon the desk and began the lesson.

"Compared with other languages, Japanese is relatively simple to speak. On the surface, it is less complex than English. There are no articles preceding nouns, no *a*, *an*, or *the*. The word *hon* may mean *book*, *the book*, *a book*, *books*, or *the books*."

Jack was already beginning to think that a Jesuit sermon would have been less painful than learning Japanese.

"There are no conjugations or infinitives of verbs . . ." Father Lucius stopped abruptly. "Why aren't you writing any of this down? I thought you were educated."

Jack begrudgingly picked up the quill as instructed, dipped it in the ink pot, and began to write.

By the time Taka-san returned to collect him, Jack's head had become a jumble of verbs and Japanese idiosyncrasies. But he refused to appear fazed by Father Lucius's teaching, and made a show of greeting Taka-san in halting Japanese.

Taka-san looked puzzled, blinked, then smiled as he recognized Jack's heavily accented Japanese greeting.

They returned to Hiroko's house, and immediately after lunch Jack was ushered into Masamoto's room.

Masamoto sat on a raised platform, dominating the room like a temple god on a sacred shrine. The black-haired boy was there too, silent and brooding by his side.

To Jack's dismay, Father Lucius entered through the other *shoji* and knelt opposite Jack. He had been summoned to interpret again.

"How was your lesson with Father Lucius?" asked Masamoto, through the priest.

"*Ii desu yo, arigatō gozaimasu,*" replied Jack, hoping he had pronounced the words correctly to say "Very good, thank you very much."

Masamoto nodded appreciatively. "Jack, you are a quick learner. That is good," he continued, his words translated by a malcontented Father Lucius, who scowled at Jack. "I have to return to Kyoto. I have my school to attend to. You will remain here in Toba until your arm has healed. My sister will look after you well, and I hope you will be fluent in Japanese by my return."

"*Hai*, Masamoto-sama," Jack replied when Father Lucius had finished translating.

"It is my intention to be back in Toba before the

winter sets in. Now I introduce to you my second son, Yamato. He's to stay here with you. Every boy needs a friend—and he will be yours. For in truth, you are brothers now."

The black-haired boy bowed curtly, his eyes trained on Jack's. Hard and challenging, they delivered a clear message: Jack would never be worthy of replacing his brother, Tenno, and he had no intention of being Jack's friend . . . *ever*.

CHAPTER 16

THE *BOKKEN*

THE CHERRY BLOSSOM tree in the center of the garden marked Jack's time in Japan. When he arrived, it had been lush and green, a cool haven where he'd sheltered from the hot summer sun. Now, three months later, his arm completely healed, the tree's leaves had turned a golden brown and were starting to fall to the ground.

The tree was Jack's place of sanctuary. He had sat there for hours studying his father's rutter, examining the meticulously drawn constellations, tracing the outlines of coastal maps, and on every page trying to unlock the secret ciphers that protected the mysteries of the seas from enemy eyes. One day, his father had promised, he would be given the answers to all these codes. But now his father was dead. Jack had only his wits to work the rest of them out, and with each one he managed to solve, the closer he would feel to his father.

The tree was also a symbolic bridge, a link through which he had slowly come to understand the Japanese culture. For it was here that he met with Akiko most afternoons to practice speaking her language.

Three days after Masamoto had left for Kyoto, she had heard Jack struggling to pronounce a Japanese phrase that Father Lucius had given him and had offered to help.

"*Arigatō*, Akiko," he had replied, repeating the corrected phrase several times to etch it into his memory.

So their afternoons had begun, and combined with Father Lucius's lessons, his Japanese improved rapidly. Akiko had been a lifeline to him. With each passing week, Jack had been able to converse more and more fluently.

Yamato, on the other hand, in spite of his father's edict, had maintained an icy distance. Jack could have been invisible, for all the boy cared.

"Why doesn't Yamato speak to me?" he had asked Akiko one day. "Did I do something wrong?"

"No, Jack," she replied with deliberate courtesy. "He's your friend."

"Only because Masamoto has ordered everyone to be nice to me," Jack shot back.

"He hasn't ordered me," she said, a flicker of hurt showing in her eyes.

Jack, realizing he had been rude, tried desperately to think of the appropriate Japanese words with which to apologize. Apologizing, Father Lucius had explained to Jack, was considered virtuous in Japan. While Europeans viewed an apology to be an admission of guilt or failure, the Japanese saw it as taking responsibility for one's actions instead of blaming others. When someone apologized and showed remorse, the Japanese would forgive and not hold a grudge.

"I'm sorry, Akiko," Jack had eventually said. "You have been very kind to me."

She bowed, accepting his apology, and they had continued with their conversation, his prickly remark forgotten.

Today, as he approached the spot to begin his studies, Jack noticed that the cherry blossom tree had shed more leaves, leaving a golden carpet beneath its branches. Uekiya was sweeping them away, stuffing the dead leaves into an old sack.

Jack picked the rake up off the ground and started helping the old man.

"This is not work for samurai," stated the gardener gently, taking the rake out of Jack's hands.

At that moment, Akiko crossed the bridge and made her way over to them. She wore a lilac kimono dotted with ivory flowers and tied with a yellow-gold *obi*. Jack could never quite get used to how well presented

Japanese women were. The linen smocks and plain-colored woollen gowns worn by English women were dull and unattractive in comparison.

Jack and Akiko settled beneath the tree, and Uekiya, bowing, moved away to tend one of his already perfectly pruned bushes. They began their afternoon lesson. But before they had progressed very far, Jack asked her about the gardener's strange comment to him.

"How can I be samurai? I don't even have a sword."

"Being samurai is not only about wielding a sword. True, samurai are warriors, for we are *bushi*, the warrior class. As Masamoto's adopted son, you are *bushi*, too." Akiko paused to allow her words to sink in. "And samurai means 'to serve.' A samurai's loyalty is to the Emperor first and then to his *daimyo*. It is about duty. And your duty is to Masamoto. Not to the garden."

"I still don't understand," he said. What other duties would Masamoto require of him? Was he tied to this samurai for life?

"You will. Being samurai is a state of mind. Masamoto will teach you this."

As Jack tried to grasp Akiko's meaning, Yamato strode out of the house carrying a shaft of dark wood. It was about the length of his arm; one-third of it rounded into a sturdy handle, the other two-thirds hewn into a long blade that curved slightly toward its tip.

"What's that he's carrying?" asked Jack.

"A *bokken*. It's a wooden sword."

Yamato saw them, bowed stiffly, then marched over to a clear patch of garden.

"What? A toy sword!" Jack laughed, seeing Yamato whirl the *bokken* above his head and execute a vicious strike on an imaginary opponent.

"Toy? No, a *bokken* is no toy," said Akiko, suddenly serious. "It can kill a man. Masamoto-sama himself has defeated more than thirty samurai using a *bokken* against their swords."

"So what is Yamato doing now? It looks like playing to me."

Yamato had repeated the strike, then followed it with a series of cuts and blocks.

"*Kata*. They are set patterns of movements that help a samurai to perfect his martial art skills. Yamato is learning the art of sword fighting."

"Well, if I am a samurai, I had better learn how to fight too," said Jack, adjusting his kimono and standing.

Ignoring Akiko's protests, Jack strode over to where Yamato was practicing. He watched with interest, studying his moves and technique. All the while, Yamato ignored him and continued to parry and thrust at his imaginary opponent.

"May I try?" asked Jack, when Yamato had apparently decapitated his attacker with a powerful crosscut.

Yamato slid the *bokken* into his *obi* and inspected

Jack as if he were a fresh recruit. For a moment Jack thought the boy would refuse in order to prove his authority over him.

"Why not, *gaijin*," said Yamato, with a look of haughty amusement. "It would be good to have a target to practice on. Jiro," he called, "fetch a *bokken* for the *gaijin*!"

The little boy came scampering out of the house, struggling with the wooden sword in his arms. Jiro gave the enormous weapon to Yamato, who, bowing with his two hands outstretched, offered the *bokken* to Jack.

Jack stepped forward to take it.

"NO! You must bow when given the honor of using another's sword."

Jack seethed at Yamato's command, but did as he was told. He dearly wanted to handle the weapon, to know how to use it the way Masamoto had wielded his two swords on the beach.

"And take it with two hands," instructed Yamato in a patronizing tone, as if Jack were a little boy.

Jack found the wooden sword to be surprisingly heavy. He could now appreciate how such a weapon could inflict damage devastating enough to kill.

"NO! Blade down," corrected Yamato, when Jack held the *bokken* out in front of him as he had seen Yamato do. He turned the *bokken* the right way up in Jack's hands.

"Don't let the *kissaki* drop!" Yamato rolled his eyes in disbelief at Jack's ignorance.

"*Kissaki?*" questioned Jack.

"The tip of the *bokken*. Keep it in line with your opponent's throat. One foot forward. One foot back. Wider. You must stand strong."

Warming to his role as teacher, Yamato paced around Jack, fastidiously adjusting Jack's stance and form until he was satisfied.

"That'll have to do. First, we will practice *kihon*— the basics. A simple parry and strike."

Yamato stood opposite Jack and lined his *kissaki* up with Jack's. An instant later he struck Jack's *bokken*. The weapon shuddered in Jack's hands, sending a wave of pain up his arm and forcing him to drop it. Yamato's blade struck forward and stopped a hair's breadth from Jack's throat. Yamato stared contemptuously into Jack's face, daring him to move.

"Don't they teach you how to fight where you come from? You hold it like a girl," admonished Yamato, who was enjoying belittling Jack in front of Akiko and Jiro. He obviously relished the feeling of superiority it gave him, so much so that he failed to notice Akiko's wide-eyed horror at his behavior.

No matter, thought Jack. He would soon learn how to use the *bokken*, and then he could teach Yamato a lesson or two.

"Pick it up. Don't grip with your thumb and fore-finger next time. That's weak; your hold can be broken easily. Look at mine. Put the little finger of your left hand around the base of the handle. Then wrap the rest of your fingers around the hilt. The bottom two fingers should be tight. Your right hand should be just below the guard, and grip it in the same manner as your left. This is correct *tenouchi*."

Once Jack had mastered the grip, Yamato repeated the attack. This time Jack kept hold of the *bokken*.

"Good. Now you try."

Jack found the movement of the strike awkward at first. It was difficult to get enough force behind the parry, but Yamato made him repeat the movement again and again until the technique began to flow.

They practiced through the afternoon, Yamato teaching Jack three other *kihon* moves: a basic cut, an evasive maneuver, and a simple defensive block. The *kata* training was surprisingly hard work, and after a while Jack began to tire. Having done little physical exercise since his time on board the ship, the *bokken* was begin-ning to feel like lead in his hands. Yamato was clearly pleased to see Jack flagging.

"Want to try some *randori* now?" challenged Yamato.

"What's that?" said Jack, out of breath.

"Free-sparring. Best out of three?"

"Excuse me, Yamato," interrupted Akiko, hoping

to avert the trouble she saw coming. "May I suggest that you both join me for *sencha*? You've practiced so much—you should rest."

"No, thank you, Akiko. I'm not thirsty. But Jack looks like he could do with a rest."

Jack knew Yamato was trying to break him. Jack recognized this moment from his time on board the *Alexandria*. The men who had not stood up for themselves during the first week ended up being the ones last in line for food; the ones shoved to the hammocks nearest the bilge; the ones lumbered with the worst duties, like scrubbing the scuppers where the crew relieved themselves. Jack had to prove he was not someone who could be beaten easily. If he backed down now, he would be trying to regain his ground forever.

"No, thank you, Akiko. I'm not tired."

"But your arm?" she insisted. "It's not wise to—"

"I'll be fine," said Jack, politely cutting her off before turning back to Yamato. "*Randori*, eh? Best out of three. Why not?"

They faced off, *kissaki* touching.

Jack's hands were slippery with sweat. He tried to remember the moves: the footwork, the parry, the block, the strike. He readied himself, but Yamato struck first. He knocked Jack's *bokken* aside and slammed his own down onto Jack's exposed fingers. Jack cried out in shock and pain, dropping his *bokken*.

"Too slow," said Yamato, a sadistic smile spreading across his face. "I could see you *thinking* the move before you made it."

Jack bent to pick up his weapon. His fingers throbbed and he had difficulty closing his hand around the *bokken*. He gritted his teeth and lined up his *kissaki* again.

This time he saw Yamato's *bokken* twitch, and stepped back to evade the first cut. Yamato brought his *bokken* around for a second time, and Jack, more by luck than design, blocked his strike. This infuriated Yamato, who piled in with a vicious thrust, which Jack only managed to avoid by twisting away. Yamato hit Jack hard across the back. The blow sent Jack to his knees, his kidneys flaring up in pain, and his lungs feeling like they had collapsed.

"Two–nothing," gloated Yamato as Jack writhed on the ground in agony. "A bit of advice. Never turn your back on your opponent."

"Enough, Yamato," broke in Akiko. "He doesn't know how to fight with a *bokken* yet. He can't defend himself!"

Winded and stiff with pain, Jack dragged himself to his feet, using the *bokken* as a crutch. He refused to give in. This was the actual moment he had to prove himself. He'd always known he wouldn't win, but *he* had to draw the line for when they stopped, *not* Yamato. With an effort, he raised his sword.

Yamato looked dumbfounded. "Don't be stupid. Best out of three. I won."

"What? Scared I might beat you?"

The direct challenge spurred Yamato into action, and he instantly fell into guard.

Knowing Yamato was watching for telltale signs of his first move, Jack feigned a strike to the left like he had seen the warrior Godai do with the *nodachi* on the beach. Yamato went to block it, and Jack switched offensive, bringing his *bokken* around hard to the right.

Yamato was thrown off guard and had to block awkwardly, so much so that Jack's sword cut across his right hand. Inflamed by the unexpected contact, Yamato retaliated with a flurry of blows. They rained down on Jack, who managed to avoid the first two and miraculously block the third, but the fourth cracked him across the face.

It was as if someone had cut the connection between his brain and the rest of his body. His legs crumpled and he collapsed to the floor. His head rang in agony, and little flashes of light sparked across his eyes.

Akiko was immediately by his side, calling for Chiro to bring water and towels to stem the blood dripping from his nose. Jiro was pulling on Jack's sleeve, upset by the unexpected violence. Even Taka-san had appeared and was bending over Jack with concern.

Jack could see Yamato standing alone, a thunderous look on his face as everyone disregarded his victory. Jack may have been beaten, but he had still won in the end.

CHAPTER 17

GAIJIN

"WHAT HAPPENED TO YOU?" wheezed Father Lucius from his bed.

"I had a fight," said Jack defensively, unable to hide the bruises ringing his eyes.

"Looks like you lost. I warned you that samurai could be ruthless."

Father Lucius sat up, hacking into his handkerchief. The coughing and yellow sputum were now accompanied by a fever and shaking chills. Mindful of Masamoto's order, Father Lucius insisted that Jack have his lessons, despite the fatigue that often overwhelmed him. But after only a few sentences, they had to stop.

"Jack, I'm afraid this sickness is defeating me in spite of all the teas, herbs, and ointments the local doctor can administer. Even their medicines are no match for this . . ."

Pain racked the priest's face as he broke into a coughing fit and put a pale hand to his chest. Slowly the coughing subsided, only to be replaced by labored wheezing.

"I'm sorry, Father," said Jack, sincerely feeling pity for the sick priest. During the course of their lessons, Father Lucius's icy demeanor toward him had thawed, allowing for a wary friendship. His apparent change of heart meant that the priest no longer called him a heretic, though Jack was still loath to trust him completely.

"No need for pity, Jack. I have done my duty on this earth and will soon be rightfully rewarded in heaven." He made the sign of the cross on his chest. "I'll be better tomorrow, but today you must teach yourself. Please hand me my book."

Jack reached across to the table and passed the priest his thick notebook.

"This is my life's work," he said, gently caressing its soft leather binding. "A Japanese–Portuguese dictionary. I have been compiling this book ever since I came to the Japans over ten years ago. It is the key to unlocking their language and their way of thinking. Using it, the Brotherhood can bring the Word of the Lord to every island of Japan."

Religious fervor shone in Father Lucius's rheumy eyes.

"It's the only one in existence," he said, fixing Jack with a grave look. He studied Jack for several moments before offering the book to him with a shaky hand.

"Would you take care of it for me, and if I am to pass from this world, will you ensure that it is placed in the hands of His Eminence Father Diego Bobadilla, in Osaka?"

"Yes, Father," promised Jack, unable to refuse the man's dying wish. "It would be an honor."

"No, it would be mine. You have been a good pupil, in spite of your beliefs. Your mother must have been a fine teacher. With Akiko's continued assistance, you'll be speaking as fluently as a natural-born Japanese boy before the turn of the year."

He smiled graciously at Jack, then continued in an unusually honeyed tone.

"Perhaps you would be so kind as to let me look at your father's diary? I fear my days on this earth are shortening, and it would give me great pleasure to read of another's worldly adventures."

Jack immediately stiffened. Had the offer of the dictionary been a ploy to get the rutter?

Jack remembered the way the Jesuit's eyes had gleamed with desire when it had first been presented by Masamoto. Since that day Father Lucius had often mentioned his father's diary during their lessons. *Was it safe? Where did Jack keep it? Would he care to regale him with one of his father's stories? Would he show him a page from the diary?* The priest clearly wanted the rutter, if not for himself, then most certainly for the Brotherhood.

Jack felt a small spike of anger at Father Lucius's request, and wondered whether the priest's change of heart had been genuine at all, or merely a ruse to obtain his precious rutter.

"I am sorry, Father Lucius," replied Jack coldly, "but as you know, it is private and the only remaining possession of my beloved father."

"I know, I know. No matter." The Father seemed too weary to pursue the issue any further. "I will see you again tomorrow?"

"Yes, Father. Of course."

That afternoon under the cherry blossom tree, Jack leafed through the pages of the dictionary. Father Lucius had been right to speak so proudly of his work. It contained reams of Japanese words together with their Portuguese equivalents, detailed notes on grammar, directions for correct pronunciation, and guidance on proper Japanese etiquette. It was truly his magnum opus.

"Excuse me, Jack," said Akiko, approaching him from across the little bridge. "I hope I'm not disturbing you."

"No, not at all," said Jack, putting the dictionary down. "I thought you were going pearl diving today."

"No, not today," said Akiko, with a soft disappointed sigh. She picked at one of the cherry blossom leaves and examined it intently.

"Why not? You usually do, don't you?"

"Yes . . ." She hesitated, clearly considering whether it was appropriate to confide in Jack. Then, apparently making up her mind, she discarded the leaf and knelt down beside him.

"Mother says that I'm too old to be associating with such people now. She says being an *ama* is not fitting for a lady of the samurai class, and she forbids it."

"Not fitting? Why would she say that?"

"Pearl diving can be very dangerous. *Ama* can get caught in riptides or attacked by sharks. That's why only lower-caste villagers do work like that."

"So why do you do it?" asked Jack, somewhat amazed by her revelation.

"I like it," said Akiko emphatically, a keen fire lighting up in her eyes. "Down there you get to see all sorts of sea creatures: octopus, sea urchins, and sometimes even sharks. Under the water, I can go where I want. Do what I want. I feel free."

"I know exactly what you mean," agreed Jack. "I felt the same way when the *Alexandria* was under full sail and I was allowed to stand on its prow. It was like riding the crests of the waves!"

They dropped into a silent reverie while gazing up at

the autumn brown leaves of the cherry blossom tree, sunlight dappling their upturned faces.

"Are you feeling better today?" asked Akiko after a while.

"I'm fine, thank you. Yamato didn't hit me that hard anyway," he replied with obvious bravado.

Akiko gave him a doubtful look.

"Well, my nose hurts," Jack finally admitted, "and I still have a headache, but I'm much better today."

"I'm responsible. I shouldn't have let you get involved," said Akiko, bowing. "I apologize for Yamato's behavior. He should not have acted like he did."

"Why are you apologizing? It wasn't your fault."

"Because it happened in my house. I'm sure Yamato didn't mean to harm you. He merely got carried away in the heat of the moment."

"Well, I'd hate to see Yamato when he did mean it," said Jack vehemently.

"I'm so sorry. You must understand, Jack, Yamato is under great pressure from his father. Ever since Tenno was killed, Masamoto expects Yamato to be as skilled a samurai as his brother was, despite being younger. But that doesn't excuse his actions or excuse him for calling you *gaijin*. I am so sorry."

"Will you stop apologizing for him!" said Jack, somewhat exasperated. "And why does it matter that he calls me *gaijin*?"

"*Gaijin* is the name we give to uncivilized foreigners—it means barbarian. It's not very nice, and now that you are a member of his family, Yamato is wrong to use such a disrespectful term. It is an insult."

At that moment, Yamato strode out of the house, *bokken* tucked inside his *obi*. He gave a purposeful bow in Akiko's direction, but disregarded Jack's presence entirely.

Jack watched Yamato begin his *kata* routine, then decided his own course of action. He packed away Father Lucius's dictionary and stood up.

"Where are you going?" asked Akiko, concerned.

"To get some more practice in," said Jack, walking over to where Yamato had commenced his second *kata*.

"Back for more?" asked Yamato incredulously, without halting the thrust to the gut of his imaginary opponent.

"Why not? I can't do any worse than yesterday."

"You certainly have spirit, for a *gaijin*," said Yamato, noting with mild amusement the effect the insult now had upon Jack.

Jack bit back a retort. He didn't want to ruin his chances of learning something from his rival.

Yamato called for Jiro to retrieve another *bokken* from the house.

"Follow what I do. Exactly," instructed Yamato when they both held weapons in hand.

Yamato stood, his feet together, heels touching. He had slipped his *bokken* through his *obi* on his left-hand side. His left hand, grasping it just below the hilt, kept it firmly in place by his hip.

"Other way up," he said, nodding at Jack's *bokken.* "The blade edge should face the sky, so that when you withdraw the sword you are immediately able to make your cut."

Jack turned the *bokken* over so that the curved edge of the wooden blade was pointing up.

"Good. Now watch me."

Yamato moved his right hand across his waist and gripped the handle. His right leg slid forward, dropping into a wide stance. Simultaneously he whipped out his *bokken*, grasping it with both hands, and sliced down. He drove forward another step, lifting the *kissaki* up to his imaginary victim's throat. The attack completed, he then twisted the *bokken* with a sharp one-handed flick to the right before stepping up carefully and resheathing his weapon.

"Now your turn."

Jack went to mimic Yamato's movements, but had not even grabbed the hilt before he was interrupted.

"No! Your hand must stay close to your body. If you have it out there, your enemy will just chop it off."

Jack began again. At every stage, Yamato stopped him to correct his movements. Jack quickly grew frustrated. There was so much to think about, and Yamato was unflinching in his criticism.

"What's the final flick for?" asked Jack irritably.

"That move is called *chiburi*," replied Yamato, giving a sadistic smile. "It shakes your enemy's blood from the blade."

The whole afternoon was spent repeating that single *kata*. Jack progressed through each step of the sequence until he was able to execute it in one complete move. He was by no means fluid, but he had learned the core techniques. The sun was already beginning to set when Yamato brought the session to an end.

"*Arigatō*, Yamato," said Jack, bowing courteously.

"*Dōmo, gaijin.*"

"My name is Jack." He held Yamato's imperious look, challenging him to show appropriate respect.

"Your name is *gaijin* until you prove otherwise," Yamato said, resheathing his *bokken*.

Yamato then spun on his heels and disappeared into the house without returning Jack's bow.

CHAPTER 18

BEST OUT OF THREE

THE NEXT DAY Jack arrived early in the garden to make sure he was practicing the *kata* before Yamato turned up. Yamato made no comment, but Jack's point had been made. He would not be put off *bokken* practice, however disrespectfully Yamato behaved.

Yamato fell in beside Jack and began to synchronize his training with Jack's.

Yamato was by no means a skilled martial artist. He had only been training properly for a year. But he had clearly inherited some of his father's ability with a weapon and knew enough to teach Jack the basics of *kenjutsu*—the art of the sword.

As autumn gave way to winter, Jack improved steadily. At first the various *kata* moves were awkward and stilted, but gradually they began to flow, and the *bokken* became a natural extension of his arms. Even Yamato could not deny Jack's progress. Their *randori* became more evenly matched, and each time, Yamato needed greater skill to defeat Jack.

Akiko, however, did not approve of Jack's decision to train with Yamato. She thought Jack should wait until Masamoto returned. Masamoto could train him properly in the art of the *bokken* and without Jack constantly getting injured. However, Akiko soon realized Jack would not be dissuaded, and resigned herself to administering herbal ointments for the numerous cuts and bruises he sustained during *randori*.

As a compromise, Akiko had insisted that if Jack was to train in the martial arts of the samurai, then he should also acquaint himself with the more refined aspects of what it meant to be a samurai: in particular, formal Japanese etiquette. She reminded Jack that Masamoto would expect him, as his adopted son, to be well versed in their ways, and that Jack should not disappoint him.

Akiko demonstrated the accepted ways of bowing, sitting, and rising in the presence of a samurai and master of the household. She showed him the correct manner in which to offer and receive gifts, using both hands. She helped Jack perfect his Japanese language skills, detailing the correct forms of address when meeting people of differing status and relationships.

Jack thought his head would explode during each and every one of Akiko's etiquette lessons. There were so many customs and codes of behavior that he was almost paralyzed for fear of offending someone.

Perhaps this was the reason why he enjoyed *randori* with Yamato so much. It allowed him to be free, to control, in some small way, his own actions and destiny.

"Best out of three?" challenged Jack one day as the first dusting of snow settled over the garden.

"Why not, *gaijin*?" said Yamato, taking up his fighting stance.

Akiko, who was teaching Jiro to trace *kanji*, the Japanese form of writing, in the snow, gave them her usual disapproving look before returning to Jiro's studies.

Jack checked his posture, adjusted his grip, and raised his *kissaki*. Yamato immediately struck, parrying Jack's *bokken* clear as he surged forward. Jack swept his body sideways, evading the blade, and brought his own weapon around on Yamato.

Yamato effortlessly blocked it and countered with a rising cut. Jack jumped back, the *kissaki* barely missing his chin. He heard Akiko let out a worried gasp.

Yamato drove forward and caught Jack on the shoulder with a downward strike. Jack winced under the blow.

"One to me," said Yamato, relishing his victory.

They faced off.

Jack did not make the same mistake this time—he came in straight for the kill. He knocked Yamato's *bokken* aside, thrusting the *kissaki* into Yamato's face. Yamato stumbled backward to avoid being stabbed. He slashed wildly with his *bokken* in retaliation, and Jack had to retreat to avoid getting caught by the flurry of blows.

Jack baited him by lowering his *kissaki*. Yamato spotted the opening and, raising his *bokken* high, sliced down at Jack's exposed head. Jack slipped to Yamato's outside and cut across his stomach. Yamato crumpled, defeated by the unexpected maneuver.

Jiro, who had lost interest in Akiko's *kanji* lesson as soon as the *randori* had commenced, let out a loud whoop, shouting "Jack won! First time! Jack won!"

"One all, I believe," said Jack as he helped the winded Yamato back to his feet.

"Lucky strike, *gaijin*," wheezed Yamato, shrugging off Jack's helping hand.

Incensed at his lapse of judgement, Yamato broke with fighting etiquette and attacked Jack without waiting to match guards.

He swiftly struck at Jack's *bokken* and cut down at Jack's neck. Jack retreated to avoid taking a blow to the head. He managed to spin out of harm's reach, backpedalling to create distance between them. Yamato cut across at Jack's feet, forcing Jack to jump the blade. Jack

lost his balance but somehow blocked Yamato's returning strike to his stomach.

"*Yamato . . . !*" reprimanded Akiko, but he resolutely
ignored her.

Yamato slammed his *bokken* up under Jack's,
knocking it out of Jack's grip. He then kicked Jack hard
in the chest, throwing him back against the cherry blossom tree.

Pressing forward his attack, Yamato swung his
weapon directly at Jack's head. At the last second, more
out of instinct than design, Jack ducked and felt the tree
shudder as the *bokken* collided with the trunk, a shower
of snow dropping from its branches.

Jack realized that the fight had turned serious, and
he charged forward with all his might, driving his
shoulder into Yamato's gut. Yamato flew back, and they
landed in a heap.

"Enough! Enough!" pleaded Akiko, while Jiro jumped
up and down with excitement at the escalating fight.

Jack rolled off, desperately searching for his *bokken*.
He saw it at the foot of the bridge and scrambled for
it. Yamato immediately pursued Jack, screaming at the
top of his lungs, his *bokken* held high and primed to
strike.

Jack snatched up his weapon and, ignoring Akiko's
cries for calm, ran past her onto the bridge. Hearing
Yamato close on his heels, Jack turned on the spot,

slicing his *bokken* through the air at Yamato's approaching head. Also aiming for Jack's head, Yamato collided with Jack's *bokken*, and the blades shuddered to a halt, inches from one another's throats.

"Draw!" shouted Jiro in delight.

At that very moment, Taka-san appeared, and the two fighters lowered their *bokken*.

"Jack-kun!" he called, approaching the three of them. "Father Lucius requests your attendance. Urgently."

Jack knew that it could only mean one thing.

He bowed to Yamato and Akiko, then hurried after Taka-san.

Entering Father Lucius's room, Jack was struck by an overpowering stench of vomit, stale sweat, and urine. It reeked of mortality.

A guttering candle feebly lit the gloom. From the far corner, he could hear the priest's labored breathing.

"Father Lucius?"

Jack edged closer to the shadowy figure lying supine on the futon. His foot came into contact with something in the darkness, and looking down he saw a small bucket brimming with vomit. Jack gagged but forced himself to bend over the bed.

The candlelight spluttered then flared, and Jack was confronted with the hollow, shriveled face of Father Lucius.

The priest's skin was a pallid blue, and moist with oily sweat. His hair, thin and streaked with gray, was plastered in limp strands over his sunken cheeks. Specks of blood mottled his cracked lips, and there were now permanent black shadows under his eyes.

"Father Lucius?" said Jack, almost hoping the priest was already dead and no longer suffering such torment.

"Jack?" croaked Father Lucius, his pale tongue running the length of his cracked lips.

"Yes, Father?"

"I must ask for your forgiveness. . . ."

"For what?"

"I'm sorry, Jack . . . son of a heretic though you are . . . you have spirit. . . ."

He spoke in short bursts, taking harsh wheezing breaths in between each utterance. Jack listened, saddened by the pitiful state of the priest. He was Jack's last link to the far side of the world, and despite the constant preaching Jack had been forced to endure during their lessons, he had come to respect the man.

"I misjudged you . . . I enjoyed our lessons . . . I wish I could have saved you. . . ."

"Don't worry about me, Father," consoled Jack. "My own God will look after me. Just as yours will."

Father Lucius let out a small sobbing moan. "I'm sorry . . . I had to tell them . . . It was my duty. . . ." he cried feebly.

"Tell who what?" asked Jack.

"Please understand . . . I didn't know they'd kill for it . . . May God have mercy. . . ."

"What did you say?" urged Jack.

The priest continued to move his lips, trying to say something else, but his words weren't audible.

With the faintest of coughs, Father Lucius exhaled his last breath and died.

CHAPTER 19

MASAMATO'S RETURN

THE CHERRY BLOSSOM tree had shed all its leaves, and its bare branches were burdened with snow, stretching like a skeleton against the sky. Jack walked through the garden, passing beneath its shadow. Death seemed to hang all around. What had Father Lucius meant, *I didn't know they'd kill for it*? Jack presumed he was talking about the rutter. If so, that meant he was in danger. But from whom?

His thoughts were interrupted by a soft voice from behind.

"I'm so sorry for the passing of Father Lucius. You must be very sad to lose your teacher."

Akiko, who was wearing a plain white kimono, appeared suddenly, like a snowflake in a world of white.

"Thank you," he said, bowing, "but I don't think he was really my friend."

"What makes you say that?" gasped Akiko, shocked at his cold sentiment.

Jack took a breath before answering. Could he trust her? Could he trust anyone here? Yet Akiko was the closest he had to a friend. He had no one else to turn to.

"When Father Lucius died," Jack explained, "he said something very strange. He implied someone wanted to kill me, then died weeping and asking for God's forgiveness."

"Why would anyone want to kill you, Jack?" asked Akiko, her nose wrinkling in bewilderment.

Jack considered her. Could his trust extend to revealing his father's rutter? No, he decided, he couldn't tell the whole truth. Not yet, anyway. His father's rutter was the only possession he had of any worth. He could only assume *they* wanted it, but since he didn't know who *they* were, the fewer who knew of its true purpose the better.

"I have no idea. Perhaps they don't like *gaijin*?" lied Jack.

"Who do you mean by 'they'?"

"I don't know. Father Lucius died before he could say any more."

"We should tell someone."

"No! Who'd believe me? They'd say it was the ravings of a dying man."

"But you seem to believe it," said Akiko, eyeing him closely. She knew he wasn't revealing everything. She was no fool, but Jack also knew that Japanese courtesy prevented her from pressing for the answer.

Jack shrugged. "Perhaps I misheard him. I'm not certain what he said."

"Clearly," she said, letting the matter go. "But just in case you did hear right, you should be careful. Keep your *bokken* with you at night. I'll ask my mother to leave a lamp burning. I'll tell her I'm troubled by nightmares. That way any intruder will believe someone is always up."

"Thank you, Akiko. But I'm sure it will turn out to be nothing," said Jack, skeptical of his own words even as he spoke them.

But Jack was right. Nothing happened.

Father Lucius was buried according to his customs, and Jack returned to his routine of Japanese study with Akiko, and *kenjutsu* with Yamato.

A few days later a mounted samurai arrived with a letter announcing Masamoto's return to Toba. He would be here within the week.

The household became a flurry of activity. Hiroko personally visited the market, ensuring Masamoto's favorites would be in the house, and hired additional help for the cook to prepare a celebratory meal. Chiro scrubbed all the floors, washed bedding and kimonos, and prepared Masamoto's room. Uekiya swept the paths and somehow made the garden appear beautiful, even in its stark winter state.

The night before Masamoto was due, the whole household went to bed early, eager to be fresh and alert for the following day. Jiro was almost bouncing off the paper walls with excitement, and it took Hiroko several attempts to settle him.

Yamato's mood, on the other hand, had darkened with his father's imminent arrival, and he practiced his *kata* late into the night, aware that he would have to impress his father greatly to gain favor.

Jack's mind whirled as he lay on his futon, staring at the muted glow of the night lamp through the *shoji*. He had no idea what was expected of him during his audience with Masamoto. Would he have to prove himself like Yamato? Did he have to fight? Was it to be a test of his Japanese language ability? Or was it all these things? Worst of all, what if he caused serious offence through a simple lapse in etiquette?

Masamoto was clearly a man who did not expect to be questioned, and had a killing streak that ran deep in his veins. He was austere and brusque, and his severe scarring put Jack on edge.

Yet all those around Masamoto honored him, and Akiko thought him to be "one of the greatest samurai to have lived." He had reset Jack's broken arm and taken him in as his own son. Jack knew there was more to Masamoto than a scarred face and a swift sword.

A shadow passed in front of the night lamp, briefly darkening Jack's room. Jack tensed, but there appeared to be no one there. There wasn't even the sound of a footstep.

Jack decided it must have been Yamato returning to his quarters, or a breeze dipping the flame. He turned over to settle down to sleep.

He closed his eyes and imagined himself, as he often did at night, standing on the prow of the *Alexandria*, returning home to England, triumphant, with his father piloting the ship, the hold crammed with gold, silk, and exotic Eastern spices, Jess waving to them from the harbor. . . .

Another shadow passed across the room.

Jack opened his eyes, having sensed the room darken. Behind him, he heard the *shoji* slide softly back.

No one ever entered his bedroom during the night. Ever so quietly, Jack reached for the *bokken* by the edge of his futon. He held his breath, listening intently.

There was the unmistakable creak of the wooden veranda and the slightest pad of a foot coming to rest on the *tatami* next to his futon.

Jack spun off of his futon, rolling to one knee while bringing the *bokken* up to defend himself. A flash of silver flew past his face, and a *shuriken* thwacked into a wooden beam behind him.

Jack froze.

Crouched in front of him was the shadow warrior, his single green eye fixed upon Jack.

"Dokugan Ryu!" uttered Jack in disbelief.

CHAPTER 20

AKIKO

DRAGON EYE momentarily faltered at the mention of his name.

Jack seized the initiative. There was no way he could defeat the ninja, but there was still a chance he could escape.

Jack flung himself hard at the outside wall of his bedroom. The thin wooden crossbeams splintered, and the fragile paper tiles disintegrated as his body ripped through the wall.

Semi-stunned by the collision, Jack staggered to his feet, snatched up his *bokken*, and without a backward glance in Dragon Eye's direction, sprinted away down the veranda.

Jack caught a glimpse of two shadows flitting

through the garden, and another entering a room farther ahead.

Akiko! He had to warn her.

The noise of the breaking *shoji* had roused the household, and the cook stepped out onto the veranda to see what was happening. Bleary-eyed and bemused at the young *gaijin* running straight at him, they almost collided, but Jack jumped aside at the last second.

As he did, a second *shuriken* flew over his shoulder and plunged into the neck of the cook. The cook registered a look of mild surprise, shock blocking out the pain of the weapon now embedded in his throat. He gurgled something indecipherable at Jack, then flopped to the floor.

Jack kept running, with Dragon Eye in deadly pursuit.

Jack switched direction and dove through an open *shoji* just as Taka-san emerged brandishing both his swords.

Dragon Eye was caught off guard by Taka-san's sudden appearance. Taka-san, battle-hardened and courageous, gauged the situation in a single glance. With calculated precision he cut at the ninja's head. Dragon Eye evaded the strike, bending as effortlessly as a blade of grass in a breeze, and Taka-san's *katana* sliced through thin air, passing just above the ninja's upturned face.

Then Dragon Eye twisted and let loose a lightning

kick into Taka-san's midriff, which sent the samurai careering into a nearby pillar.

Dragon Eye drew his own sword from the *saya* strapped to his back and advanced on Taka-san.

The *ninjatō*, with its distinctive square *tsuba*—hand guard—had a straighter, shorter blade than the *katana* of the samurai, but was no less deadly. Dragon Eye attacked without remorse.

Taka-san blitzed Dragon Eye with his own barrage of lethal blows, and drove the ninja back along the veranda.

Meanwhile, Jack escaped into another room, only to be confronted by a second ninja. Fortunately for Jack, he was focused on fighting someone else and had his back turned. The ninja's victim suddenly lost his footing and dropped to the floor. Jack glimpsed Yamato's face, drained white with fear, staring up at his assailant. The ninja raised his *ninjatō* to deliver the killing strike.

"Nooooo!" screamed Jack.

All the confusion, fear, pain, and anger he had suffered since his father had been murdered welled up like a volcano.

The ninja were responsible for the death of his father, his friends, his crew, and now they were attacking the only other family he knew. Jack's muscles exploded with burning aggression, and, without thinking, he charged the ninja.

Startled, the ninja spun around, his *ninjatō* at the

ready, but Jack drove his *bokken* down onto the ninja's sword arm with every ounce of strength he possessed. Jack heard a sickening crack as the ninja's wrist snapped. The man howled in pain.

Jack brought his weapon around for a second attack, trying to recall everything Yamato had taught him. He aimed for the ninja's head.

The ninja ducked, then flung himself out of the way, picking up the dropped sword with his undamaged left hand as he rolled. He snarled at Jack, his broken wrist hanging useless by his side.

Jack backed away, suddenly aware of the danger he was in. He was trying to fight a ninja!

The ninja shifted his grip on the sword, and Jack noted that his opponent wasn't comfortable using his left arm. Realizing he would only get one shot at this, Jack prayed that this small advantage would give him the opening he needed. *But where should I strike?* Every time he moved, the ninja countered instantly.

Then Masamoto's duel flashed before his eyes—the bluff that had made Godai overconfident and permitted Masamoto to win.

Jack let his *kissaki* drop, feigning defeat exactly as Masamoto had done.

The ninja, sensing an easy kill, hissed and slid forward. He drew his weapon back to deliver a back-handed slice to Jack's head. At the last second, Jack sideslipped the sword and brought his own *bokken* straight across the man's gut. The ninja buckled to the floor on all fours, heaving like a felled boar. Jack spun around on his heels and brought his *bokken* down hard onto the back of the man's head. With a *thunk*, the ninja dropped unconscious to the *tatami*.

Jack stood over the prone body, astounded at his own strength, his *bokken* trembling uncontrollably in his hands, the adrenaline pumping through his veins.

"Where did you learn that move?" asked Yamato, hurriedly getting to his feet.

"From your father," said Jack, his mouth thick and dry with shock.

"*Arigatō, gaij*—Jack," said Yamato, deliberately correcting himself and giving a brief but respectful bow. Their eyes locked, and for a second an unspoken bond of comradeship passed between them.

"We need to find Akiko," said Jack urgently, breaking the moment.

"*Hai!*" agreed Yamato, running out onto the veranda and along to Akiko's room, Jack following close behind.

Taka-san could still be heard battling with Dragon Eye, and Jack glanced over his shoulder to see Taka-san driving the ninja back toward the little bridge.

"Listen," breathed Yamato, but from the outside, Akiko's room was ominously silent.

Yamato pulled back the *shoji* to reveal the inert body of a girl, her blood spreading in a large red pool on the *tatami*.

"NO! Akiko!" Jack shouted.

She lay facedown on the floor, her arms outstretched as if still trying to hang on to life. Jack knelt beside the body, his eyes welling with hot, angry tears. He reached over and pulled back the hair from her face, revealing the porcelain features of Chiro.

Jack glanced up anxiously at Yamato. Where was Akiko?

They heard movement in the adjoining room. They flung open the inner *shoji* to discover Akiko facing not one but two armed ninja. She held a short staff in one hand and her unwrapped *obi* in the other.

One of the ninja wielded a short *tantō*, the other a *ninjatō*. They attacked simultaneously.

Akiko did not hesitate. She flicked the long band of her *obi* into the eyes of the ninja with the sword. It cracked across his face like a whip, momentarily blinding him. The ninja with the *tantō* surged forward and slashed at her face. In one flowing motion, Akiko blocked it with her short staff, stepped between the two ninja, and chopped her *obi* hand down onto the neck of her assailant. The man, stunned by the blow, dropped his *tantō* and staggered back against the far wall.

The other ninja let out a venomous hiss and ran

at her with his sword. Akiko spun on her attacker and, rapidly twirling her *obi*, wound it around the man's outstretched sword arm. She tugged hard on her *obi*, but in so doing drew his weapon straight toward her.

Jack shouted a warning. But she deftly evaded the blade and purposefully guided it in the direction of the other ninja, who was now so off balance that he couldn't stop his forward momentum, and his sword sunk deep into his comrade's chest.

Akiko had been so quick that Jack and Yamato had barely stepped into the room before it was all over. The ninja withdrew his sword too late. His comrade, choking with blood, slumped dead on the *tatami*.

Turning, he faced the three children—a girl, a boy, and a *gaijin*! They stood their ground, raising their weapons as one. Unnerved by their daring, he shot one glance at his fallen comrade and fled.

"How . . . did you do *that*?" stammered Jack, astounded at Akiko's lightning skills.

"Japanese women don't just wear kimonos, Jack," she replied, indignant at his incredulity.

Outside they heard Taka-san shouting.

"Quick! Taka-san needs help," she said, hurrying to the door ahead of the two boys.

They raced out into the garden just in time to see Dragon Eye run Taka-san through with his sword. The three of them screamed and charged Dragon Eye.

Dragon Eye stepped away from Taka-san's body, pulling his sword out, then turned to confront them. Taka-san crumpled to the ground, clutching his bleeding stomach and hacking up blood. Jack, Akiko, and Yamato formed a protective ring around their wounded friend.

"Young samurai! How novel!" Dragon Eye laughed, amused at the sight of three children wielding weapons.

"Not too young to die, though," he added with sinister malevolence.

Two other ninja emerged from the darkness, weapons at the ready. Jack noted that one of them cradled a broken wrist to his chest. Clearly didn't hit him hard enough, thought Jack bitterly.

"Rutter," hissed Dragon Eye, his solitary green eye flaring at Jack. "Where is it?"

CHAPTER 21

NITEN ICHI RYŪ

"I DON'T KNOW what your talking about," said Jack, thinking on his feet.

Akiko and Yamato exchanged puzzled glances. Jack was the reason for the attack?

"Liar!" countered Dragon Eye. "We wouldn't be here unless we knew you had it."

Suddenly there was a high whistling in the air and the soft sound of a weapon meeting flesh. The ninja with the broken wrist fell facedown on the snowy ground, an arrow quivering in his back.

"Masamoto!" spat Dragon Eye.

Masamoto, swords drawn, charged into the garden with four of his samurai. Three more of his men thundered across the veranda, stringing fresh arrows onto their bows.

"Another time, *gaijin*," promised Dragon Eye, before fleeing over the bridge with the remaining ninja.

Yamato dragged Akiko and Jack to the ground as arrows shot overhead. The first arrow caught the trailing ninja in the leg. The second pierced his throat. The third was targeted at Dragon Eye, who leaped catlike into the cherry blossom tree, the arrow flying beneath him and embedding itself in the trunk. Dragon Eye swung from the lower branch, dislodging a thick curtain of snow, and deftly flipped himself over the wall before escaping into the night.

"By *Akuma*! Who was that?" demanded Masamoto as he leveled with them.

"Dragon Eye," said Jack, getting back to his feet.

"Dokugan Ryū?" echoed Masamoto, incredulous, then shouted at the nearest samurai, "Captain! Fan out. Secure the house. Raise all our samurai from the village. By the memory of my son Tenno, find this so-called Dragon and destroy him!"

The captain barked orders at his retinue of samurai, who silently disappeared into the night. Masamoto, beckoning a heavyset samurai and a distraught Hiroko over from the house, turned to Jack, Yamato, and Akiko—who was kneeling upon the ground cradling the wounded Taka-san in her arms.

"Kuma-san here will look after you all. He is one of

my most loyal men. Don't worry about Taka-san, Akiko," he said, noting the pleading look in her eyes. "I will have him tended to. Now go!"

The next day, Jack, Akiko, and Yamato were summoned to see Masamoto in his chamber.

"Be seated," he ordered curtly.

Masamoto was sitting in his usual place on the raised platform. He appeared to Jack to be less composed than on previous occasions; his scarring was more inflamed and his voice tight and hoarse.

Hiroko poured him *sencha*.

"Dokugan Ryu has not been found," he said bluntly, clearly displeased at his samurai's failure. "My scouts had word of a sighting of ninja from Matsuzaka village, ten *ri* from here. We came as fast as we could, but our horses were not swift enough to save Chiro."

Hiroko stifled a sob, and Masamoto signed for her to make a discreet exit. They all knew she was grief-stricken by the loss of her faithful maid.

"Masamoto-sama, may I ask how Taka-san is?" Akiko asked.

"He is comfortable, Akiko-chan. His wound is deep, but I have been told he will recover. Dokugan Ryu is a formidable enemy and Taka-san fought with valor."

Masamoto scrutinized all of them.

"Taka-san was fortunate, though, to have you three

by his side. You acted with true *Bushido*. Do you know what that is, Jack-kun?"

"No, Masamoto-sama," replied Jack, and bowed as he had been taught by Akiko.

"*Bushido* means 'Way of the Warrior,' Jack-kun. It is our samurai code of conduct. It is unwritten and unsaid. It is our way of life. *Bushido* is only known through action."

Masamoto took a deep draft of his *sencha* before continuing.

"The seven virtues of *Bushido* are rectitude, courage, benevolence, respect, honesty, honor, and loyalty. Last night each of you demonstrated these virtues through your actions."

He let the weight of his words hang in the air. All three bowed low in appreciation.

"I have one question, though. For I'm mystified as to why Dokugan Ryu should rear his head again. I cannot believe he's still under the employ of my *daimyo's* enemies. That threat has passed. The men responsible for that assassination attempt are now all dead, by my own hand. I can only assume he has a new mission, but how that involves my family, again I do not know. So did Dokugan Ryu give you any indication as to why he dares attack the sanctity of this house?"

Jack remained silent, suddenly feeling hot and uncomfortable under his kimono. He could sense

Masamoto's eyes on him. Should he reveal the truth about the rutter? Chiro had died because of it, yet his father had commanded that he keep it secret. The rutter was his lifeline home, and until Jack knew who wanted it, he could not reveal the book's true purpose to anyone, not even to Masamoto.

"Jack . . ." began Yamato.

But Akiko glared at Yamato, her eyes clearly stating that it was Jack's duty to tell Masamoto if he knew anything. Not Yamato's.

"Yes, Yamato?"

"Jack . . ." Yamato wavered, "saved my life. He defeated a ninja with his *bokken.*"

"Jack-kun, you have skill in weaponry? My, my, you have surpassed my expectations," said Masamoto with a surprised expression, his question about Dokugan Ryu momentarily forgotten. "I sensed from the first time I laid eyes upon you that you possessed strength of character. Indeed, the essence of *Bushido* spirit."

"It was Yamato's training that made it possible, Masamoto-sama," replied Jack, keen to give Yamato the credit in order to impress his father. He also hoped it would lead the conversation away from the rutter.

"Excellent. But he is no teacher," stated Masamoto. Although he meant no harm, his blunt comment cut deep at Yamato's pride.

Jack felt sorry for Yamato. Nothing he did ever

seemed good enough to gain Masamoto's respect. Jack's own father, on the other hand, had always been quick to recognize his achievements. A bitter pang of grief swept through Jack as he thought how proud his father would have been of him defeating a ninja.

"Jack-kun. You have proven yourself worthy to follow the Way of the Warrior. I decree, therefore, that you are to train at the Niten Ichi Ryū, my One School of Two Heavens. Whatever Dokugan Ryu's intentions are, you'll be safer under my direct supervision. Tomorrow we shall leave for Kyoto."

CHAPTER 22

THE TOKAIDO ROAD

DAWN HAD BARELY broken when Jack was roused from his bed by the noise of horses' hooves and the curt shout of a commanding samurai bringing his troop to a halt outside the house.

Jack gathered together what few possessions he had: his spare kimono and *obi*, extra *tabi*, a pair of sandals, his *bokken*, and most important of all, his father's rutter. He picked up the priest's dictionary, not forgetting his promise to deliver it to Father Bobadilla in Osaka when the chance arose, and stuffed it along with the other items in a shoulder bag. With a final check to ensure that the rutter was safely stored at the bottom, away from prying eyes, he stepped out onto the veranda.

A thin orange haze lit the winter sky, and Jack could

make out the tracery of the cherry blossom tree, its branches silhouetted against the crisp white landscape. The samurai's arrow was still buried in its trunk, a deadly reminder that Dragon Eye was out there somewhere, bent on stealing the rutter. Jack shuddered and hugged himself against the chill of morning.

"Good morning, Jack-kun." Uekiya had shuffled up to Jack, and was bowing low by Jack's side.

"Good morning, Uekiya-san, what are you doing up so early?"

"Jack-kun, please accept this humble gift."

The old man handed him a small wooden carrying case and opened up the lid to reveal a tiny potted plant within.

"What is it?" asked Jack.

"It is *bonsai*," explained Uekiya, "a miniature *sakura* tree, just like the one you sit under in this garden."

Jack examined the little plant. It was a perfect cherry blossom tree, yet not much larger than the span of his hand.

"*Sakura* bloom in April," explained Uekiya with tenderness. "The blossom is brief but beautiful. Like life."

"*Arigatō*, Uekiya-san. But I don't have anything to give you in return."

"That is not necessary. You have given me great pleasure every day you have enjoyed my garden. That is all an old gardener could wish for."

"Jack-kun! Jack-kun!" beckoned Hiroko, scurrying out of the house. "You must hurry. It is time to go."

"In Kyoto, look upon this *bonsai* and remember old Uekiya and his garden?"

"I will," said Jack, bowing his gratitude. He realized that he would miss everything in this garden: the wooden bridge spanning the stream, the trickle of the waterfall, and most of all the shade and shelter of the cherry blossom tree itself.

Hiroko ushered him toward the front of the house. Jack glanced over his shoulder one last time and saw the old man bow low, holding it to mark respect. He was so still it was as if he grew out of the very earth itself.

"How do I look after a *bonsai*?" called Jack.

Uekiya looked up. "Prune it and water a little every day, but not too much . . ."

The old gardener clearly wished to say more on the subject, but he could see Hiroko was impatient to get Jack going. She led him through the front gate, where a troop of samurai and their horses were gathered. Final preparations were being made for the journey, and Jack could see Yamato mounting a horse at the head of the column, next to Masamoto.

"Just a moment, Jack-kun," said Hiroko, disappearing back into the house.

She returned almost immediately with a neatly wrapped kimono made of a rich, burgundy-colored silk.

"You will need this for ceremonies and festivals. It bears the phoenix *kamon*, the family crest of Masamoto," she said. Tears welled in her eyes. "You will be safer under Masamoto-sama's watchful eye in Kyoto than you can be here."

"*Arigatō*, Hiroko-san," said Jack, taking the gift with both hands and admiring it. "It is truly magnificent."

A heavyset samurai, with dark bushy eyebrows and a large mustache that appeared to grow directly from his nostrils, approached on a horse. He was dressed in a dark brown kimono and riding coat. As he drew closer, Jack recognized him. It was one of Masamoto's trusted samurai, Kuma-san.

"Jack-kun! You are to ride with me," he commanded, patting the back of his saddle.

Jack placed the new kimono in his shoulder bag, together with the *bonsai* tree, and secured them in an empty saddlebag. Kuma-san offered his hand, and Jack mounted the horse. He passed Jack a thick cloak to ward off the cold.

"And remember to bathe!" admonished Hiroko, giving the departing Jack a rueful smile.

As they trotted to the front, Jack's eyes suddenly burned, and he had to blink back tears. He would be sad to leave Toba, which had become his home since he'd arrived that summer. He had no idea when or if he would ever return. He waved good-bye to Hiroko, who bowed back. Then he realized he had not seen Akiko. *Where is she?* He had to say farewell. Jack desperately looked around, unable to get down from the horse.

Eventually he spied her behind a group of mounted samurai. She was riding her own white stallion, the same one Jack had seen her with his first morning in Japan.

"Akiko!" called Jack. "I was worried I wouldn't see you to say good-bye."

"Good-bye?" She gave Jack a perplexed look and trotted over. "Jack, I'm coming to Kyoto."

"What? But we're going to train to be samurai warriors."

"Women are samurai too, Jack," said Akiko. She gave him an affronted look, then spurred her horse onward before he could reply.

There was a cry of *"Ikinasai!"* and the column of horses set off.

Jack became aware of someone sprinting up alongside his horse.

"Bye-bye, Jack Furesha!" shouted Jiro enthusiastically.

"Good-bye, Jiro," replied Jack, waving back.

Then the samurai took off up the hill, leaving the little boy lost in a flurry of snow.

The troop of samurai rode up out of the harbor and wound their way through the terraced paddy fields to join a narrow dirt road. At the lip of the hill, Jack looked back on the port of Toba. It appeared so small now, the boats like petals on a pond. The *torii* gateway in the harbor glowed fire-red in the early morning light—then was gone, lost behind the rise of the hill.

Kyoto was forty *ri*, some ninety miles, from Toba, Kuma-san told Jack. They would ride until midday, rest, then push on to the village of Hisai. From there they would head to Kameyama and join the main Tokaido Road, striking inland to approach Kyoto from the southern end of Lake Biwa. The whole journey would take three days.

The route itself was empty of traffic, though little pockets of life came in and out of view along the way. Coastal villages with boats tied to stakes at the shoreline, and fishermen repairing their nets. Paddy fields dotted with farmers tending the frozen rice terraces. A local vegetable market. A roadside inn opening up for the day's business. Half-wild dogs that barked and chased the horses. A lone merchant making for the Tokaido Road, his back laden with goods.

As Masamoto and his entourage passed through, each villager bowed in deep respect, keeping their heads low until the whole train had gone by.

When they halted for lunch at an inn, Jack sought out Akiko and found her tending her horse.

"That's a fine horse," said Jack, not knowing quite what else to say, still embarrassed by his tactless remark earlier that morning.

"Yes, Jack. It was my father's," she replied, refusing to look at him as she loosened the straps on the saddle of her horse.

"Your father's? What happened to him?"

"My father was Dāte Kenshin. He was a great warrior, but he died at the hands of his enemies. He wasn't allowed to commit seppuku and was therefore shamed in death."

"I'm sorry . . . I didn't realize . . ." stumbled Jack. "What's *seppuku*?"

"Ritual suicide. It would have been an honorable death for my father. But don't be sorry. It happened many years ago. This horse and the swords in my mother's house are all that's left of him."

Jack recalled the red-and-black swords that hung on the wall in Hiroko's dining room. It made him think about the only evidence he possessed of his father's existence—the rutter. He recognized in Akiko's eyes the same bitter sense of loss that he experienced each day.

"Well, I am still sorry," he said, wishing he could comfort her more. "I also apologize for this morning. I upset you. I had no idea a woman could be a samurai. In England it is only the men who do the fighting."

"I accept your apology, Jack," she said, bowing. Her

face brightened. "Sometimes I forget you are not Japanese."

"How can you? Who else here has blond hair and a big nose!" he said, pointing at the throng of samurai all with dark hair and small features. They both laughed out loud.

A samurai came over, a bemused look on his face, and handed them each a bowl of rice and smoked fish. Taking the dishes, they sat down together under the lee of the little inn and began to eat, watching the snow settle over the paddy fields.

"There have always been female samurai, Jack," began Akiko. "Six hundred years ago, at the time of the great Gempei War, Tomoe Gozen lived. Her courageous deeds are honored with a verse in the *Heike mono-ga-tari*."

"The *Heike* what?" asked Jack, through a mouthful of rice.

"The *Heike mono-ga-tari* is the epic tale of the struggle between the Taira and Minamoto clans for the control of Japan. Tomoe Gozen was a female general for the almighty *daimyo* Minamoto Yoshinaka. She rode into battle and fought as skillfully and valiantly as any male samurai."

"Go on," encouraged Jack, taking another portion of smoked fish with his chopsticks. "What was she like?"

"The *Heike* describes Tomoe as exceptionally beautiful, with white skin and long dark hair. She was an outstanding archer, and as a swordswoman she was a warrior worth a thousand men, ready to confront god or demon, mounted or on foot."

"She sounds invincible," said Jack.

"To many samurai she was. Some thought her so powerful that they believed she was the reincarnation of a river goddess."

Akiko put down her bowl and looked directly at Jack.

"She could break wild horses with unparalleled skill and ride down perilous descents without falling. Whenever a battle was imminent, Yoshinaka sent *her* out as his advance guard. She wielded a *katana* and a mighty bow, and she performed more deeds of valor than any of his other warriors."

Jack was stunned into silence. There was more to Akiko's fervor than a simple respect for Tomoe Gozen's achievements. Akiko clearly had something to prove—as a female samurai herself.

"What did Dragon Eye mean by a . . . rutter?" asked Akiko suddenly, keeping her voice low so that the samurai eating nearby wouldn't overhear.

"Err . . . I don't know," mumbled Jack, taken off guard by her directness. He knew this was a poor answer. He had been struggling with his conscience ever since he'd decided to keep quiet about the rutter.

"But Dragon Eye demanded it from you. What is it?"

"It's nothing. . . ." Jack made a move to leave. He was not used to such forthright questioning from Akiko.

"Jack, it is a mighty *nothing* for Dragon Eye to risk his life for . . . and for Chiro to lose hers!"

Her voice had risen in frustration, and several of the samurai glanced up from their bowls. Akiko forced a serene smile, bowing her head slightly by way of an apology for her outburst, and they returned to their meals.

Jack considered Akiko for a moment. *Can I really trust her?*

He had to. She was his only friend.

"It's my father's diary," he finally admitted.

"A diary?"

"Well, not exactly. The rutter is a guide to the oceans of the world. My father said the person who possesses it rules the seas," explained Jack. "Its knowledge is priceless."

"So why didn't you tell Masamoto?"

"Because it's the only hope I have of ever getting home," said Jack emphatically. "Furthermore, my father swore me to secrecy. Men will kill to own this rutter, as you've seen. The more people who know of its survival, the more dangerous it is for all of us. I don't know who I can trust, and until I do, this rutter has to remain hidden."

"Well, you can trust me. I remained silent on your

behalf—and if you're honor-bound to your father to keep it secret, and if what you say is true—that it will be safer hidden—then you can trust me to stay silent."

"But what about Yamato? Can I trust him?" enquired Jack.

A cry from the head of the column interrupted them.

The samurai rapidly regrouped in preparation for departure.

"We must go," said Akiko, leaving the question unanswered.

Akiko mounted her stallion, and Kuma-san rode up before Jack could press Akiko further. Then, in a long disciplined file, two abreast, they set off down the road.

By nightfall they had reached the coastal village of Hisai. The main street boasted two rest houses, and Kuma-san had secured lodgings in the better of the two for the night.

The next day they rose early and made rapid progress to Kameyama, a bustling stopgap of a town on the main route between Edo and Kyoto. This was the station at which they joined the Tokaido Road.

The main Tokaido Road was little more than a wide track, but it was busy with foot traffic. Merchants. Samurai. Travelers. Exhausted porters warming themselves by fires. Some wore round-domed straw hats and carried large square backpacks. Others had slung cloth bags over their shoulders and wrapped their heads against the cold with large patterned bandanas. There were few women on the road, but those who did travel were escorted by manservants. Only the samurai were on horseback, and the scene struck Jack as a little odd, for there were no carts or horse-drawn vehicles of any kind, unlike the thoroughfares back in England.

As they journeyed along the road, which weaved snakelike into the distance, Jack noticed that they frequently passed small mounds with two trees planted on either side.

"What are those, Kuma-san?" asked Jack, pointing at one.

"Distance markers. We are now seventeen *ri* from Kyoto," explained Kuma-san.

Near these markers was the occasional merchant plying his wares, or a small inn offering refreshment and lodgings. They had just passed a very old merchant, who was selling freshly brewed *sencha* from a teapot hanging in the branches of a tree, when the pedestrian traffic in the distance began to scatter. Jack heard a far cry of "Down! Down!" and the road ahead became lined with Japanese prostrating themselves on the ground

"Jack-kun, off the horse and bow. Now!" commanded Kuma-san.

Jack did as he was told, and Kuma-san joined him.

Clearly deaf, the old tea merchant had not heard the

warning, and was so involved in preparing another brew that he didn't notice the approaching convoy. Everyone was bowing except him.

Jack raised himself up and tried to get the attention of the old man, but Kuma-san yanked Jack's head back down just as the leading samurai swept past on his horse, his sword passing within a hair's breadth of Jack's head.

The mounted samurai glared at Jack; then, without breaking pace, he raised his sword again to chop the old merchant's head off.

The contingent of mounted samurai powered past, heralding a procession of ceremonial samurai, uniformed marching men, and attendants holding colorful blue, yellow, and gold banners aloft. In the midst of this convoy was a brilliantly lacquered palanquin, borne by four sweating men in loincloths.

As it passed by, Jack caught a glimpse of a man ensconced inside, his haughty face turned away from the old tea merchant's body flopped in the dirt.

"Who was that?" whispered Jack, breathless with shock.

"The *daimyo* Lord Kamakura Katsuro returning to Edo," said Kuma-san, with venom in his voice. "He *insists* on utmost respect."

The procession plowed on down the Tokaido Road, scattering pedestrians like autumn leaves.

CHAPTER 23

BUTOKUDEN

"JACK-KUN! KYOTO!" said Kuma-san the following afternoon, nudging Jack from the doze that the
gentle rocking of the horse had lulled him into. "The Heart
of Japan, where the great Emperor himself resides!"

Jack opened his eyes. The Tokaido Road had ended in
a magnificent wooden bridge that spanned a wide, lazy-
flowing river. The bridge streamed with people coming
and going, an exotic flood of color and noise. But as soon
as they saw Masamoto and his samurai approaching, the
crowd parted like a wave breaking upon a rock, and a uni-
form bow rippled along as the troop passed through.

Beyond the bridge, Jack could see the broad expanse
of Kyoto.

A vast city of villas, temples, houses, gardens, shops,

and inns filled the valley floor. Bound by mountains on three sides, the rising slopes were swathed in cedar trees and dotted with shrines. Soaring up to the northeast of the city was the most magnificent of these peaks, upon which the desecrated remains of a massive temple complex perched.

"Mount Hiei," said Akiko as she and Yamato joined Jack on the bridge. "It was the site of Enryakuji, the most powerful Buddhist monastery in Japan."

"What happened to it?" asked Jack, surprised at the hundreds of burned-out buildings, temples, and structures littering its slopes.

"The great General Nobunaga invaded the monastery forty years ago," said Kuma-san. "Burned every temple to the ground. Executed every monk."

"Why?"

"When Kyoto was first built," replied Akiko, "Emperor Kammu established a monastery on Mount Hiei to protect the city from evil spirits. It was the monks' responsibility to guard Kyoto."

"They even had their own army of *sohei*," added Yamato.

"*Sohei*?"

"Warrior monks trained in martial arts," explained Kuma-san. "Nobunaga challenged their control of Kyoto. His forces stormed the mountain and conquered the *sohei*."

"But why did Nobunaga destroy them if they were the guardians of Kyoto?" asked Jack.

"Nobunaga was not the destroyer of this monastery," said Kuma-san vehemently. "The monks had become too rich, too powerful, too greedy. The destroyer of the monastery was the monastery itself!"

"So who protects Kyoto from evil spirits now?"

"There are many other monasteries, Jack," explained Akiko. "Kyoto is a city of temples. See there on that steep slope, peeking just above the trees? That is Kiyomizu-dera Temple, the Temple of Clear Water. It protects the source of the Kizu river, the Otowa-no-taki."

"What's Otowa-no-taki?"

"The Sound of Feathers waterfall. It is said that to drink from its waters will help cure any illness."

Jack gazed at the towering pagoda temple until it disappeared from view.

Akiko pointed out the various shrines and temples as they wended their way through the narrow streets and byways of Kyoto. Every street appeared to have its own shrine. Finally the road opened out on to a large paved thoroughfare dominated by a magnificent wooden gateway with a large curving roof decorated in gold leaf. Pale earthen walls, topped with jade green tiles, stretched out on either side for over half a mile, completely encircling the buildings hidden within.

"Kyoto Gosho," breathed Akiko with utter reverence.

"The Imperial Palace," explained Yamato, seeing Jack's bafflement. "We are passing by the home of the Emperor of Japan, the Living God."

Masamoto bowed briefly in its direction, then bore left along the palace's walls. They followed him down the wide boulevard and back into the narrowing streets of the city. It was not long before they emerged in front of another fortified enclosure.

Thick white walls upon great stone foundations surrounded a three-tiered castle with a large curving roof. The fortifications sloped into a wide moat, and large defensive turrets guarded the main gate and thoroughfares at each corner. The castle exuded an air of impregnability.

"We are here," stated Kuma-san.

"We are staying in the castle?" said Jack in astonishment.

"No! That is Nijō Castle, home to *daimyo* Takatomi. We are going to the Butokuden," he said with immense pride.

They dismounted, and Jack, unloading his saddlebag, turned to Akiko.

"What is the Butokuden?" he whispered, not wishing to offend Kuma-san.

"It is the Hall of the Virtues of War. The Butokuden is Masamoto's *dojo*—his training hall," Akiko explained quietly, and nodded in its direction. "It is the home of the Niten Ichi Ryū, the greatest sword school in Kyoto and the only one sponsored by the *daimyo* Takatomi himself. It is the place where we will be trained in *Bushido*, the Way of the Warrior."

On the opposite side of the street was a large rectangular building constructed of dark cypress wood and white earthen walls, crowned with two tiers of pale russet tiles. Jutting out from its center was an intricately carved entranceway bearing a large phoenix *kamon*. Masamoto stood beneath its flaming wings, waiting for Akiko, Yamato, and Jack to join him.

"Welcome to my school, the Niten Ichi Ryū," said Masamoto magnanimously.

Akiko, Yamato, and Jack all bowed, and Masamoto led the way into his One School of Two Heavens.

Even before Jack had set foot inside the Butokuden, he could hear the shouts of *"Kiai"* emanating from the *dojo*.

There was a sharp cry of *"Rei"* as Masamoto entered the great hall, and the entire group of trainee warriors instantaneously ceased their practice. The room became so quiet that all Jack could hear was the sound of their breathing. As one, the entire class bowed and held their bow as a mark of utmost respect.

"Continue your training," commanded Masamoto.

"ARIGATŌ GOZAIMASHITA, MASAMOTO-SAMA!" they thundered, their salutation rolling and rebounding around the *dojo*.

The forty or so students returned to their various activities of *kihon*, *kata*, and *randori*. The late afternoon sun filtering through the narrow papered windows gave an almost mystical quality to their movements. As the warriors sparred, their shadows fought in unison across the honey-colored wood-block floor that defined their training area.

Jack was overawed. From its rounded pillars of cypress to the elevated paneled ceiling, to the ceremonial throne set back in a curving alcove, the Butokuden radiated an aura of supreme power. Even the students kneeling in orderly lines around the edge of the *dojo* exhibited complete focus and determination. This was truly a hall of warriors in the making.

Masamoto, his back turned, was conversing with a stern-looking samurai who had a sharp spike of a beard.

Slowly, like the sound of a receding storm, the *dojo* fell silent again. Jack wondered who had entered this time, but with increasing alarm he realized that every student had stopped their training to stare at *him*. They met his gaze with a mixture of amazement, disbelief, and open contempt.

The hard stares of the students impaled Jack like arrows.

"Why have you stopped?" demanded Masamoto, as if unaware of Jack's presence. "Continue your training."

The students resumed their activities, though they

continued to steal furtive glances in Jack's direction.

Masamoto addressed Jack, Akiko, and Yamato. "Come. Sensei Hosokawa will show you to your quarters. I have business to attend to, so I won't see you again until the reception dinner tonight in the Chō-no-ma."

They bowed to Masamoto and left the *dojo* through a door in the rear of the Butokuden. Sensei Hosokawa led them across an open courtyard to the Shishi-no-ma, the Hall of Lions, a long building that housed a series of small rooms. They entered through a side *shoji* and, leaving their sandals at the door, walked down a narrow corridor.

"These are your sleeping quarters," said Hosokawa-sensei, indicating a number of small unadorned rooms barely big enough for three *tatami* mats. "The bathhouses are at the rear. I will collect you for dinner once you have washed and changed."

Jack stepped inside his room and closed the inner *shoji* behind him.

He put down his shoulder bag and placed the *bonsai* tree on a narrow shelf beneath a tiny lattice window. Looking around, he searched for a safe place to hide his father's rutter, but with no furnishings to speak of, his only option was to slip it beneath the futon spread out on the floor. Patting back the mattress, he then collapsed on top of it.

As he lay there, exhausted from three days of hard

travel, a sense of dread shuddered through his body, and he couldn't stop his hands from shaking. What was he doing here?

He was no samurai.

He was Jack Fletcher, an English boy who had dreamed of being a pilot like his father, exploring the wonders of the New World. Not a trainee samurai warrior stranded in an alien world, the prey of a one-eyed ninja.

Jack felt like a lamb going to the slaughter. Every single one of those students looked as though they wanted to tear him limb from limb.

CHAPTER 24

SENSEI

"**Y**OUNG SAMURAI!**"** boomed Masamoto down the Chō-no-ma, the Hall of Butterflies, a long chamber resplendent with panels of exquisitely painted butterflies and *sakura* trees.

Masamoto sat cross-legged at the head table, a black lacquered slab of cedar that dominated the end of the room. Raised upon a dais, he was flanked on either side by four samurai in ceremonial kimonos.

"*Bushido* is not a journey to be taken lightly!"

Jack, Yamato, and Akiko listened along with a hundred other trainee warriors, all of whom had requested to study under Masamoto Takeshi.

"To train to be a samurai warrior, one must conquer the self, endure the pain of grueling practice, and cultivate a level mind in the face of danger," declared Masamoto. "The way of the warrior is lifelong, and mastery is often simply staying the path. You will need commitment, discipline, and a fearless mind."

He took a measured sip from a cup of *sencha*, letting his words settle in the minds of the students, who knelt in neat rows along the length of the chamber.

"You will also need guidance. For without it, you will perish! You are all blinded by ignorance! Deafened by inexperience! Voiceless with incompetence!"

Masamoto paused again and took in the whole room, ensuring his speech had had the intended effect. Jack could feel the gravity of his stare upon him, even though he was at the very back of the chamber.

"From every tiny bud springs a tree of many branches," he continued, his austere tone thawing slightly. "Every castle commences with the laying of the first stone. Every journey begins with just one step. To assist you in making that first step and the many others you will take, I present your sensei. *REI*!"

All the students bowed, their heads touching the *tatami* mat as a mark of the complete respect they had for their teachers.

"First, Sensei Hosokawa, master of *kenjutsu* and the *bokken*."

Masamoto acknowledged the samurai to his immediate right, the one who had directed Jack to his room earlier that day. Hosokawa was a fierce-looking warrior with jet-black hair swept up into the customary topknot, and dark, piercing eyes. He tugged thoughtfully at his point of a beard.

"Together, we will train you in the Art of the Sword, and should you demonstrate excellence, we will impart to you the technique of Two Heavens."

Sensei Hosokawa stared at each student in turn, as if assessing their right to be there. He then bowed his head, apparently satisfied. Jack wondered what the Two Heavens technique was, and looked across to Akiko to ask, but she, like everyone else, was staring resolutely in the direction of the sensei.

"To Sensei Hosokawa's right is Sensei Yamada, your sage in Zen and meditation."

A bald man with a long, wispy, gray beard and a crinkled old face dozed at the far end of the table. He was thin and reedy, as if grown from a bamboo shoot, and Jack guessed he was at least seventy years old, for even his eyebrows had gone gray.

"Sensei Yamada?" asked Masamoto gently.

"*Hai! Dōzo*, Masamoto-sama. It's good to have an end to journey toward," said the old man with considered care, "but it is the journey that matters, in the end."

"Wise words, Sensei," responded Masamoto.

Sensei Yamada then nodded forward and appeared to drift back to sleep. Jack wished he could fall asleep so easily in that position. His knees were already stiffening up, and his feet ached.

"You need to stop fidgeting," whispered Akiko, seeing Jack shift his weight around. "It is disrespectful."

No sympathy from her, thought Jack. Perhaps the Japanese were born kneeling!

Masamoto turned to a young woman on his left. "Now I present Sensei Yosa, mistress of *kyujutsu* and horsemanship."

The sensei wore a shimmering bloodred-and-ivory kimono adorned with a *kamon* of a moon and two stars. Her black hair glistened in the light of the numerous lanterns hanging from the walls of the Chō-no-ma, giving it the appearance of a cascading waterfall. Jack quickly forgot his kneeling misery as, like the rest of the students, he was immediately captivated by this female warrior.

"She is undoubtedly one of the most prodigious talents in the Art of the Bow," explained Masamoto. "I would go so far as to say she is the finest archer in all the land. I truly envy those who benefit from her tutelage."

Her chestnut-colored eyes never left her students as she bowed. They darted to each as if calculating distance and trajectory. She reminded Jack of a hunting hawk: elegant and graceful, yet sharp and deadly. Then, as she straightened up, she drew her hair behind her ears and revealed an ugly ruby-red scar that cut the entire length of her right cheekbone.

"Finally, may I introduce Sensei Kyuzo, master of *taijutsu*."

A small man perched at the end of the table to Sensei Yosa's left. He had black specks for eyes, and a tuft of a mustache beneath a flattened pudgy nose.

"He is your authority on all matters of hand-to-hand combat: kicking, punching, grappling, striking, blocking, and throwing. The skills you will learn from Sensei Kyuzo will feed into everything you do here."

Jack was amazed. The sensei could not have been much bigger than a child, and seemed an extremely odd choice for a tutor of hand-to-hand combat. Many of the other new students wore similar looks of disbelief.

The small man gave an irritable bow. Jack noticed he was crushing nuts with his bare hands. Methodically and without haste, Sensei Kyuzo would pick up a large unhulled nut from a red lacquered bowl and squeeze it between his fingers until it split. He would then pick at the pieces before moving on to the next nut.

With the introductions over, Masamoto indicated that all the students should bow once more in honor of their new sensei.

"The Way of the Warrior means more than martial arts and meditation," continued Masamoto. "It means living by the samurai code of honor—*Bushido*—at *all* times. I demand courage and rectitude in all your endeavors. I expect honesty, benevolence, and loyalty to be demonstrated daily. You must honor and respect one another. Every student of the Niten Ichi Ryū is personally chosen by me, and thus *every* student is worthy of your respect."

Jack felt the last comment had been said directly for his benefit, and a number of the students turned their heads in his direction. One of them, an imperious-looking lad with a shaved head, high cheekbones, and dark hooded eyes, shot him a look of pure malevolence. He wore a jet-black kimono with a red sun *kamon* emblazoned on the back.

"Tomorrow you will begin your formal training. Those of you who have been students a season or more, you too will need to refresh the skills you've acquired. Do not think for one moment that you know it all. You have only taken your *first* step!" proclaimed Masamoto, slamming his fist down on the table to emphasize the point.

"Given enough time, anyone may master the physical. Given enough knowledge, anyone may become wise. It is only the most dedicated warrior who can master both and achieve true *Bushido*. The Niten Ichi Ryū is your path to excellence. Learn today so that you may live tomorrow!"

Masamoto bowed to his students, and everyone let loose a resounding chorus. "MASAMOTO! MASAMOTO! MASAMOTO!"

As the salutation died away, the large entrance *shoji* slid back, and servants entered bearing several long lacquered tables. The students rose to allow the tables to be placed in two rows down the length of the Chō-no-ma.

An unspoken but rigid system of hierarchy dictated the seating arrangement. The most advanced and eldest students assembled nearest the head table, while the newest recruits sat closest to the entrance. Jack, Yamato, and Akiko, who wore a jade green ceremonial kimono with her father's family *kamon* of a *sakura* flower, went to seat themselves with seventeen other new recruits at the very end.

Jack had dressed in the burgundy kimono Hiroko had presented him before leaving Toba. Somehow wearing Masamoto's family *kamon* had given him the strength to subdue his fears. The phoenix *kamon* had acted like invisible armor and discouraged the other students from approaching or physically challenging his presence. They had merely observed him with guarded suspicion.

As Jack went to seat himself, though, the student with the red sun *kamon* strode over.

"That's my seat, *gaijin*," he challenged.

All the students turned to see what the blond-haired *gaijin*'s reaction would be.

Jack squared up to the boy.

They held one another's stares, the seconds seeming

to stretch into infinity. Then he felt Akiko's hand on his elbow, and she gently pulled him away.

"It's all yours," said Jack. "I didn't like the smell over here anyway."

The boy's nostrils flared at the implied insult of his cleanliness, and he shot a scathing look at two trainees who had smirked at Jack's retort.

"You shouldn't offend people like that, Jack," whispered Akiko, hurriedly leading him over to the table where Yamato had seated himself. "You do not want to be making enemies—certainly not within the Niten Ichi Ryū."

CHAPTER 25

THE SHINING ONE

"I WASN'T THE ONE who confronted him," said Jack, sitting cross-legged between Akiko and Yamato.

"It doesn't matter," stressed Akiko. "It's all about face."

"Face?" queried Jack, but before Akiko could reply, they were interrupted by several servants laden with trays of food.

The servants meticulously arranged the dishes on the tables. Bowls of miso soup, fried noodles, pickled vegetables, different varieties of raw fish, some soft white cubes that were called *tofu*, little dishes filled with a dark salty liquid—soy sauce for dipping, informed Akiko helpfully—and a number of heaped servings of steaming boiled rice. Jack had never seen so many different types of food to choose from. The sheer variety of dishes implied that this was a highly prestigious event.

"*Itadakimasu!*" cried Masamoto, now that the banquet had been served.

"*Itadakimasu!*" responded all the students, who began to help themselves to the food.

With so much on offer, it was difficult for Jack to know where to start. He picked up the *hashi* and carefully adjusted his grip. Although he was getting used to the little chopsticks, he still found small morsels tricky to eat.

"You were saying it's all about face," prompted Jack, selecting a good-size piece of *sushi*.

"Yes. It's very important for a Japanese person never to lose face," Akiko replied.

"How can you lose a face?" asked Jack incredulously.

"It's not a physical thing, Jack," explained Yamato. "Face is our perception of another person's status. It's crucial to maintain face. Face translates into power and influence. If you lose face, you lose authority and respect."

"You made him lose face in front of his fellow students," explained Akiko.

"So, he lost face," said Jack, shrugging and pointing his *hashi* at the boy with the red sun *kamon*. "Who is he anyway?"

The boy stared directly at Jack, his eyes narrowing aggressively.

"Don't do that!" scolded Akiko.

"Do what?"

"Point your *hashi* at him. Don't you remember what I taught you? It is considered very rude," said Akiko, exasperated at Jack's continual uncivilized behavior. "And don't leave them sticking up in your bowl of rice, either!"

"For heaven's sake, why not?" exclaimed Jack, immediately retrieving his offending *hashi* from the rice bowl. He would *never* get Japanese etiquette right. There was just so much to think about for each and every action and occasion, however insignificant or senseless it seemed.

Suddenly he realized that everyone at his table was staring at him. He dropped his eyes to the dish in front of him and started picking at its contents.

"Because it means someone has died," said Akiko in a hushed tone, bowing. "Only at a funeral service are *hashi* stuck into the rice. The bowl is then placed at the head of the deceased so that they won't starve in the next world."

"Why didn't you tell me that before?" fumed Jack under his breath. "Everything I do here is rude. Come to England and your habits would be thought of as very odd, too. I'm sure even *you* could offend somebody!"

"I'm sorry, Jack," said Akiko timorously, bowing her head. "I apologize. It's my fault for not teaching you properly."

"And will you stop apologizing!" shouted Jack,

holding his head in his hands with sheer frustration.

Akiko went very quiet. Jack glanced up. The students at his table were pretending to ignore them, but it was clear that his tone with Akiko had been entirely inappropriate. Yamato glared at him but said nothing.

"I'm sorry, Akiko," Jack mumbled. "You're only trying to help me. It's just *so* difficult speaking, thinking, and living like a Japanese person all the time."

"I understand, Jack. Now please enjoy the meal," she replied flatly.

Jack continued to work his way through the various bowls, in rotation, but they had lost their flavor. He hated that he had upset Akiko, and even worse, he had shouted at her in front of other people. He was sure she had lost face by his behavior. When Jack looked up again, the boy with the sun *kamon* was still staring at him, a belligerent scowl on his face.

"Akiko," he said, bowing his head and speaking loudly enough for those around them to hear. "Please accept my humblest apologies for my behavior. I'm still tired from our journey."

"Thank you for your apology, Jack," she said, and with the apology formally accepted, the atmosphere around the table lightened, and everyone resumed their polite conversations.

"Please, would you tell me who that boy is?" asked Jack, nodding toward the boy with the sun *kamon*. He was relieved that he had managed to restore some degree of accord. Maybe he was beginning to appreciate the intricacies of Japanese etiquette after all.

"I don't know," she replied.

"I do," offered an enthusiastic lad opposite Jack. "He's in the same year as us. His name is Oda Kazuki, son of *daimyo* Oda Satoshi, second cousin to the Imperial Line. That is why he bears the *kamon* of the Imperial Sun. Some would consider the Oda family to be rather high and mighty. Maybe that's why his father named him Kazuki. It means 'Shining One.'"

They all stared at the jovial boy with growing amazement as he continued to talk unabated. He was rather plain-looking, with a chubby face whose only outstanding feature was the eyebrows: thick black caterpillars fixed in a permanent expression of surprise.

"I apologize," he said, bowing. "I didn't introduce myself. My name is Saburo. I am the third son of Shimazu Hideo. Our *kamon* displays two hawk feathers—it symbolizes the swiftness, grace, and dignity of the hawk. My brother is Taro. You can see him near the top table. He is one of the best students of *kenjutsu* in the school. This year he will be learning the Two Heavens technique—"

"It's an honor to meet you," interrupted Yamato politely. "I am Yamato, son of Masamoto Takeshi. This is my cousin, Akiko. And this is Jack. He is from the other side of the world."

They each bowed in turn as Yamato introduced them

"Ahh! The *gaijin* Masamoto saved," said Saburo, warily acknowledging Jack, then ignoring him in favor of Yamato. "It is truly an honor to meet you too, Yamato. I cannot wait to inform my mother that I dined opposite Masamoto's surviving son. It was tragic what happened to Tenno. My brother knew him. They sparred together many times—"

"And who is your friend?" asked Akiko quickly, seeing Yamato's mood darken at the mention of his brother's death. A small girl with shoulder-length black hair framing an oval face sat to Saburo's left. But Saburo answered for her before she could reply.

"This is Kiku, second daughter of Imagawa Hiromi, a famous Zen priest." They all bowed as Saburo continued. "So who do you think will be teaching us first? Do you think it will be Sensei Yosa? I hope so. Surely she has to be reincarnated from a goddess. Our very own Tomoe Gozen, *neh*?"

Jack could see that Akiko was affronted by Saburo's offhand comments about her idol, and hurriedly thought of a question to move the conversation on.

"Saburo, what are the Two Heavens?" asked Jack, who was honestly interested.

"Ahh, the Two Heavens is Masamoto's secret—"

But before Saburo could elucidate, Masamoto

brought a formal end to the dinner with a cry of *"Go-chiso-samakohaita!"* He commanded everyone to get an early night, for their first day's training would be far from easy.

There was a shout of *"REI SENSEI!"* and the whole room stood and bowed. Masamoto and his sensei rose and made their way down the center of the Chō-no-ma and into the night. The students filed out silently behind them, in order of seniority.

Jack emerged into the cold, clear night air, relieved to be getting away from the constant eyeballing he'd endured in the Hall of Butterflies. Each time Jack had looked up from his bowl, Kazuki had shot him a contemptuous look, while the students around him laughed at something or other he had said regarding the *"gaijin."*

Jack ambled behind Akiko, Yamato, and Kiku, who were closely pursued by the talkative Saburo as they made their way to the Hall of Lions. He gazed up at the star-filled sky, trying to recognize the constellations his father had taught him. Orion's Belt, The Plow, Bellatrix . . .

Suddenly Kazuki materialized in front of him, blocking his path.

"Where do you think you're going, *gaijin*?"

"To bed, Kazuki. Like everyone else," replied Jack, attempting to step around him.

"Who gave you permission to use my name, *gaijin*?" said Kazuki, pushing Jack.

Jack stumbled and fell against another boy, who had sidled up behind him. Jack rebounded off the boy's impressively large belly.

"Now you have insulted Nobu too. You owe us both an apology."

"Apology for what?" exclaimed Jack, trying again to get past, but Nobu's *sumo*-like bulk refused to budge.

"How rude! Not willing to apologize. You should be punished," said Kazuki darkly.

Jack heard Nobu cracking his knuckles, as if limbering up to hit him, but Jack stood his ground.

"You wouldn't dare!" said Jack defiantly.

He glanced over Kazuki's shoulder. Akiko and Yamato, along with everyone else, had already disappeared into the Hall of Lions. His bravado was slipping rapidly.

"There's no one here, *gaijin*," sneered Kazuki. "See? You're not *always* under Masamoto's protection. Who'd believe a *gaijin* anyway?"

Kazuki's hand shot out and grabbed Jack's left wrist, twisting it. The pain was instant. His whole arm contorted, and Jack dropped to his knees, desperate to relieve the agony.

"First, you took my seat. Second, you insulted me in front of my friends. Third, you offended me greatly by pointing your *hashi* at me. Apologize!" said Kazuki, rotating Jack's wrist farther with each demand, sending bolts of burning pain through his arm.

"Apologize, *gaijin*!"

"*Go to hell!*" spat Jack in English.

"What did you say?" said Kazuki, baffled by the strange-sounding words. "You'd better be careful, *gaijin*. You wouldn't want to injure yourself before you start your training, would you?"

Kazuki applied even more pressure. The pain seared white-hot through Jack's arm, and Kazuki drove him facefirst into the ground. Jack was unable to move. Kazuki forced Jack's arm up and behind his back, and purposefully rubbed Jack's face in the dirt.

"Enjoying the worms, *gaijin*? It's all your kind deserve to eat!" taunted Kazuki. "*Gaijin* aren't worthy to be taught our secrets. *Our* martial arts. You don't belong. Go home, *gaijin*!"

He twisted Jack's arm one notch farther, and it felt like it was about to break.

"Sensei!" warned Nobu.

Kazuki jumped to his feet, releasing his grip on Jack.

"Another time, *gaijin*!"

Then both Kazuki and Nobu were gone, fleeing around the corner of the Chō-no-ma.

Jack lay there, clutching his arm to his chest. He trembled as he thought of Kazuki's final words—

Another time, gaijin!—ominously echoing Dragon Eye's threat.

The pain subsided, and he tested his arm cautiously. It wasn't broken, but it still hurt a great deal when he moved it. Sensei Yamada shuffled up as Jack lay there nursing his aching arm. The sensei leaned upon a bamboo walking stick and looked down at Jack like he was inspecting an insect with a broken wing.

"In order to be walked on, you have to be lying down," he said matter-of-factly, before resuming his unhurried journey across the courtyard toward the sleeping quarters.

"What's that supposed to mean?" Jack called after him, but the old sensei gave no reply. The only response was the diminishing click of the walking stick as it echoed around the stone courtyard.

CHAPTER 26

DEFEATING THE SWORD

"O wwww!"

Jack rubbed his shins and hobbled into the Butokuden. He laid his *bokken* along the edge of the hall with the other students' weapons, then gingerly knelt in line beside Yamato.

Akiko entered with Kiku and bowed. Saburo hurried in behind them.

"Owwww!" cried Saburo.

He came hopping across the floor and eased himself into line, biting his lip against the pain.

Sensei Hosokawa stood by the main entrance brandishing a *shinai*, a bamboo sword. He scrutinized the remainder of the new students making their way across the courtyard to the *dojo* for their first period of the day—a morning session of *kenjutsu*. Three more got struck across the shins upon entering.

"Martial arts does *not* begin and end at the gate of the *dojo*!" thundered Sensei Hosokawa as the last student joined the nervous rank of kneeling boys and girls. "Always bow with your sword raised high when you enter the *dojo*. Anyone caught dragging their feet, slouching, or being inattentive will feel the edge of my *shinai*!"

The whole line immediately stiffened to avoid any possibility of slouching. Sensei Hosokawa paced the hall, inspecting each prospective samurai. As he leveled with Jack, he stopped.

Jack glanced up. Hosokawa appeared to be sizing him up.

"I hear from Sensei Masamoto," he began, "that you fought a ninja and defeated him with a *bokken*. Is this true?"

"Umm . . . *hai* . . . sort of . . ."

"*Hai*, SENSEI!" he thundered at Jack.

Jack quickly apologized and bowed lower. *Idiot!* He had forgotten the proper etiquette when addressing a person of higher status. "*Hai*, Sensei. I was helping Yamato—"

"Excellent," he said, cutting Jack off. "Were you afraid?"

Jack didn't know what answer Hosokawa was expecting. He glanced down the line of students, who were all gawking at him. *Should he admit that he was terrified? That he thought the ninja was going to run him through with his sword? Or else throttle him just like his father had been?*

Jack could see Kazuki sneering at him, eager to hear the *gaijin* admit his weakness to everyone. Then he caught Akiko's eye; she was nodding.

"*Hai*, Sensei," said Jack cautiously.

"Absolutely," agreed Hosokawa. "One should be afraid when facing a ninja."

Jack breathed a sigh of relief as the sensei retraced his steps along the line.

"Courage is not the absence of fear, but rather the judgment that something else is more important than fear. Jack valued his loyalty to Yamato above fear. An ideal worthy of a samurai."

Jack swelled with pride at the unexpected compliment and caught Kazuki looking thoroughly annoyed at the sensei's praise.

Sensei Hosokawa continued, "Jack showed courage, conquered fear, and so defeated his opponent. A fine lesson to start your training in the way of . . ."

He stopped midsentence. Nobu was laboring across the courtyard, late for the lesson. He was tucking in his kimono as he went, his *bokken* shoved awkwardly under his armpit. The sensei strode across to the door and waited.

Every student knew exactly what was coming. Nobu

kept running, oblivious to his inevitable punishment.

"Owwww!"

Sensei Hosokawa's *shinai* rapped Nobu so sharply across both shins that his feet went out from under him, and the boy fell flat on his face, his *bokken* clattering across the wooden floor. There was the sound of stifled laughter from the other students before Sensei Hosokawa cut them short with a stern look.

"Get up! Never be late for my class again," Hosokawa ordered, kicking Nobu firmly in the rear. "And never present yourself like that in my *dojo!*"

Nobu scrambled to his feet, looking like he was going to explode with shame, then scurried over to the rest of them, bowing and scraping all the way.

"Right. Now that we're all here, we can begin your training. Pick up your *bokken*, then line up in three rows down the *dojo*. Give yourself enough space to swing your weapon."

They all bowed and got to their feet, haphazardly forming themselves into three ragged lines.

"What is this?" screamed Hosokawa. "Everyone ten push-ups! Kazuki, count off!"

The whole class dropped to the floor and commenced their punishment.

"One! Two! Three! Four! Five! . . ."

"Next time I say, 'Line up,' I expect you to run! And form ordered lines!"

Jack's arms shook a little with the effort, but despite last night's torture, two years of climbing the rigging had strengthened him enough to cope without breaking a sweat. Some of the students, though, began to skip counts, and several gave up completely. Kazuki continued unabated, not even out of breath.

". . . Eight! Nine! Ten! Now line up!"

Everyone got to their feet and sprinted into position.

"Better. First, I want you to simply hold your *bokken* in your hands."

Jack adjusted his wooden sword until it was positioned exactly as Yamato had shown him back in Toba.

"Where is your *bokken*?" Hosokawa suddenly demanded of a small, mouselike boy who stood quietly at the back.

"Sensei, I left it in the Shishi-no-ma," he said, cringing.

"What's your name?"

"Yori, Sensei."

"Well, Yori-kun, what sort of samurai will you make?" asked Hosokawa in disgust.

"I don't know, Sensei."

"I'll tell you—you'll be a dead one. Now get a spare from the weapons wall."

Yori scampered over and retrieved one from the back wall, where the wooden panels were loaded with weapons—swords, knives, spears, staffs, and half a dozen weapons Jack had no name for.

"To begin with, class, I want you simply to get a feel for the *bokken*. Hold it. Get an idea of its weight, its shape, its point of balance. Swing it around—without hitting the walls, the floor, or anyone else!"

Jack shifted the *bokken* in his hands, juggling it between his left and right. He tried some basic cuts, then spun himself around. He held it over his head and swung it in a great arc. Saburo was doing the same, but failing to pay enough attention, struck another student on the back of the head.

"I said without hitting anyone else!" shouted Hosokawa, who rapped his *shinai* across Saburo's shins again. "The sword is an extension of your arm. You should instinctively know where its *kissaki* is, the reach of its blade, and where it is in relation to your own body at all times."

Without warning, Hosokawa brought his *shinai* up and struck at Yamato's head with lightning speed, stopping within a hair's breadth of his nose. Yamato flinched at the unforeseen attack, his eyes wide open in shock.

"What is the use of power if there is no control?" Hosokawa said, letting his weapon drop. "Now hold your *bokken* out in front of you. Both arms out straight, your weapon resting horizontally upon the edges of your hands."

Jack stood there, the weight of the *bokken* gently

pushing down on his outstretched hands. Not too hard, he thought.

"Keep holding it there until I tell you to stop."

Sensei Hosokawa began to pace the room thoughtfully. Like an army turned to stone, every student held their arms out, *bokken* on top, and waited for his command to stop.

One by one, the arms started to quiver. Two up from Jack, Kiku began to drop her arms.

"Did I say you could lower your arms?" barked Hosokawa, and Kiku instantly straightened, her face pinched and straining at the effort.

A few minutes later, a girl in the far corner dropped her *bokken*, unable to continue.

"Given up?" asked Hosokawa. "Go sit at the side. Who's next?"

Several students immediately gave up, including Kiku and Yori. Akiko was beginning to strain. Jack, however, was still feeling quite fresh.

Five others lowered their arms, breathless with the effort, and left the training area.

"Beaten so easily?" Hosokawa said with obvious derision, as Saburo gave up at the same time as Nobu.

"Excuse me, Sensei?" asked Saburo with appropriate deference, while massaging the aches out of his arms.

"Yes?"

"What is the purpose of this exercise?"

"The purpose?" Hosokawa said, incredulous. "I would have thought that was obvious. If your own sword can defeat you in your own hands, what hope do you have of defeating your enemy?"

The revelation of the point of the exercise renewed the efforts of all those who were still standing. Everyone was keen to impress the sensei in their first lesson, so they pushed through the pain.

A few minutes later, two others dropped out, leaving only five students standing—Jack, Kazuki, Yamato, Akiko, and Emi, an elegant but haughty girl, whom Jack had been told was the first daughter of the *daimyo* Takatomi, the sponsor of the school.

Akiko's arms were beginning to shake, but she appeared determined to beat the remaining girl. Emi, however, was the more stable of the two. She looked over at Akiko and gave her a strained but victorious grin. She clearly didn't wish to lose face either. Akiko began to take shallow breaths, willing herself to keep going. Out of the corner of Jack's eye, he could see Emi's arms beginning to drop. But then Akiko reached her physical limit and dropped her *bokken*.

Barely a second later, Emi's arms collapsed too.

"Excellent," commented Hosokawa. "Emi, you demonstrated strong fighting spirit. You earned my respect."

They both went to sit down. On the way, Emi, with

a triumphant smirk on her face, brushed into Akiko. Evidently wanting the chance to wipe away the girl's supercilious expression, Akiko restrained herself and bowed politely.

"We still have three valiant warriors left," announced Hosokawa. "*Kohai*, this is no longer about strength or stamina. This is about willpower. Mind over matter. It's about testing the very limits of your endurance."

Yamato was shaking like a tree in a storm. Jack knew he would not last much longer, but that didn't matter. *He* was intent on outdoing Kazuki.

Kazuki, though, appeared as steady as a rock.

A few moments later, Yamato's arms failed him, and he had to join the others at the edge of the *dojo*.

Jack and Kazuki continued to battle it out—the fight as much in their own minds as with one another.

Kazuki's arms suddenly shuddered under the weight of the *bokken*.

"Kazuki!" shouted Nobu in support, and several other students immediately joined in. "Kazuki! Kazuki! Kazuki!"

Kazuki, revived by the support, straightened his arms out again. He grinned at Jack, confident of his victory over the *gaijin*.

Then Saburo blurted, "Come on, Jack!" and Akiko, Yamato, and Kiku added to the chorus "Jack! Jack! Jack!"

The two boys stood in the center of the Butokuden, warriors fighting an invisible war, their armies chanting from the wings.

Jack thanked the Lord for all the hours he had spent as a rigging monkey on board the *Alexandria*. He was used to hanging on with his arms for hours at a time in wind, rain, or snow.

Yet he also knew his limits and recognized the signs that he was approaching the end of his endurance. He had perhaps another minute or so before his arms gave up entirely.

Kazuki, however, was once more as steady as a rock.

CHAPTER 27

A REASON TO TRAIN

A SINGLE BEAD of sweat rolled down Kazuki's face, and his arms began to tremble.

That was all the incentive Jack needed. Kazuki was fading fast.

"Jack! Jack! Jack!"

The shouts kept coming.

"Kazuki! Kazuki! Kazuki!"

No, he wasn't going to be beaten by Kazuki! He would *not* be defeated by the sword. He could see Akiko willing him on from the sidelines, and he fought the *bokken* in his hands. Gritting his teeth, he closed his eyes and called upon every last drop of strength he had.

Suddenly, like the breaking of a wave, his body flooded with a curious energy. He experienced an infinite nothing, his arms seeming to stretch on forever, weightless, almost numb.

There was a loud wooden clatter as a *bokken* fell to the floor of the *dojo*; then an explosion of clapping and cheering and only the sound of his name.

"Jack! Jack! Jack!"

"Well done, Jack-kun. You defeated the sword," said Sensei Hosokawa.

Jack opened his eyes to see Kazuki fuming, his arms limp by his side, his *bokken* lying on the floor.

With utter relief, Jack lowered his aching arms. They felt heavy as lead, but he had won. He had beaten Kazuki—in front of everyone. Relishing his very public triumph, he bowed to Kazuki.

Kazuki, imprisoned by etiquette, was forced to acknowledge Jack's victory with a lower bow.

At lunch that day, Akiko, Yamato, Kiku, and Saburo crowded around Jack at the table at the far end of the Chō-no-ma. Kazuki sat rigid at the opposite table, fixing Jack with a thunderous expression and ignoring the attempts of Nobu and Emi to lighten his mood.

"How did you manage it, Jack?" pestered Saburo between slurps of noodle soup. "Your arms were dropping. Then BANG! They went straight as an arrow."

"I don't know," said Jack, who was still trying to massage the remaining tension from his shoulder muscles. "I just had a rush of energy, and my arms became weightless. I've never felt that way before"

"*Ki!*" said Kiku.

Jack looked at her, baffled.

"*Ki* means 'life force.' My father explained it to me once. It's your spiritual energy. With training, samurai can channel it into their fighting," explained Kiku.

"Of course!" interrupted Saburo enthusiastically. "The *sohei* monks of Mount Hiei were legendary for being able to harness their *ki*. Supposedly they could defeat their enemies without even drawing their swords."

They all gave Saburo a collective look of disbelief.

"No, really! Sensei Yamada will probably teach us how to use our *ki*. We have his Zen class this afternoon. We could all learn to defeat our swords."

"It's unlikely he'll be any help," mumbled Jack, more to himself than anyone else, but Akiko overheard him.

"What makes you say that?" she asked.

"Well, last night Kazuki decided he wanted me to apologize and tried to break my arm."

Everyone stopped eating and stared at Jack.

"Why didn't you report him?" Akiko asked, putting down her soup and inspecting his arm.

"What's the point? Kazuki stopped before anything happened. But only because Sensei Yamada showed up.

Sensei wasn't much help, though—he just spouted some meaningless saying at me."

"What was it?" asked Yamato, returning to his lunch and slurping appreciatively.

"'In order to be walked on, you have to be lying down.' Some sage he is! What help is that?"

"Excuse me." A tiny voice piped up, and Yori, the boy who had forgotten his *bokken*, peeped around from behind Saburo. "Sensei Yamada may be suggesting you learn to defend yourself."

It took a moment for the meaning to sink in before Jack realized Yori was right. It was suddenly so obvious. If he could master the sword and *taijutsu*, and be stronger, faster, and better than Kazuki, then it would be Kazuki lying down, not him.

With the right skills, he could defend himself against anyone, maybe even Dokugan Ryu.

Now that was a reason worth training for.

"Are you all right, Jack?" asked Akiko, curious at the look of determination fixed upon Jack's face.

"Absolutely. I was just thinking about what Yamada said. It makes sense now. Complete sense."

There and then, after just one lesson at the Niten Ichi Ryū, Jack vowed to devote himself to the Way of the Warrior.

CHAPTER 28

THE DARUMA DOLL

"COME. COME. *Seiza*!" encouraged Sensei Yamada as they hovered at the entrance to the Butsuden, the Buddha Hall, on the east side of the courtyard.

Sensei Yamada beckoned them in. He was perched on a raised dais at the rear of the hall, sitting upon a small around *zafu* cushion, which in turn was set upon a larger square *zabuton*. He wore a simple robe of charcoal blue and sea green and sat cross-legged, his hands laid gently in his lap, the tips of his fingers touching. He reminded Jack of a genial toad on a lily pad.

The afternoon light fingered its way into the hall through slatted windows, catching smoky trails of incense and giving Sensei Yamada's beard the appearance of a finely woven spider's web. The air was heady with the scent of jasmine and sandalwood, and Jack soon felt calmed by the aroma.

The class settled themselves upon cushions set out in semicircular rows. Jack found a *zabuton* near the front with Akiko, Yori, and Kiku. As Jack made himself comfortable, he saw Kazuki and Nobu enter last and sit at the back of the class. Kazuki caught Jack's eye and shot him a venomous look.

"Please. Sit as I do," gestured Yamada.

There was much shuffling as the students rearranged themselves to mirror Sensei Yamada's pose.

"This is a half-lotus position. Good for meditation. Encourages the circulation of your *ki*. Everyone comfortable?" he enquired, and then took a long measured breath. "Now in front of each you is a gift to welcome you to my Zen class."

Jack looked at the wooden object by his feet. It appeared to be a small, egg-shaped doll without arms or legs. Painted in a vivid red, it had a bright, surprised face with a black mustache and beard. Curiously, its white eyes had been left blank.

"Can anyone tell me what it is?" Yamada asked.

Kiku raised her hand. "It's a Daruma doll. It's modelled on Bodhidharma, the founder of Zen. You write your name on its chin and fill in one of its eyes with black ink while you make a wish. If the wish comes true, you color in the second eye."

"Yes, that is what it is, but it is much more than that," said Yamada, lightly pushing the Daruma doll that sat in front of him.

The doll lolled to one side, slowed, then rolled the opposite way and slowed, before continuing the motion in smaller and smaller sways.

The class waited patiently for Sensei Yamada to continue, but the old man appeared to have fallen into a trance. Only when the doll had completely stopped moving did Sensei Yamada look up, blinking as if surprised they were all still there.

"So who can tell me what the Nine Views are?" he continued, apparently unaware he had not explained his last statement.

Nobody raised a hand.

Sensei Yamada waited.

Still no one offered an answer. Still Yamada waited, as if the answer simply needed to settle in the minds of his students, like dust on an old book.

At last, Kiku tentatively raised her hand.

"Yes, Kiku-chan?"

"Is it the nine rules to achieve enlightenment?"

"Not exactly, Kiku-chan, but a worthy summation," said Yamada, obviously pleased with her effort. "It is an ascending sequence of nine stages, or views, that a samurai needs to pass through during meditation. Proper understanding of the Nine Views ultimately leads to *satori*, enlightenment."

An enigmatic smile appeared on his lips, and his eyes sparkled like sunlight on a stream. Jack felt himself being drawn into the old man's gaze, as if he were a leaf floating upon that same stream.

"This meditation process is called *zazen*. The aim of *zazen* is sitting and opening the hand of thought. Once your mind is unhindered by its many layers, you will be able to realize the true nature of things and thereby gain enlightenment."

Sensei Yamada's voice was the sound of a babbling brook, the hum of bees in summer, and the soft tenderness of a mother all rolled into one. So while Jack did not really understand what the sensei was talking about, he drifted effortlessly along with the hypnotic ebb and flow of the old man's speech.

"Today we will practice *zazen* on the Daruma doll. We will meditate for one stick of time," he said, lighting a short length of incense that would measure their progress.

"The first View is to adopt the proper meditative posture, as you are all doing now—seated, legs folded, back straight but relaxed, hands on top of one another, eyes half closed."

Everyone resettled themselves into the position.

"The second View is to breathe from the *hara*. Aim

just above your navel. This is your center. Breathing should be slow, rhythmic, and calm. *Mokuso*," he said, beginning the breathing meditation.

Jack concentrated on his breathing, but found it difficult to shift his breath from his chest down to his stomach.

"From the *hara*, Jack-kun. Not the chest," said Yamada softly.

How on earth could he tell? thought Jack, astounded. He refocused on his breathing, trying to push out his stomach rather than raising his chest.

Sensei Yamada let the whole class slow their breathing for several minutes.

"The third View is to soothe the spirit. Let go of any trivial thoughts, distracting emotions, or mental irritations. Imagine they are snow in your mind. Let them all melt away."

Jack became aware that his mind was crammed with thoughts. They buzzed in his head like wasps—*Kazuki, the rutter, Dragon Eye, Akiko, home, Masamoto, his father, Jess . . .* He tried to calm his mind, but as he pushed one thought away, another instantly took its place.

"The fourth View is fulfilment. As your worldly thoughts dissipate, begin to fill your body with *ki*. Envision yourself as an empty vessel. Pour in your spiritual energy as if it were honey. Let it fill you from the bottom of your feet to the top of your head."

It was impossible for Jack to concentrate on this next stage while he was still struggling with the last one. He found his mind constantly being dragged away by random thoughts.

"The fifth View is natural wisdom. When one is calm, undisturbed, and at peace, things can be seen in their true light. This naturally leads to the development of wisdom."

Sensei Yamada's mellifluous voice continued to lull everyone into a dreamlike state. He let them float for a while longer before continuing. Jack was still trying to clear his mind so that he could fill himself with *ki* and once again experience the energy he had stumbled upon during the *bokken* test.

"For today we will remain at this fifth View and begin with a basic *koan*, a question for you to answer for yourselves. Focus your attention on your Daruma doll and start it rocking. We all know what it is, but what is it?"

It was clear Sensei Yamada didn't want to hear an answer to his *koan*, but only for them to ponder on an answer. Unfortunately for Jack, he was still unable to focus properly, and no solutions were forthcoming. The Daruma doll still looked like a Daruma doll, its sightless eyes as blank as Jack's answer.

Jack's mind wandered from the doll, thoughts flickering like shadows, until the incense stick had burned through and Sensei Yamada chimed, *"Mokuso yame!"*

Everyone ceased their attempts at meditation, and there was an audible sigh of relief now that the task was over.

"Well done, everyone. You have just learned an important ideal of *Bushido*," said Sensei Yamada, a smile of contentment spreading across his face, as if the answer to the *koan* were as clear as daylight.

Jack still didn't understand what the sensei was talking about. He glanced around and saw that many of the other students also had confused expressions on their faces. Enlightenment had clearly not graced them either. Kiku and Yori, however, appeared quite satisfied with their experiences.

"Tonight I want you all to continue your meditation upon the doll. See what else you can learn from it." Sensei Yamada nodded sagely, suggesting there were many more truths to be discovered from the wooden toy. "The key to the art of Zen is daily regularity, so discipline yourself by meditating every morning and night for half a stick of time. Soon you will see life for what it is."

He bowed, signifying the end of the lesson. The students got to their feet and bowed back, departing with their Daruma dolls in hand.

Jack shook the blood back into his legs and went to join Akiko, Kiku, and Yamato.

"Remember to paint in the first eye and make a

wish!" Sensei Yamada called cheerily after them, remaining perched upon the dais of cushions, still the genial toad on a lily pad.

Emerging from the dim Butsuden into the main courtyard, Jack had to shade his eyes against the winter sun, which had dipped low in the evening sky.

"So, what was that all about?" asked Saburo, who came shuffling down the Butsuden steps behind them.

"I don't know," replied Yamato. "Why not ask Kiku? She seems to know everything."

"You're supposed to work it out yourself," said Kiku.

"I still don't get it," said Saburo. "It's just a wish doll."

"No it's not. It's more than that," responded Kiku, rolling her eyes in exasperation.

"That's exactly what Sensei Yamada said. You're just repeating his words. I reckon you don't have a clue either," challenged Saburo.

"Yes I do," she replied primly, and refused to say any more.

"Will *someone* tell me what he meant?" pleaded Saburo. "Akiko? Yamato?"

They both shrugged.

"I would ask you, Jack, but you probably don't even know what Zen is."

He was right. Jack didn't know. He had hoped

someone would tell him, but hadn't dared ask, for fear of appearing even more stupid.

"Seven times down, eight times up," said a tiny flutelike voice.

They all turned to see Yori coming down the steps toward them.

"What?" said Saburo, confusion crinkling his bushy eyebrows.

"Seven times down, eight times up. No matter how often you are knocked down, get up and try again. Like the Daruma doll."

They all stared at Yori in bewilderment.

"Sensei Yamada taught us a vital lesson in *budo*. Never give up."

"Why didn't he just tell us that?" said Saburo.

"That's not the way Zen works," said Kiku, clearly annoyed at Yori for revealing the answer. She turned to Jack, as if offering the explanation for his benefit only. "Zen emphasizes the idea that ultimate truth in life must be experienced firsthand, rather than pursued through study."

"Sorry?" said Jack, desperately trying to grasp the concept.

"Sensei Yamada is meant to guide us, not instruct us. You are meant to discover the answer for yourself. If Sensei Yamada had just told you the answer, you wouldn't have understood its true meaning."

"I would have!" interrupted Saburo. "It'd save me a lot of brain ache too!"

That night, Jack lit a short stick of incense and sat cross-legged in the half-lotus position in his room, contemplating the red doll. He pushed it over and watched it wobble. He waited patiently for enlightenment.

A stick later, an answer wasn't forthcoming, so he lit another and poked the Daruma doll again. Its gentle movement began to lull him. He pushed it once more, and without anyone there to distract him, Jack felt himself drift. The doll continued to sway.

Jack's posture relaxed . . . his eyes half-closed . . . his breathing slowed . . . his mind calmed . . . his thoughts became less chaotic . . . his body gradually filled with a soft warm glow . . . *ki* . . . Then a single thought burned bright in his mind.

He *knew* what to wish for.

Jack painted in the first eye.

CHAPTER 29

SENSEI KYUZO

JACK WAS FLYING through the air.

The floor rushed up to meet him. With a sickening crunch, he landed on his back, the wind completely knocked out of him. He lay there, gasping for breath.

A second later, Yamato crumpled in a pile next to him, followed by Saburo, who dropped on top of them both, pinning them to the floor.

"Idiot!" they both barked at Saburo.

"Sorry. His claims just seemed a little . . . unbelievable," replied Saburo, rolling off them and rubbing his chest.

"Well, now you know they weren't!" said Yamato, kicking him away.

Jack shot Saburo a resentful look. It was his fault

that they were in such trouble. Sensei Kyuzu had been introducing himself and listing his victories over various renowned warriors, when Saburo inadvertently snorted his disbelief and Sensei Kyuzu had stormed over.

"What was that? Think I'd lie for the benefit of a sniveling *kohai*? Think someone my size cannot defeat a six-foot Korean warrior? Get up! You, Yamato, and the *gaijin* there," he said, stabbing a gnarled finger at Jack. "Attack me. All of you at once."

They had stood awkwardly in the middle of the Butokuden, looking like startled rabbits. The old man was smaller than all of them, but appeared as dangerous as a rattlesnake.

"Come on. I thought you were samurai!" he taunted. "I'll even it up a little. I promise only to use my right arm."

The class had snickered at this outlandish gesture.

"Attack me now!" he screamed.

They had stared at one another, then, as one, charged at Sensei Kyuzo. Jack had not even touched the sensei before he was flung through the air, crash-landing on the *dojo* floor seconds before Yamato and Saburo joined him in humiliating defeat.

As Jack knelt back in line, he noticed Kazuki smirking at him.

"I am grateful to my parents for giving me a small body. Warriors underestimate me. You underestimate me," said Sensei Kyuzo defiantly. "Have I knocked belief into you yet, Saburo-kun?"

"*Hai*, Sensei," said Saburo, bowing so forcefully that his forehead struck the floor.

Sensei Kyuzo continued to lecture them while he punched and stabbed at a wooden post with his fingers. Hard as iron, they made the post shudder each time he struck it.

"In order to overcome bigger opponents, I have had to hone my techniques to perfection and train twice as hard."

His voice pummeled their ears in short bursts, keeping time with his punching.

"If my enemy trains one hour, I train two. If they train two hours, I train four. The key to *taijutsu* is hard work, constant training, and discipline. *Hai*?"

"*Hai*, Sensei," said each student.

"I asked if you understood. The gods in heaven need to hear your answer. *Hai*?" demanded Sensei Kyuzo again.

"*HAI*, SENSEI!" they yelled in unison, their shout resounding off the walls.

"Every time you step out that door, you face ten thousand foes. *Hai*?"

"*HAI*, SENSEI!"

"Regard your hands and feet as weapons against them. *Hai*?"

"*HAI*, SENSEI!"

"Tomorrow's victory is today's practice. *Hai?*"

"*HAI*, SENSEI!"

"Your first year of *taijutsu* will be devoted to basic techniques."

Sensei Kyuzo continued to punch the air with his words while slamming the wooden post with his fist.

"Master the basics. They are all that matter. Get your stances right. Make your moves precise. Then you can fight. Fancy techniques are for traveling fairs and impressing ladies. The basics are for battle."

Suddenly he stopped his pounding of the post.

"You, *gaijin*! Come over here," ordered Sensei Kyuzo.

"My name is Jack, Sensei," replied Jack stiffly, taken aback at the sensei's insulting use of the term.

"Fine. *Gaijin Jack*, come here," he said, beckoning him with one sharp flick of his hand.

Kazuki let out a snort of laughter, whispering "*Gaijin Jack*" under his breath to Nobu.

"Kazuki!" said Sensei Kyuzo, without taking his eyes off Jack. "I trust that you will live up to your father's reputation as a samurai. Pay attention!"

Jack got up and stood opposite Sensei Kyuzo. He didn't know what to expect; the sensei was clearly ruthless. Jack certainly wasn't going to underestimate him again.

"Before we deal with kicking, punching, or throwing, you must be able to control your enemy. We are going to start with grabs and locks, since it is easier for you to feel the energy lines in a hold than a strike."

He squared up to Jack, eyeing him meanly.

"Grab my wrist as if you were trying to prevent me from drawing my sword. Attack me!" he ordered Jack.

Jack stepped up and warily took hold of the sensei's arm. His own wrist instantly flared with pain, and he involuntarily dropped to his knees to relieve the agony. Sensei Kyuzo had merely wrapped his hand over Jack's arm and twisted it toward him, but the effect was overpowering.

"This is *nikkyō*. It applies painful nerve pressure to the wrist and forearm," explained Sensei Kyuzo. "Tap your hand on your thigh or the floor when it gets too unbearable, *gaijin*."

Sensei Kyuzo then rolled Jack's wrist a notch farther, and Jack was blinded with agony. Jack frantically slapped his thigh and the technique stopped. Through eyes watery with pain, Jack could see Kazuki thoroughly delighting in his public suffering.

"Get up and attack me as hard and fast as you can," he ordered.

Jack did, but was immediately driven to the ground again by the same simple move. Jack's hand thrashed wildly on his thigh and the pressure was released.

"You see, the soft controls the hard. The harder *Gaijin Jack* tried to attack, the easier it was for me to defeat him," he said, a callous smile on his lips as he demonstrated the technique several more times for the benefit of the class.

Sensei Kyuzo then performed further techniques on Jack, flinging him around like a puppet, using him as a punching bag, pushing him over for having a poor stance. By the end, Jack was exhausted, bruised, and aching.

"Now I want all of you to practice *nikkyō*. Partner up—decide who is the *tori*, executing the technique, and who is the *uke*, receiving the technique. Kazuki, why not train with my *uke*? He should be nicely warmed up for you."

Jack groaned inwardly at the unfairness, but was determined not to let his frustration get the better of him in front of Kazuki.

"Since you are my *uke*, *Gaijin Jack*, I go first," said Kazuki, offering his arm for Jack to grab.

"Remember, everyone," warned Sensei Kyuzo, "if the technique is applied too severely, tap the floor or your thigh to let your partner know. They *must* release you."

Jack clamped his hand over Kazuki's wrist, confident that Kazuki's inexperience would mean he would not be able to apply the technique. But Kazuki had clearly practiced *nikkyō* before. Jack dropped to his knees, his body instinctively reacting to avoid the pain.

Jack tapped his thigh.

Kazuki applied more pressure.

Jack tapped harder.

Kazuki twisted Jack's wrist as far as it would go. So acute was Jack's agony that tears streamed down his face. Kazuki looked on, a vindictive glee in his eyes.

"Change partners," commanded Sensei Kyuzo.

"Good training with you, *Gaijin Jack*," spat Kazuki, dropping Jack's wrist and striding off to find his next victim.

Jack fumed. He hadn't even been given the chance to retaliate.

When class came to an end, Jack was the first to leave.

Akiko came hurrying out and chased after him.

"Are you all right, Jack?" she asked.

"Of course not! Why couldn't Sensei Kyuzo pick someone else to demonstrate on?" he said, exploding with pent-up rage. "He's just like Kazuki. He hates *gaijin*."

"No, he doesn't. Sensei Kyuzo will probably use someone else next time," she said, trying to placate him. "Anyway, it is good to be *uke*. Masamoto told me that it's the best way to learn. Then you'll know how the technique should feel when applied properly."

Jack could hear the taunts of "*Gaijin Jack*" and their accompanying giggles from the passing students as they left the Butokuden and headed to the Chō-no-ma for lunch.

"And what is it with the *Gaijin Jack*? I don't go around insulting them!"

"Ignore them, Jack," said Akiko. "They don't know any better."

But they should, thought Jack. They're all supposed to be samurai.

CHAPTER 30

TARGET PRACTICE

A SPECK OF WHITE, no bigger than an eye, flared brightly in the midday sun. A temple gong chimed, sending its sound shimmering over the school's rooftops.

A streak of feathers, with the speed of a hawk swooping down on its prey, shot through the air accompanied by a high shrill whistling, then a resounding thump like the single beat of a heart as the arrow penetrated the very center of the white target.

A second arrow struck a moment later, parallel to the first, sending both feathered flights quivering.

The students applauded. Sensei Yosa maintained her stance a moment longer, the intensity of her concentration palpable. Then she lowered her bow and approached her students.

"*Kyujutsu* demands a unique combination of talents in a samurai," she began. "The determination of a warrior, the grace of a dancer, and the spiritual peace of a monk."

The students listened intently, all gathered at one end of the Nanzen-niwa, the Southern Zen garden behind the Butsuden. It was a garden of beautiful simplicity, designed around a long rectangular stretch of raked white sand, and decorated with monolithic stones and carefully cultivated plants. An ancient pine tree, twisted and bent by the elements, stood in the opposite corner. Like a frail old man, its trunk was propped up by a wooden crutch. The target was under this tree, and being at the other end of the garden, it appeared no larger than Jack's own head, its central white bull's-eye almost undetectable within the two concentric rings of black.

"The bow is the weapon of choice for long-range fighting. It can be fired by both man and woman, girl and boy, with equally devastating results."

Jack knelt between Yamato and Akiko, in awe both at the lithe beauty and the supreme skill of Sensei Yosa. He was being taught by a lethal angel.

"All the *daimyo* have been trained in *kyujutsu*, from Takatomi Hideaki to Kamakura Katsuro, to Masamoto Takeshi himself. And, of course, it was the weapon that made Tomoe Gozen a legend."

Akiko was transfixed by Sensei Yosa's words. The

mention of Tomoe Gozen had delighted Akiko so much that Jack thought she might burst into applause at any second.

"Unlike the sword, the fist, or the foot, the bow resists you. At full draw the bow is nine-tenths toward actually snapping in half!"

The students gasped in astonishment. Kazuki, though, gazed around, appearing a little bored with it all. Perhaps there wasn't enough violence for him, mused Jack.

"Mastering the Way of the Bow is akin to a pyramid, where the finer skills sit atop a very broad and firm base. You must take the requisite amount of time to build up a strong foundation. We will develop each stage in turn over the coming months," she said, tenderly caressing the feathered flight of an arrow between thumb and forefinger. "Today, though, I simply want everyone to get a feel for the bow. If you're able, maybe even shoot an arrow."

There was a murmur of excitement at the possibility of shooting at a target. Akiko knelt even more erect, a wound-up spring ready to jump to her feet at the first opportunity.

"To begin with, please watch closely, so you can copy my movements," said Sensei Yosa, stepping up to the firing mark. "The first principle in *kyujutsu* is that the spirit, bow, and body are as one."

Sensei Yosa positioned herself carefully, her shoulders

in line with the target, and settled herself into a wide stance, forming an A-shape with her body.

"The second principle is balance. Balance is the foundation stone to *kyujutsu*. Picture yourself as a tree. Your lower half is the trunk and roots, stable and solid. Your upper body forms the branches, flexible yet retaining their form and function. This balance is what will make you a great *kyudoka*!"

Sensei Yosa held her bowstring with her right hand, then positioned her left carefully on the bow's grip. She raised the bow, which was taller than she was, above her head and prepared to draw.

"There is a constant struggle between the mind and body to control the flow of the draw. To strike a target with any degree of precision, absolute focus is required. This is the third principle. The slightest imbalance, a wrong breath, any loss of concentration will result in a miss."

Sensei Yosa brought the bow down, drawing the string past her cheekbone and the arrow in line with her eye, so that her ruby red scar was framed between them.

"When your spirit and balance are correct, the arrow will strike its target. To give yourself completely to the Way of the Bow is your spiritual goal."

Sensei Yosa completed the draw in a single fluid movement. The arrow soared through the air and struck the center of the target once again.

"Who would like to go first?" asked Sensei Yosa.

Akiko's hand shot straight up. Emi, seeing an opportunity to outshine Akiko again, raised her hand too.

"Well, let us begin with you two. Please use these bows. They should be of a suitable size and draw strength," said Sensei Yosa, indicating the lower part of a rack behind her.

"Good luck," said Akiko genially to Emi as the girl rose to take up her position.

"Luck is for the inept," Emi said, dismissing Akiko as she strode up to the firing line.

"Ladies, I would like you to draw the bow as I demonstrated, but do not release until I say so."

They both raised their weapons and drew back, framing themselves within the curve of their bows. Standing beside Akiko, Emi was noticeably taller, her slender figure accentuated by unusually long, arrow-straight hair. Her face had a sharp beauty, highlighted by a pinprick of a mouth. In all, Jack thought, she mirrored her family *kamon*, the crane—tall, slim, and elegant.

"Good. You both show acceptable form. You may fire in your own time; aim at the nearest target." She pointed to one only ten or so paces away.

Emi released, but the bowstring caught on her arm, and her arrow fluttered weakly through the air before landing short of the target.

Akiko's shot was more impressive, flying true but wide of the target.

"That was a fair first attempt," said Sensei Yosa. "You have both done this before?"

"*Hai*, Sensei," admitted Emi with a sour look on her face.

Akiko shook her head, much to Emi's displeasure. "*Iie*, Sensei."

"I am most impressed, Akiko-chan," said Sensei Yosa. "You demonstrate natural aptitude for the bow."

"I want to try again with my second arrow," Emi said petulantly.

Sensei Yosa, slightly taken aback by the girl's haughty tone, appraised both the girls before replying. "I'm not against a bit of a competition. It encourages talent. Please, both of you step up to the mark. Let's see if you can hit the target this time."

Emi lined up again, drew her bow, and fired cleanly. The arrow struck the outer black ring of the target. She looked down her nose at Akiko, assured of her victory.

"Very good, Emi-chan. Let's see if Akiko-chan can improve on that."

Akiko stepped up to the firing line.

Jack held his breath as Akiko positioned herself and took hold of the bowstring. He could see her hands shaking slightly as she reached for the bow grip. Her face became fixed with a steely determination. She steadied herself, raised the bow above her head, and lowering it slowly, drew back on the string. Jack could see Emi willing Akiko to miss. And with the bull's-eye appearing so small, how was Akiko ever going to hit it?

Pulling the bowstring past her cheek, she released the arrow. It cut through the air and struck the target a thumb's width closer to the center than Emi's shot. Jack let out a celebratory yell, and immediately the other students joined in. Akiko beamed with a mixture of delight and astonishment.

"Excellent, Akiko-chan. You may both sit down," said Sensei Yosa. "Who would like to be next?"

Several other students immediately threw up their hands, while a disgruntled Emi and a jubilant Akiko knelt back in line.

Jack watched as each student took his or her turn.

When Kazuki and Nobu stepped up, they both selected the biggest bows they could find from the rack, despite Sensei Yosa's warning that they would be too powerful for them. Nobu immediately proved her right. He lost his grip on the bow, the string snapped back into place and caught him hard across the cheek. Nobu howled in pain, much to everyone's delight. Even Kazuki laughed at his friend's misfortune.

Then it was Jack's turn.

He stepped up to the mark, nocked an arrow, and drew back his bow. Out of nowhere, something struck him on the cheek. Distracted, he lost his grip and the arrow flew off out of control. It hit a large standing stone and ricocheted toward Sensei Yosa, who was standing to one side. The arrow landed at Sensei Yosa's feet, snagging the edge of her *tabi*.

"STOP!" she shouted.

No one moved. A deathly silence fell upon the garden. Jack could clearly hear the scrape of the arrow tip as Sensei Yosa tugged it out of the ground, then the crunch of the gravel as she approached.

"Jack-kun," she breathed into his ear, "did I say you could release your arrow?"

"So sorry, Sensei, but it wasn't my fault."

"Take responsibility for yourself! You are the bow. You had control. See me after class when I will prescribe your punishment."

"Excuse me, Sensei Yosa," Yori said timorously.

"What is it, Yori-kun?"

"It was not Jack, Sensei Yosa. Someone threw a stone at him."

"Is this true?" she demanded of Jack. "Who did that?"

"I don't know," he replied, although he was certain he could guess.

"Yori? Who was responsible?"

The little boy bowed and nervously whispered Kazuki's name.

"What was that, Yori?" asked Sensei Yosa, not hearing his first attempt.

"Kazuki, Sensei . . ." And Yori's voice trailed off.

Kazuki's eyes flared with anger at this open betrayal,

and he made to move on Yori, but shrank back as Sensei Yosa thundered, "KAZUKI! You will see me after class when we will discuss *your* punishment. Now fetch my arrows from the target!"

Kazuki swiftly bowed and dashed to the target. He was so terrified of her wrath that he struggled to pull the arrows out. He had just managed to retrieve the first one when an arrow shot by his ear and impaled the sleeve of his kimono to the target. He spun around, eyes bulging, mouth open in silent horror.

"Arouse a bee, Kazuki-kun, and it will come at you with the force of a dragon!" she called down the garden as she nocked another arrow in her bow. "*Kyujutsu* is highly dangerous for a student. Do not fool around. Do you understand, Kazuki?"

She let the second arrow fly. Kazuki didn't even have time to blink. The arrow clipped him just above the head, parting his hair before striking the target. Kazuki, writhing to escape like a worm impaled on a hook, was desperate to end his humiliation.

"*Hai*, Sensei Yosa! *Moushiwake arimasen deshita!*" he blurted, expressing the highest form of apology possible.

Jack relished his enemy's comeuppance. Perhaps next time, Kazuki would not be so eager to harass him.

Jack turned to Yori to bow his appreciation, but the little boy didn't acknowledge him. He merely knelt there, with blank eyes, biting his lower lip anxiously.

CHAPTER 31

KAZUKI'S WAR

KAZUKI WAS not present at dinner that evening.

For the first time since his arrival in Kyoto, Jack relaxed. Clearly Kazuki was still carrying out Sensei Yosa's punishment. Jack's only concern was that Yori had not turned up for dinner, either. Akiko said she had seen him heading over to the Buddha Hall and thought he may have gone there to see Sensei Yamada. However, when dinner started, Sensei Yamada shuffled in alone.

There was still no sign of Yori when the meal drew to a close, and Jack was certain something had happened to him. He grew even more anxious when he saw Nobu waddle out the door in a hurry.

"Akiko, I'm worried about Yori. He never came to dinner."

"I'm sure he's fine, Jack. He's probably meditating somewhere. I see him meditating in his room morning, noon, and night. He has some lovely sandalwood incense. He even let me try some—"

"I'm serious, Akiko. After *kyujutsu* today, surely he has made an enemy of Kazuki."

"Jack. Kazuki lost face, but he wouldn't dare do anything to Yori. It would be against his honor."

"Honor? What honor? He attacks *me* without any problem."

"That is true, but you're"—Akiko appeared suddenly uncomfortable—"*gaijin* . . . a foreigner. He doesn't see you as an equal. Yori, however, is Japanese, from a samurai family with a long and honorable history."

"But Masamoto has adopted me; surely I deserve the same respect . . ." but he trailed off.

Jack could see it in her eyes. He was not equal. He never would be. Not in hers or Kazuki's eyes. He looked around the table. Saburo and Kiku politely avoided his gaze. Yamato stared coolly back. It was apparent to Jack that Yamato still only tolerated him because his father had commanded him to, despite Jack having saved his life.

"So honor is only reserved for the Japanese, is it?" Jack said, challenging them. Akiko's face crumpled like a snowdrift, and she bowed to avoid his furious glare. "Fine. Well, at least maintain your honor for Yori and help me find him."

"Yes, good idea," said Saburo, attempting to diffuse the situation. "Perhaps Yamato and I can go and look for him in the Niwa? Akiko and Kiku can try to find him in the Shishi-no-ma. Jack, you can check out the Butsuden. Akiko's right, he's probably just meditating somewhere."

Saburo quickly got to his feet, urging everyone to begin searching, and they all hurried out of the Chō-no-ma.

It was another cold starry night, and a half-moon hung in the heavens, illuminating the courtyard in a ghostly pale light as Jack's lone figure climbed the stone steps to the Butsuden's entrance.

Jack wanted to scream at the moon. His frustration at being in Japan simmered like hot oil beneath his skin. He could handle most of it, even Kazuki, but the thing that had hurt him most was Akiko's reaction and the realization that she also saw him as beneath her. Jack thought they were friends. But friends don't divide by difference. They unite because of it.

Jack gave a humorless smile. Now he was starting to sound like Sensei Yamada spouting some Zen proverb. He swallowed down his bitterness. At least Yori had stood up for him. Jack just hoped the boy wasn't in trouble.

Reaching the top step, he peered into the Butsuden's gloomy darkness. Shafts of moonlight cut across the hall like the bars on a cell. He was about to call out Yori's name, when he heard subdued voices, tense and angry.

"I had to spread the night soil from the toilets onto the garden," said the voice. "I've missed my dinner and I stink!"

"So sorry, Kazuki. But it was wrong to . . ."

Jack peered around the door and saw Kazuki standing over the trembling form of Yori. Nobu was looming behind him, his shadow spread fat and bulbous across the floor. Jack pressed himself flat against the wall and, hidden by the darkness, edged closer.

"Wrong? What do you care? He is *gaijin*! He is not worthy of being one of us," spat Kazuki. "I dare not believe that you, Yori, first son of the Takedas, whose ancestors fought and defeated the Mongols, stood up for a mere *gaijin*!"

"But he is really no different from us, Kazuki. . . ." pleaded Yori.

"What? You have much to learn. We are the descendants of Amaterasu, the sun goddess. The samurai are the chosen ones, the warriors of the gods. *Gaijin* are nothing. *Gaijin* are to be ruled over."

Jack was astounded at Kazuki's self-importance. His blood boiled at the boy's ignorance. No one person was better than another. Only different. Kazuki, however, clearly saw difference as a weakness, a flaw, a mistake. Jack steeled himself to intervene. Just as he was about to make his move, Kazuki changed tack.

"But I can be reasonable, Yori," continued Kazuki in an almost appeasing tone. "In recognition of your family's ancestors, I will give you a chance to escape your punishment."

Jack checked himself. Maybe Akiko is right, thought Jack. Perhaps he will honor Yori as a samurai. Yori blinked up at Kazuki in the darkness, confused and anxious.

"You appear to know a lot about Zen. I want you to answer this *koan*. It's a riddle I'm sure you can solve easily. But if you don't, then you will accept your punishment gratefully, although you may find eating a little hard tomorrow."

Nobu chuckled at the threat, cracking his knuckles, the sound reverberating throughout the hall. Yori whimpered.

"Here is your *koan*. Two hands clap and there is a sound. What is the sound of one hand clapping?"

Yori said nothing for a moment, nervously wringing his hands on his kimono, his forehead creased in panicked concentration.

"What is the sound of one hand, Yori?" demanded Kazuki.

"Please. Please. I need silence to think."

"Sorry, but I'm hungry and have little patience. Answer me!"

"It refers to the *koan* itself," blurted Yori. "When

the two hands clapping are seen as the seeking of the answer, the hands themselves become the *koan*. . . . It then follows that you as the meditator . . . become the *koan* that you are trying to understand. That is the sound of one hand clapping."

Yori looked up hopefully at Kazuki, certain his answer was right.

"Excellent. Sensei Yamada would approve of such a philosophical muddle of an answer. But wrong! This is the sound of one hand clapping," said Kazuki, and he raised his own hand and slapped Yori hard across the face. Yori fell to the floor, whimpering.

"No!" shouted Jack, who without a second's thought, flew from the shadows and slammed into Kazuki.

He drove his shoulder into Kazuki's gut, and they both rolled into the middle of the hall. Kazuki was severely winded and couldn't move. Jack punched him in the mouth.

"That one's for Yori," said Jack. "And this is for me!"

Akiko and Kiku came flying into the Butsuden just as Jack raised his fist for the second time.

"Jack!" cried Akiko.

Jack glanced up. It was the split second Kazuki needed. He drove his own fist into Jack's chin, sending Jack backward. Kazuki scrambled to his feet as Jack lay sprawled across the stone floor. Kazuki stood over him, his burst lip trickling blood.

"Bad move, *gaijin*," he spat, lifting his leg to strike.

"No!" warned Akiko, launching herself at Kazuki in an attempt to stop him. But Nobu grabbed her by the hair and pulled her back sharply.

Jack, fired up by Nobu's assault on Akiko, rolled into Kazuki and drove hard into his legs.

Pushed off balance, Kazuki crashed to the floor.

The two boys wrestled, each trying to get the upper hand.

Kazuki managed to roll on top of Jack, trapping his left arm. Jack felt pressure being applied and was immediately paralyzed with pain. He tried to move, but each time he did, Kazuki pressed down harder.

Yamato ran in with Saburo.

"Yamato, help Jack!" cried Akiko, who struggled against Nobu's grip.

Nobu, scared that Yamato might attack him, immediately released Akiko. Kiku ran to her aid, but Akiko didn't need any help. She elbowed Nobu hard in the stomach, causing him to double over in agony.

"Why would you want to help a *gaijin*, Yamato?" shouted Kazuki, breathless from the fight. "Especially one who has usurped your brother's place. I am right, he is Masamoto's adopted son, isn't he?"

Yamato faltered, stalling his approach, and stared at

Jack, who lay pinned down under Kazuki.

"How could you let that happen, Yamato? A *gaijin*, part of your family. The disgrace!"

Kazuki's words rebounded off the walls of the Butsuden, echoing "Disgrace! Disgrace! Disgrace!" in Yamato's ears.

"I can end this dishonor. I can break his arm so badly that even your father couldn't fix it. I don't know many one-armed samurai, do you, Yamato?"

Jack could see Yamato weighing his options. On the one hand, how much better it would be for Yamato if he was gone, and on the other, there was the debt of honor he owed Jack for saving his life. But that was not the real issue here; the wrath of his father would be the deciding factor.

"Masamoto won't punish us," egged on Kazuki, as if reading Yamato's thoughts. "Nobu is my witness. He saw the *gaijin* strike me first. I have every right to defend myself."

Yamato stepped back a pace.

"That's right, Yamato, let me rid you of this *gaijin*. You and I both know he's been a thorn in your side."

Kazuki twisted Jack's wrist a notch farther to emphasize the point. Jack cried out, the pain searing through his arm like a hot iron rod. Then suddenly the pressure disappeared.

Akiko had slammed her foot into Kazuki's back,

using a *mae-geri*, the simple but effective front kick they had been taught that day in *taijutsu*. Kazuki was sent sprawling across the floor.

He flipped over and started toward Akiko.

Instinctively she threw up her guard to counter his attack, but Kazuki checked his strike at the last moment.

"This is foolish," he said, stepping away and raising his hands in a sign of peace. "We're fighting over a *gai-jin*. Masamoto decreed that we should be loyal to the samurai of this school. I will not fight you."

"Yet you would fight Jack, and he is samurai too," Akiko retorted.

"No, he isn't. He never will be, and he knows it. Just look at him."

Jack lay on the floor, cradling his arm, his face bruised and swelling where Kazuki had struck him. Akiko looked down at Jack, her eyes filled with pity.

Jack didn't want pity. He was hurt and ashamed, but not beaten. What he wanted was acceptance, but perhaps that was too much to ask. He turned away from her.

Kazuki bowed and calmly walked over to the door, Nobu following faithfully behind him, still clutching his stomach. Kazuki wiped the blood from his lip with the back of his hand, then turned to face them all.

"I don't want any of you telling the sensei about tonight."

"I'll tell Masamoto—if you ever touch Jack again," threatened Akiko.

"No, you won't. If you do, we'll all be thrown out of the school. Fighting within the Buddha Hall is forbidden."

"Jack is my friend, and I'll defend him—whatever the cost."

Jack couldn't believe his ears. Akiko had declared her loyalty publicly. The significance of her pronouncement was not lost on any of the others present, either.

She helped Jack to his feet.

"Don't be a *gaijin* lover, Akiko! I can't promise to hold back next time you stand in my way," warned Kazuki.

"Harm him and I'll tell. The choice is yours."

Kazuki faltered.

Jack guessed that he couldn't afford to gamble on Akiko's threat. Being thrown out of the Niten Ichi Ryū would be highly inappropriate for a boy of imperial blood, and a permanent loss of face.

"I don't wish to see you disgraced, Akiko, so I'll make you a promise in return for forgetting this night. I'll not fight the *gaijin* again within the walls of the Niten Ichi Ryū. Agreed?"

Akiko looked at Jack before nodding her acceptance.

"*Gaijin!*" snarled Kazuki. "You and I aren't finished. Our war has barely begun."

CHAPTER 32

HANAMI PARTY

A glorious butterfly with iridescent blue wings rested on the pink blossom of a cherry tree. It sipped the sweet nectar of the flower, gaining nourishment and growing strong. Its antennae twitched as the breeze shifted.

Out of nowhere a heavy iron bar came crashing into the blossom. The butterfly flitted away, escaping death only by a fraction of a second. A giant red demon came thundering from the undergrowth, maniacally swinging the bar, intent on catching the butterfly as it settled upon each blossom.

The butterfly effortlessly avoided the blows time and time again. Sweat rolled down the face of the red demon, frustration etched on its brow. The demon, boiling with rage, thrashed at the butterfly again and again, until it collapsed on the barren earth, defeated by its own efforts. The butterfly—with its iridescent blue wings still intact—fluttered away. . . .

JACK'S EYES fluttered open.

A languid trail of incense smoke curled its way to the ceiling of his tiny bedroom. The red Daruma doll sat perched upon the narrow windowsill next to the *bonsai* tree. The doll's solitary eye fixed Jack with an innocuous stare.

Jack breathed heavily, reeling from the clarity of the vision.

Jack could regularly attain the third View—a pure mind—during his morning meditations. It allowed him to think clearly for the rest of the day, but he had never experienced a vision like this before. *What made me see a demon and a butterfly? What did it mean, if it meant anything at all?* This was far beyond anything he had been taught. He would have to speak to Sensei Yamada.

Jack got to his feet and stretched. Taking a small jug from beneath the window, he poured a little water onto his *bonsai* tree. He had done this every morning, as Uekiya had instructed. The old gardener would be pleased.

As Jack tended to the *bonsai*, he spotted tiny pink flower buds emerging. The same as those in his vision. *Sakura* blossom.

The blossom meant it was spring.

Jack couldn't believe it. He had been training at the Niten Ichi Ryū for more than three months. He had been in Japan almost nine months. He had not set foot on English soil in nearly three years! His life was so different from what it had been. He was no longer a child dreaming of being a pilot like his father. He was a boy training to be a samurai warrior.

Every morning he rose before dawn to meditate for

half a stick of time. Then he joined the others for the same bland breakfast of rice and pickled vegetables. What he would give for some English bacon and fried eggs!

After breakfast they embarked upon their lessons for the day. Two long sessions, one in the morning, and one in the afternoon. Some days it was *kenjutsu* and Zen; others it was *kyujutsu* and *taijutsu*. Following training, he would gather with the students in the Chō-no-ma for dinner, the sensei all seated at the head table, like a row of esoteric warrior gods looking over their charges.

After dinner, they would be expected to practice by themselves, perfecting the skills they had learned. *Learn today so that you may live tomorrow* was the mantra that was constantly drilled into them.

Despite the regimented routine and rigorous discipline of this life, Jack had to admit that he was more at peace with himself than he had been for a long while. The routine was a comfort in itself. He was not a free wheel spinning without purpose or direction. He was learning how to defend himself, to live by the code of *Bushido*.

He could now wield a *bokken* with power and accuracy and had mastered the first three attacks—*The only ones you will ever need*, Sensei Hosokawa had said.

He could shoot an arrow, although he had only hit the target a couple of times, unlike Akiko, who had taken to *kyujutsu* as if she had been born with a bow in her hand.

He could now kick, punch, block, and throw. Admittedly, he only knew the very basic techniques, but he was no longer powerless. The next time he met Dragon Eye, he would not be the helpless little boy who failed to save his father.

Since the fight with Kazuki in the Buddha Hall, many things had changed. Akiko, having declared her friendship, was Jack's closest ally. Yori had become a constant companion, but he was so reserved that Jack still didn't really know him. Kiku was pleasant enough to him, though Jack thought that was more for Akiko's benefit than out of any real desire for friendship. Saburo sat on the fence. He was everyone's friend. He would talk to anyone who listened.

Yamato, however, had distanced himself completely. He now sat at the other table with Kazuki, Emi, and Nobu. He still spoke to Akiko and the others, but blatantly ignored Jack. That suited Jack just fine.

On the upside, Kazuki had kept his word. He left Jack alone. He still threw intimidating looks and called him *"Gaijin Jack"* along with the rest of his cronies, but he didn't lay a finger on him. Except when training in *tai-jutsu*.

That was no-man's-land.

During the *kihon* and *randori* sessions in those classes,

Sensei Kyuzo would often turn a blind eye to Kazuki's excessive use of force. One time they had been practicing *ude-uke*, inside forearm blocks, and the power behind each block had escalated until they were both hammering at each other's forearms. The bruises didn't fade for more than a week. Jack had tried to complain about Kazuki's behavior, but Sensei Kyuzo shot him down, saying, "It's good conditioning for you. If you can't take a little pain, you are clearly too much *gaijin* to be a samurai."

Akiko's voice interrupted his thoughts.

"Jack, are you coming?"

She had appeared at his door in a sky blue kimono decorated with butterflies. Jack blinked. She was like the butterfly from his vision! Then Kiku sidled up to her, wearing a light green spring kimono and carrying a small bag.

"Coming where?" Jack asked.

"*Hanami!*" Akiko sang, and hurried off with Kiku in tow.

"What's *hanami*?" Jack called down the hallway after her.

"A flower-viewing party," said Saburo, who had popped his head around the corner. Jack could see Yori waiting silently in the background.

"*A flower-viewing party?* Sounds absolutely thrilling," said Jack with forced enthusiasm. Still, he put down his watering jug and followed them. At least it would make a change from training, he thought.

"This certainly *is* a change," said Jack, letting out a long contented sigh as he lounged on the grassy banks of the Kamogawa River, shaded from the sun by *sakura* trees that literally drooped under the weight of their blossom.

Akiko, Kiku, Yori, and Saburo were sitting beside Jack, equally enjoying the bliss of the moment. This was the first time the students had been allowed out of the school complex, and they were all relishing the freedom.

"So how do you like our *hanami* party?" asked Akiko.

"Well, if all it involves is eating, drinking, and relaxing under cherry blossom trees, Akiko, then this is the best *hanami* party I've ever been to!" Jack replied.

"It's much more than that, Jack!" admonished Akiko, with a good-natured smile.

"You're starting to sound like Sensei Yamada with one of his *koan*!" replied Jack lightheartedly, and they all laughed.

"Seriously, Jack, *hanami* is very important to us," said Akiko. "The cherry blossom marks the start of the rice-planting season, and we use the flowering to divine the success of the harvest. Judging by the fullness of the blossom already, this will be a good year."

"The blossom also signals a beginning, a new stage

in life," added Kiku, "so we make offerings to the gods who live inside the trees. See those samurai over there?"

"Yes," said Jack, peering over at three samurai who were sprawled around the base of a cherry blossom tree. They were passing an extremely large ceramic bottle between them and appeared to be heavily intoxicated. One of the samurai had jumped up and was performing an ungainly dance, kicking his legs high into the air, while the others sang and laughed loudly as their companion repeatedly fell over.

"They have made the traditional offering of *saké* to the *sakura* and are now partaking of the offering."

"What's *saké*?" asked Jack.

"Rice wine!" said Saburo buoyantly. "Want to try some?"

Akiko shot Saburo a disapproving look, which made Jack feel hesitant, but he was also intrigued. "Why not?"

Saburo ran over to the drunken samurai and quickly returned with a wooden, box-shaped cup brimming with clear liquid. He offered some to Jack.

Jack took a swig. The *saké* tasted sweet and watery, but became sharper and more potent as he swallowed. He hacked as the *saké* burned the back of his throat.

"What do you think?" asked Saburo eagerly.

"Well, it's not as rough as the drink on board the ship, but I'll stick to water if you don't mind."

Saburo shrugged indifferently, finishing off the rest

of the cup in one gulp. He went to return the cup to the samurai, only to come back with another full cup. He offered it to the girls this time.

"Saburo, you know we're not allowed to have *saké*," scolded Kiku.

Saburo ignored her and merrily drank the entire cup on his own.

They spent the rest of the day relaxing under the tree, occasionally dipping their toes into the cool waters of the Kamogawa, Saburo getting the occasional refill of *saké*.

As the sun began to set, paper lanterns were lit and hung from the branches of the *sakura* trees, floating like glowing fruit above the walkways. With dusk settling in, it was time for them to return to the Niten Ichi Ryū.

"So, Jack," asked Akiko, "what do you think of the blossom now?"

"Beautiful but brief, like life," said Jack, echoing Uekiya's words.

"No! Fleeting like a woman's beauty!" blurted Saburo, the excess of *saké* having gone to his head. His legs collapsed beneath him as he tried to stand. Kiku and Yori helped him back up.

"Yes, Jack. Like life," agreed Akiko, ignoring Saburo's drunkenness. "You really are beginning to think like a Japanese."

They walked back along the river path, the branches of the *sakura* forming an enchanted bower of blossom and lamplight. Jack and Akiko wandered ahead, while Kiku and Yori juggled the intoxicated Saburo between them.

Under the soft glow of the lanterns, Akiko was even lovelier than usual. Jack remembered the moment he'd first seen her by the headland temple, her white stallion tethered to the standing stone. She had been the one constant since he'd arrived in Japan—nursing him through his fever, helping him to learn the language, teaching him their customs, then defending him from Kazuki. How could he ever repay her for all that she'd done?

He turned to speak, but the words jumbled in his throat, and all he could do was look at her.

She stopped and returned his gaze, her ebony eyes glimmering in the half-light.

"*Eh, Gaijin Jack!*" snarled a voice. "What do you think you're doing?"

Jack felt his blood run cold.

CHAPTER 33

THE *TARYU-JIAI*

KAZUKI'S FACE leered at him from across the path.

"Didn't you hear me, *gaijin*? I said, what are you doing *outside* school?"

"Leave him alone, Kazuki. You promised!" said Akiko, stepping between them.

"Oh, it's the *gaijin* lover! Still can't defend himself, is that it?" taunted Kazuki, who held his hands up in mock defeat. "Need a girl to fight for you, *gaijin*? Did you hear that, boys? The *gaijin* has to have a girl for a bodyguard!"

Snorting with amusement, Kazuki glanced over his shoulder at the four lads who were with him. Nobu rolled with laughter, his large belly heaving. Two boys, whom Jack didn't recognize, jeered approvingly, but the fourth member of Kazuki's gang looked decidedly uncomfortable, suddenly finding his *tabi* of great interest. It was Yamato.

"Well, Akiko beat you, didn't she?" said Jack. One of the boys chortled.

"Only because I had my back to her," snapped Kazuki. "Anyway, I'd be far more concerned about your welfare than mine, *gaijin*. We've got a score to settle."

"No!" exclaimed Akiko, her cheeks flushing with anger. "I warned you, I'll tell Masamoto."

"Tell him what? That a few moons ago we had a little argument in the Buddha Hall? I don't think so. Bit late for that."

He took a step closer to Jack, goading him to make a move.

"You forget, Akiko. My promise only extended to the school walls. Outside, he's fair game. We're not governed by Masamoto here."

"Come on, then," dared Jack. "Let's get it over with."

Jack was fed up with the taunts, the whispering behind his back, the bullying in the *taijutsu* classes, and the constant intimidation and threats. It was like living under a permanent shadow. He couldn't be free of it until the matter between him and Kazuki was settled, once and for all.

"I'd think carefully, *gaijin*, before entering a fight you can't win," said Kazuki. "I don't believe you've ever met my cousins. This is Raiden. His name means Thunder God."

One of the boys stepped forward and bowed. When he righted himself, Jack was astounded at his size. Raiden was a good head taller than Jack. His arms were thick and meaty, and he had tree trunks for legs. He was also unusually hairy for a Japanese person. His eyebrows, dark and bushy, hung off a pronounced forehead, and a profusion of chest hair was trying to escape from inside his kimono.

Jack would have been completely intimidated by Raiden's thunderous appearance, if his eyes hadn't been slightly too close together. They made him look like an overgrown ape, but a bit less intelligent.

"And this is his twin brother, Toru. You don't want to know what his name means, I assure you."

He was identical. Only even more stupid-looking, Jack thought.

"They're from Hokkaido, but you wouldn't know where that is, would you, *gaijin*?" said Kazuki. "Let me enlighten you. It's the north island of Japan, and these boys are from the Seto clan. They're the toughest, most ruthless samurai you'll ever come across. That's why they're enrolled at the Yagyu school here in Kyoto. It's renowned for producing some of the most fearsome warriors in Japan. Sponsored by the great *daimyo* Kamakura Katsuro himself, no less!"

"This is just between you and me, Kazuki," interrupted Jack, fed up with Kazuki's attempts to terrorize him. "Send your apes home!"

Raiden and Toru snarled at the insult, lumbering forward with the clear intention of pulling Jack limb from limb.

"Eh? Whass's going on 'ere?" slurred Saburo, stumbling from Kiku and Yori's grasp and planting himself between Jack and the two approaching giants. "Leave my friend alone. . . . We at a *ha- ha- hanami* party and you 'aven't been invited."

Saburo wobbled slightly, like a Daruma doll, then fell forward, his head thumping against Raiden's chest. Raiden slapped him away as if he were swatting a fly.

"Oww!" said Saburo, reeling from the blow, blood dripping from his nose. "You fat oaf! That hurt!"

Kiku and Yori ran to his aid, but Saburo shrugged them off and wound himself up to take a swing at his assailant. Raiden simply raised his great slab of a fist and drove it at Saburo's face.

"Oi! Pick on someone your own size!" said Jack, and let loose a *yoko-geri*, a side kick, his heel striking directly into Raiden's ribs.

Raiden grunted and staggered sideways, his fist

sailing past Saburo's startled face and straight into the trunk of a nearby *sakura* tree. Raiden howled in pain. Furious, he attacked Jack with a series of wild, swinging punches.

Jack backpedaled to avoid getting caught in the head.

"Watch out!" Akiko cried.

But it was too late. Toru had come up from behind and grabbed Jack in a bear hug, pinioning Jack's arms to his side.

"What are you going to do now, *Gaijin Jack*?" taunted Kazuki, who was watching with unrestrained glee. Behind him, Yamato backed away into the shadows in an attempt to distance himself from the escalating fight.

Toru's grip tightened, and Jack's breath was crushed from his body. Jack felt himself passing out, but Toru's grip eased as the great brute let out a wounded groan.

Akiko had kicked him with *ushiro-geri*, a spinning back kick—the most powerful kick in *taijutsu*. It had struck Toru straight in the side. Any normal person would have crumpled under such a direct hit, but Toru only loosened his grip slightly and glared at Akiko.

So she followed it up with a *mawashi-geri*, a round-house kick. Ready for the attack this time, Toru spun around and put Jack directly in its path. Akiko, desperately attempting to avoid Jack, lost her balance. Toru trapped Akiko's flailing leg with one arm, while keeping hold of Jack with his other.

Once he had them both under his control, he slipped his left arm up Jack's chest and encircled his throat. Toru then began to throttle Jack.

"Stop it!" cried a distraught Kiku, Yori frozen in wide-eyed alarm next to her. "Yamato, help them!"

But Yamato ignored her pleas and retreated farther away from the brawl. Meanwhile, Kazuki and Nobu were delighting in the spectacle, urging the cousins on.

"Haven't you learned anything, *gaijin*? Any real samurai would be able to fight their way out of that," Kazuki sneered.

"Come on, Toru, snap him in half!" Nobu shouted.

Toru tightened his grip around Jack's throat, and Jack choked. But Toru's throttling was the least of Jack's worries. Raiden was heading straight for him with both fists raised.

Jack was still pinioned by Toru's iron grip. Realizing he only had his legs to defend himself, he clamped his hands on Toru's arm, pulling it down just enough to snatch a breath. Then, using Toru's arm for support, he lifted himself off the ground, simultaneously firing off a double *mae-geri*, a front kick, from each leg. The move was totally unexpected, and Raiden, being a fraction too slow to react, was pummeled in the face. He stumbled, bringing his hands up to his flattened, bloodied face.

Saburo spotted his chance and shot out a foot. He caught the back of Raiden's legs, making him trip and bounce off a *sakura* tree. The tree shuddered. The force of the impact dislodged a paper lantern, which dropped straight onto Toru's head.

Its flimsy frame split apart on impact, and the little candle inside fell on the boy's greasy hair, which instantly caught fire. Toru released Akiko and Jack and began to leap around like a dancing bear. He flapped frenetically at his flaming crown, trying to extinguish the fire.

Saburo, Kiku, and Yori broke into peals of laughter at the dancing Toru, but their joy was short-lived.

In the chaos, Raiden had regained his footing and grabbed Saburo by his hair, winding up to knock him out. The incensed Toru, his head smoking like a chimney, bore down on Akiko and Jack.

Their playtime over, the two Seto twins were determined to end the fight with the next strike.

"*YAME!*" boomed a voice with such unquestionable authority that even a passing group of drunken samurai halted in their tracks.

"What in the name of Buddha is going on?" the voice demanded.

Masamoto stepped out of the darkness, his scarred face glowering. The retreating Yamato immediately went pale and bowed his head in shame, while Kazuki and Nobu dropped to their knees in supplication.

"Leave my students alone!" Masamoto ordered, and his hand shot out a *nukite-uchi* at Raiden's neck with lightning speed.

Masamoto's spear-hand thrust struck a hidden pressure point at the back of the neck, causing Raiden's knees to buckle. He collapsed like a puppet whose strings had been cut.

Saburo, rubbing his head where a big clump of hair was missing, scurried over to Kiku and Yori. Then they all bowed in deference to Masamoto.

"Masamoto! Leave *my* students alone," said a voice that came from behind Masamoto.

A samurai in a blue, yellow, and gold kimono strode down the path. As he got closer, the lanterns illuminated his face. Jack immediately recognized him. It was the *daimyo* from the lacquered palanquin on the Tokaido Road, Kamakura Katsuro.

The man was a little shorter than Masamoto, but he still attempted to look down his nose at him. Kamakura had a cruelly pointed face with a stringy mustache that flicked up from a tight mouth. He surveyed the scene with an air of arrogance, his eyes pitilessly examining each of Masamoto's students, as if they were vermin to be exterminated. Kamakura gave off an air of pomposity and self-righteousness. Jack thought of the old tea merchant who had been beheaded simply because he hadn't bowed in time.

"Maintain better control of your students, or I will," Masamoto firmly replied. "It appears to me that you have a discipline problem in your school."

"*We* have no problem with discipline," said Kamakura haughtily. "It seems *your* school has a problem with training. I have never seen such poor technique."

"There was nothing wrong with their technique! Akiko executed an outstanding *ushiro-geri,* and I'd like to see any of your students deliver a *mae-geri* while being strangled!"

"Masamoto, please. We are old comrades in arms," said Kamakura in a falsely conciliatory tone. "This is not a matter to be settled in a public park. Let us do this in the proper tradition. I propose a *Taryu-Jiai* between our two schools."

"A *Taryu-Jiai?*" repeated Masamoto, taken off-guard.

"Those three," said Kamakura, indicating Jack, Akiko, and Saburo with a dismissive wave of his hand, "against Raiden, Toru, and one of my girl samurai, any of whom could outperform your *ushiro-geri* girl!"

"What disciplines do you propose?" queried Masamoto, disregarding the insult directed at Akiko, but warming to the idea.

"*Kenjutsu, kyujutsu,* and *taijutsu.*"

"Agreed," said Masamoto, without showing the slightest hint of concern on his scarred face.

Jack had no idea what it was, but Akiko's face had gone pale, and Saburo had instantly sobered up at the mere mention of it. It seemed like a *Taryu-Jiai* was not a promising prospect.

"Any preference as to the timing of this little contest?" asked Kamakura.

"How about the day before the Gion Festival?" Masamoto replied nonchalantly.

"But that's three moons away!" said Kamakura, incredulous.

"By the look of their performance tonight, your students will need the extra training. We want this to be a real competition, don't we?" replied Masamoto, giving Kamakura a broad smile as he bowed. "Besides, I always like to celebrate my victories with a good festival."

CHAPTER 34

YAMADA'S SECRET

"**W**HY WEREN'T YOU defending their honor?" thundered Masamoto.

The muffled reply couldn't be heard.

"I saw you retreat! Tenno would never have done such a thing," continued Masamoto, spitting anger like fire. "Why didn't you help Jack-kun? Correct me if I'm wrong, but don't you owe Jack-kun a life? He saved you. He's proving to be more samurai than you've ever been."

There was the sound of sobbing and a mumbled apology.

"Where is your courage, your valor, your honor? It is you who should be fighting at the *Taryu-Jiai*, defending the name of my school. Not Jack-kun!"

Masamoto's voice cracked. "You have brought dishonor on this family and on yourself! Think about what it means to be a Masamoto, then come back when you have an answer! Now get out!"

The *shoji* slid open, and Yamato emerged, his face red and wet with tears. He avoided the startled stares of Jack, Akiko, and Saburo, who knelt outside the Hō-Oh-No-Ma, the Hall of the Phoenix. This was Masamoto's personal training hall, where only students good enough to be taught the Two Heavens technique were ever summoned.

"Yamato, I'm sorry . . ." began Jack, wanting to help him in some way.

Yamato just gave him a ferocious glare and hurried off without looking back.

"It's not your fault, Jack," Akiko said quietly.

"Yes it is. If I'd never come here, he wouldn't be in this—"

"ENTER!" Masamoto boomed.

They looked at one another, terrified. After the *hanami* fight, Masamoto had marched them back to the school and ordered them straight to bed. They had hardly slept; Masamoto had demanded to see Jack, Akiko, and Saburo at first light. Akiko had explained to Jack that a summons to the Hall of the Phoenix before breakfast meant only one thing—they were to be punished. They just didn't know how severely.

"*Seiza!*" he said as they entered, all bowing as low as possible.

Masamoto was sitting upon a dais, a small black lacquered table at his side. A maid was clearing up a broken teacup, while another set up a fresh pot of *sencha* for him.

Behind him, painted in vivid colors upon a silk screen, was the image of a flaming phoenix, its wings dripping fire and its beak thrusting up toward heaven. Masamoto fumed like a live volcano, his scar crimson as molten lava. He waited until the maids had departed before speaking. Jack, Akiko, and Saburo trembled and kept their heads low to the ground.

"Sit up!"

Masamoto examined each of them carefully, as if he were measuring the suitability of the punishment with their capacity to withstand it. Masamoto breathed deeply, and Jack's mouth went dry with dread.

"Excellent!" he said, a faint smile breaking through his fiery demeanor. "I was most impressed with the way you handled yourselves last night."

They stared at one another in confusion. Were they not going to be punished?

"Saburo, you are forgiven for your less than sober state. But only because you showed loyalty to your fellow samurai, and your quick-witted sweep of that Raiden character proved to me that even in your drunken condition you could function as a warrior."

Saburo bowed profusely, unable to contain his relief at his pardon.

"Akiko, you are truly a lady of the Niten Ichi Ryū. It is only the bravest of warriors who stand tall in the face of danger," he said, glowing with pride. "Jack's assailant must have been twice your size, but you didn't hesitate. It was unfortunate that he was so bullish that he wasn't felled by your *ushiro-geri*, but don't worry, he'll be waking up very sore this morning."

Akiko bowed and let out a quiet sigh.

"Now to you, Jack," he said, and sipped his cup of *sencha*.

Jack knew that since he was the cause of the quarrel, he would not get away so lightly. He would undoubtedly suffer the full consequences of Masamoto's wrath.

The moment of judgment drew on as Masamoto took his time appreciating his tea. Jack's stomach tightened into a knot of iron.

"You surpass my expectations every time," he finally said. "You have developed your martial skills considerably. You are loyal to your friends. And you have the spirit of a lion. Are you sure you weren't born samurai?"

"No, Masamoto-sama," said Jack, a wave of relief rushing through him at the reprieve.

Bowing, Akiko asked, "Excuse me, Masamoto-sama?"

"Yes, Akiko?"

"Are you telling us that you saw the whole thing?"

"Yes."

"Then why did you not prevent the fight from happening?" interrupted Jack, astonished at this revelation.

"You appeared to be handling yourselves well enough," Masamoto said, tugging at the sleeves of his kimono to straighten them. "Besides, I wanted to see how you would perform under pressure. The ultimate measure of a samurai is not where he stands in the comfort of his *dojo*, but where he stands at times of challenge and threat. I must say, while untidy, your *mae-geri* was inventive and proved effective."

Jack, Akiko, and Saburo looked at one another, aghast. Masamoto had viewed the whole episode as a martial arts test, while for them it had been a matter of life and death.

"Now, on to the *Taryu-Jiai*. I am sure Akiko has told you what a *Taryu-Jiai* is?"

Yesterday on the march back to the school, Akiko, highly alarmed by the whole idea, had explained it to Jack in a tremulous voice: "A *Taryu-Jiai* is a competition between different martial arts schools. Participants fight in selected disciplines to establish which school is the best, but there is much more at stake than a simple match. A *Taryu-Jiai* is a matter of honor. The winning school will be crowned the best in Kyoto, and the founder of that school has the rare privilege of an audience with the Emperor. It is unthinkable to Masamoto that we should lose."

Jack nodded his understanding to Masamoto.

"Good," said Masamoto, putting his teacup down. "You therefore understand the importance of such an event and why we *must* win."

"But how could we ever win?" blurted out Saburo. "As you say, they are twice our size and would have killed us if you hadn't—"

"Enough!" said Masamoto, cutting dead Saburo's outburst. "Defeat is not an option! Wipe out all thoughts of losing. I do not wish to hear the word 'lose' uttered again. Besides, the greater the obstacle, the more glory in overcoming it."

"*Hai*, Masamoto-sama," they agreed doubtfully.

"We are fortunate that I managed to negotiate enough time for you to develop your skills. True, they are bigger than you. But the bigger your enemies are, the harder they fall; and with the appropriate techniques, they *will* fall."

Akiko had been right, thought Jack. Defeat was a concept alien to Masamoto's mind. He expected nothing less from them.

"I have arranged with your sensei for extra classes every night until the contest. You will be required to train twice as hard and twice as long as anyone else."

"But—" protested Saburo.

"Enough! You *will* act like samurai and you *will* be victorious."

Masamoto dismissed them, and, bowing, they left the hall.

Outside, Kazuki and Nobu were waiting on their knees. Nobu looked pale with anguish, and for once Kazuki didn't have the nerve to taunt Jack. He was far more concerned with his own predicament.

Jack, Akiko, and Saburo made their way in silence to the Chō-no-ma for breakfast, too stunned at the task ahead of them to utter a single word.

Throughout the day, Jack, Akiko, and Saburo were swamped by students demanding to know if it was true that they would be fighting in a *Taryu-Jiai* for the honor of the school. The rumor had spread rapidly, and now that it was confirmed, everyone wanted to be their friend, hoping to increase their status by association.

Jack was suddenly accepted as a fellow samurai. No longer did they call him *Gaijin Jack* or whisper behind his back when he passed. Everyone had heard how bravely he had fought against the Seto twins from Hokkaido, and they wanted to be linked with his courageous deed.

By dinner that night the *hanami* fight had become legend. The Seto twins were giants, twice the height of anyone, and carrying staffs. Akiko had flown through the air, executing scissor, crescent, and axe kicks in every direction. Jack was now the samurai who could fight without needing to draw breath. And Saburo had become the drunken warrior who defeated Raiden the Thunder God with his eyes closed.

Jack suspected that many of these exaggerations originated with the garrulous Saburo, who never tired of recounting the story, the attention he received swelling his ego. He was clearly allowing his bravado to get the better of him. Akiko and Jack, however, were more subdued on the matter, anxious for what the ensuing months had in store.

After dinner they made their way up to the Buddha Hall for their first *Taryu-Jiai* lesson with Sensei Yamada. As they entered the courtyard, Kazuki and Nobu were heading their way. They crossed paths, yet Kazuki and Nobu resolutely ignored them.

"Where are they going?" asked Jack, surprised Kazuki hadn't spat his usual taunt of "*Gaijin Jack*."

"To the Butokuden," replied Akiko.

"What? Are they training, too?"

"No!" Saburo laughed. "Didn't you hear? Masamoto has punished them for dishonoring the school. He ordered them to polish the entire hall, floor to ceiling."

"Really? That's going to take days!" said Jack, unable to refrain from a gleeful smile.

"Not as long as it will take them to clean every brick of this courtyard," said Saburo with equal glee. "And then they have to rake the gravel in the southern Zen garden, but they can only use their *hashi*! It will take them weeks!"

That would keep Kazuki out of his way, thought Jack with relief.

They reached the top of the stairs and entered the Buddha Hall. Sensei Yamada was already perched upon his cushioned dais, incense burning, surrounded by candles.

"Come. Come. *Seiza!*" welcomed Yamada, his voice resonating in the vast expanse of the hall.

Jack, Akiko, and Saburo sat on the three cushions laid out at Sensei Yamada's feet.

"So you are the three mighty warriors?" Yamada said, his eyes sparkling with mischief. "And it is my honor to prepare your minds for the great battle?"

Sensei Yamada lit another incense stick, a mix of cedar and a red resin he called Dragon's Blood. Extracted from rattan palm trees, it had a heavy, woody aroma, and Jack felt quite light-headed with its potency.

Sensei Yamada then half closed his eyes and hummed lightly to himself, drifting into another one of his trances. They were all familiar with these by now, and Jack, Akiko, and Saburo each settled into their own meditations.

"What are you afraid of, Jack?" Sensei Yamada asked after several minutes.

"Umm," said Jack, the unexpected question interrupting his own meditation as he slipped into the fifth View—natural wisdom—the stage when things can be seen in their true light.

"Come. Come. Tell me exactly what you see. What are you afraid of?"

Sensei Yamada's voice thrummed in Jack's head, the incense amplifying his senses, and out of the swirling murkiness of his mind, images materialized, faces floated, and nightmares appeared.

"Drowning . . . I was always . . . afraid of drowning . . . being dragged . . . to the bottom of the ocean," said Jack, expelling his words like a bad dream.

"Good. Good. What else do you see?"

"My mother . . . I'm scared . . . She's leaving me . . . dying . . . alone." Jack moaned, then twitched a little in his trance. "Ginsel . . . I see Ginsel. . . . There's a knife in his back. . . ."

Then in the darkness of Jack's mind, a green mist condensed into a single eye.

"A green eye . . . Now I see a green eye . . . like a dragon's. Dokugan Ryu's eye . . . floating over my father . . . I can't help him . . . He's dying," stammered Jack, his eyes bursting open to escape the haunting image. "Death . . . I'm afraid of . . . death!"

"Jack, there's no need to be afraid of death," said Yamada calmly, opening his own eyes and drawing Jack so far into them, Jack felt he was falling down a deep well.

"Death is more universal than life," continued Yamada, his voice a warm hum in Jack's ears. "Everyone dies, but not everyone lives. Your mother. Ginsel. Your father. Let them go, Jack."

"I . . . I don't understand," stammered Jack, overwhelmed with the magnitude of Sensei Yamada's words. He tried to stifle his sobs of anguish, fearful the others would think him weak.

"Death is not the biggest fear you should have. Your biggest fear is taking the risk to be truly alive. It is about how you live, Jack, even in death," explained Yamada, his eyes brimming with wisdom. "That is what's most important. Masamoto-sama told me your father lived and died protecting you. There is not a more worthy cause. You need not fear for him, for he lived and still lives in you."

Tears coursed down Jack's cheeks as Sensei Yamada's words reverberated in his mind. Months of loneliness, pain, and sadness flowed out of him like a river. He no longer cared if Akiko or Saburo heard him.

Gradually his sobs subsided.

Jack wiped his eyes and discovered that he felt lighter, calmer, and more at ease, as if an unseen weight had been lifted from his shoulders and he had been wrapped in a great blanket of peace.

Akiko and Saburo, brought out of their own meditations by Jack's suffering, observed him with quiet compassion. Sensei Yamada leaned forward, an expression of serene triumph upon his face, and addressed them all.

"I know not how to defeat others; I only know how to win over myself," he whispered, drawing them closer with his words. "The real and most dangerous opponents we face in life are fear, anger, confusion, doubt, and despair. If we overcome those enemies that attack us from within, we can attain a true victory over any attack from without."

Sensei Yamada gazed at each student in turn, ensuring they had understood his meaning.

"Conquer your inner fears and you can conquer the world. That is your lesson for today."

Sensei Yamada gave a small bow and dismissed them. Akiko and Saburo bowed back, then started for the door, but Jack remained sitting.

"I need to ask Sensei Yamada something," said Jack, in reply to their questioning looks. "I'll join you in a minute."

"We'll wait for you on the steps," said Akiko, turning away.

"Yes, Jack," acknowledged Sensei Yamada. "Something troubling you?"

"Well . . . yesterday morning, I had a . . ."

"Vision?" finished Sensei Yamada.

"Yes. How did you know?"

"Often happens around this time. Once freed, the mind is more powerful than you can ever imagine. What did you see?"

Jack described his dream of the red demon attacking the butterfly.

"There are many ways to interpret such revelations," said Sensei Yamada, after some contemplation. "Its true meaning will be hidden under the many layers of your mind, and only you will be able to unwrap them all. You need to find the key that unlocks the secret."

Jack was profoundly disappointed. Sensei Yamada was being as obscure as ever. He had hoped the old monk would have been able to tell him the answer.

"Perhaps the key is *chō-geri* . . ." murmured Yamada, more to himself than to Jack.

"*Chō-geri?*" prompted Jack, suddenly hopeful.

"Yes, *chō-geri*. Sometimes the way through to understanding the mind is through the body. Your vision contained a butterfly. Its movements evaded the demon. Perhaps *chō-geri* will enlighten you further."

"So where do I find the *chō-geri?*"

"It is not a matter of *where*, Jack. It is a matter of *how* to find it. *Chō-geri* is an ancient Chinese martial arts technique that's been lost to time. It is named the Butterfly Kick because it is a flying kick in which all the limbs are extended in a position similar to that of a butterfly's wings in flight. It's a highly advanced maneuver that will cut a swathe through any attack. *Chō-geri* is rumored to be indefensible."

"So why tell me about the key, if no one has it?"

said Jack, frustrated with Yamada's continual enigmas.

"I didn't say no one," he replied. He studied Jack for a long time. Jack felt distinctly uncomfortable, as if the sensei were somehow peering into his soul.

"I could teach it to you," he said eventually, "but it may be far beyond your abilities."

"B-but . . ." stuttered Jack in disbelief. "Pardon my disrespect, Sensei, but aren't you too old for martial arts?"

"Oh, the blindness of youth," said Yamada, getting to his feet with the help of his walking stick.

Jack was about to apologize when, without warning, Sensei Yamada let go of the stick and sprang into the air.

The old man's torso twisted, his arms swung in an arc, and both his legs shot out, striking high over Jack's head. Sensei Yamada rotated all the way around before landing lightly back upon his dais.

Jack sat openmouthed as Sensei Yamada nonchalantly readjusted his kimono, picked up his walking stick, and prepared to depart.

"How on earth did you do that? How could you?" stammered Jack, flabbergasted at the old man's incomprehensible agility.

"Never judge a sword by its *saya*. I am a monk, Jack. But what am I?" he said, before blowing out the candles and shuffling off into the darkness.

The remaining trails of incense smoke spiraled like ghosts into the air, and the old man was gone.

Jack left the Buddha Hall in a daze, astounded by the old monk who had flown through the air with the grace of a butterfly, then left on a riddle.

Jack found Akiko and Saburo sitting on the steps. He slumped down next to them.

"Are you all right?" asked Akiko, clearly concerned that the lesson had taken a great toll on Jack.

"Fine. But you won't believe what I just saw. . . ." replied Jack, before telling them about Sensei Yamada's startling abilities.

"In the name of Buddha, Jack! Even I can work that one out," said Saburo dumbfounded. "He is *sohei*!"

"*Sohei*? But I thought all the warrior monks had been killed by Nobunaga."

"Clearly not all of them," said Saburo, gazing in awe at the Buddha Hall. "I bet you Sensei Yamada can strike a man dead just using his *ki*!"

"Here comes Kiku," said Jack, seeing the little girl emerge from the Hall of Lions and run across the courtyard toward them.

Kiku raced up the stone steps.

"What is it?" asked Akiko, worried by Kiku's obvious urgency.

"Yamato has run away!"

CHAPTER 35

THE SWITCH

"*J*ACK-KUN! JACK-KUN! JACK-KUN!*"

Jack blinked into the bright summer sunlight. It was going to be another scorching day, he thought, as he was drawn out of the cool shade of the Hall of Lions and into the baking courtyard by the cheers of the gathered students.

The past three months had been a grueling schedule of relentless training for Jack, Akiko, and Saburo. Yamato, whose absence had been keenly felt by all of them at first, had almost been forgotten in the face of such an onslaught of instruction. Jack had lost count of the number of cuts they had practiced with the *bokken* to improve their *kenjutsu*, the quantity of arrows they had shot, lost, or broken in *kyujutsu*, and there was not a single part of their bodies that hadn't been bruised during *taijutsu*.

On top of that, Jack had needed to fit in clandestine training sessions with Sensei Yamada in his attempt to learn *chō-geri*, with the hope of revealing the meaning of his vision. But the intricacies of the complex technique still eluded him. He had done everything Sensei Yamada instructed, but was simply not good enough. At the rate he was going, it would take him years to master *chō-geri*.

"I won't ever be able to do this," Jack had said in despair as he'd landed on his back for the fifth time, barely a week before the *Taryu-Jiai*.

"Whatever you believe, will be, Jack-kun," replied Sensei Yamada matter-of-factly. "It's not the technique you need to master, it is yourself."

That was all he had proffered as encouragement. This had left Jack more frustrated than ever at the sensei's garbled teachings. Could the old monk not see that the technique was beyond his abilities? Yet still Sensei Yamada demanded he practice *chō-geri* every night until his body ached with the effort.

Standing in the boiling courtyard, surrounded by a throng of well-wishers, Jack just hoped all the pain and effort would be worthwhile. But it was too late to worry about such things now.

The day of the *Taryu-Jiai* had arrived.

"Jack-kun! Jack-kun! Jack-kun!"

The chants filled his ears, and he was funneled across the courtyard and into the Nanzen-niwa, the Southern Zen garden. Akiko and Saburo were already there, waiting for him by one of the large standing stones. Masamoto and Kamakura sat upon a shaded dais at the north end of the garden. They were flanked on either side by the sensei of their schools, all wearing full ceremonial kimonos. Students lined both sides of the garden in neat, disciplined rows, the Niten Ichi Ryū on the east side, and the Yagyu Ryū on the west.

Jack's heart pounded in his chest.

"Samurai of the Niten Ichi Ryū. We salute you!" shouted a bald official in a stark white kimono.

There was thunderous applause from the crowd. Jack, Akiko, and Saburo instinctively drew closer together in a protective huddle.

As the applause faded, Masamoto and Kamakura conversed politely, but their outward civility did little to hide the underlying animosity between them. Masamoto was especially grim. The absconding of his son had aged him more than any battle scar could have. He bore the shame of his son's desertion like a wound that would never heal.

"Samurai of the Yagyu Ryū. We salute you!" shouted the official.

The students on the west side of the garden applauded and let out a battle cry of "Yagyu! Yagyu! Yagyu!"

The monstrous form of Raiden strode into the garden. He took his place by the standing stone opposite them. Jack had forgotten just how big the boy was. Raiden had looked like an oversized ape at the *hanami* that spring, but now he looked like a bull: brutal and terrible. The *Taryu-Jiai* wasn't going to be a contest. It would be a slaughter.

The lean figure of a girl with raven-black hair emerged from behind Raiden. She moved in a quick, calculated manner, as if every step were part of a *kata*. Her eyes were sharp black diamonds, and her thin-lipped mouth was a red slash across her powdered white face. She was enticing in a deadly way, Jack thought—like a viper poised to strike. Then the girl cracked a smile, exposing her teeth.

They were painted entirely black.

Jack had barely gotten over the shock, when the final Yagyu warrior entered. The whole of the Niten Ichi Ryū erupted in astonishment. It was not Toru.

It was Yamato.

Jack couldn't believe Yamato was standing with the Yagyu school. He hadn't seen him since spring. There had been rumors among the students that he had joined Yagyu, but competing against his father's school was beyond comprehension.

When Masamoto recognized the final participant, he sprang to his feet, eyes bulging with outrage. He spun on

Kamakura, but was stymied by anger and could only stand there glaring at his rival. Kamakura sat, unflinching, relishing the moment. The great Masamoto had been unhinged.

"This was not what we'd agreed upon. Where is the other samurai?" Masamoto asked, his voice barely controlled.

"Did I forget to tell you? I'm so sorry. Toru was called away by his father, and we had to replace him with one of my *other* students," replied Kamakura, deliberately lingering over his final words.

"*Your* student? This is unacceptable."

"I'm afraid the rules of the *Taryu-Jiai* clearly state that the competition is between the two schools, not individual students. I am perfectly at liberty to switch my warriors any time prior to the contest. Isn't that right, Takeda-san?" Kamakura said to the official.

"*Hai*, Kamakura-sama, that is correct," replied the official, avoiding Masamoto's glare.

"So unless you wish to forfeit the *Taryu-Jiai* . . ."

"We will continue." Masamoto sat down, fuming like a boiling pot.

The official held up his hand for silence. The murmurings of the crowd ceased.

"I am Takeda Masato," the official said. "I am the independent adjudicator for this *Taryu-Jiai*, appointed by the Imperial Court. I will referee all matches. My decision is final and irrefutable. The first round is *kyu-jutsu*. Samurai, prepare yourselves!"

The two schools gave a round of applause as the archery targets were set out in the garden.

"What is Yamato doing?" Jack demanded as they huddled around their standing stone. "How can he fight us?"

"You heard Masamoto's words just as we did," said Akiko. "Masamoto disowned him after the *hanami*. He ran away because he'd lost face. He couldn't deal with the shame."

"But why join the Yagyu school?"

"Surely that is obvious, Jack," said Akiko. "He wants his father to lose face too."

"Enough!" interrupted Sensei Yosa, who had come over to break up their discussion. "You must concentrate on the competition at hand. Don't allow yourselves to be distracted by such underhanded tactics. Remember what I taught you—you need absolute focus for *kyujutsu*. Balance is your foundation stone. The spirit, bow, and body are as one."

Sensei Yosa had drilled those three principles into them every day for the past three months. They had spent the first month just learning to stand and hold a bow correctly. Only then had she taught them how to fire an arrow. Akiko was the first to manage the technique properly, but Saburo and Jack still had difficulty striking the target with any degree of consistency.

In the final weeks, Sensei Yosa had made them shoot until their fingers bled from blisters. One time, she even came up to Akiko and tickled her ear with the feathered flight of a spare arrow. Akiko had been so shocked that she had missed the target entirely and almost struck a bird nesting in an old pine tree. All Sensei Yosa had said was, "You cannot allow yourself to be so easily distracted. Absolute focus, remember?" During the next lesson she had shouted in Saburo's ear, sending his arrow skyward. "Focus!" Sensei Yosa repeated.

"Let us begin. First round. Targets set at one hundred *shaku*," called the official.

"One hundred *shaku*!" Saburo exclaimed as he gathered his bow and arrows. "I can barely hit one at fifty!"

"The school to score the most points from six arrows will be deemed the winner of this match," continued the official. "One point for striking the target. Two points for the center. Yagyu goes first."

The girl with the black teeth stepped up to the mark. Silence descended upon the crowd. She nocked her first arrow, then barely glancing at her target, let it fly.

It struck the center, and the Yagyu school cheered. Without a moment's pause, the girl shot her second arrow, which sank into the inner white ring, missing the center by a finger's width. She grimaced in frustration.

"Three points. Yagyu."

Saburo went to position himself on the line. Even from where Jack was standing, he could see Saburo's hands shaking. He could hardly even nock his arrow.

Saburo's first shot went so wide that it almost hit a student standing in the crowd. A ripple of laughter rolled through the Yagyu school. Saburo's second shot was no better, landing short.

"Zero. Niten Ichi Ryū."

"Don't worry, Saburo," said Jack, as he saw the mortified look on his friend's face. "I'm sure the ape boy won't do much better."

Thankfully, Jack was right. Raiden could barely grip the bow properly. Both shots sailed away without even worrying the target.

"Zero. Yagyu."

Jack was up next. He double-checked his posture, calmed his breathing, and moved meticulously through each motion. He loosed his first arrow, and it just caught the target on the outer ring. There was a great cheer.

Jack tried to keep his focus, waiting for the noise of the crowd to settle into respectful silence.

He took aim and fired.

It missed.

There was a groan from the Niten Ichi Ryū side, and the sounds of celebration coming from the other school. The official put his hands up for silence.

"One point. Niten Ichi Ryū."

"Sorry," said Jack, returning to their standing stone.

"No. It was good. We still have a chance," said Akiko, a slight tremble in her voice. *She* was the chance.

Yamato stepped up to the mark. His basic technique was good, and his first arrow struck the target, but was wide of the bull's-eye. The Yagyu school sensed victory and began to shout. Yamato, however, was too bold with his second. He drew back with such force that the arrow shot past the target and embedded itself in an old pine tree at the far end of the garden, much to the relief of Jack, Saburo, and Akiko.

The match was not over.

"One point. Yagyu."

Yamato ignored Jack and the others as he sat down, clearly displeased with his performance.

Akiko advanced to the firing line.

"She's got to hit two bull's-eyes to win!" whispered Saburo in despair. "When has she ever done that?"

"Today?" said Jack hopefully, seeing Akiko draw a long, slow breath to calm her nerves.

Jack had witnessed Akiko hit the center once before at this distance, but that had been the only time during their entire period of training. Could she score twice in a row when it mattered most?

As Akiko prepared for the shot, the noise of the crowd faded to a low murmur, like the sound of a receding wave. She loosed her first arrow in one fluid movement. It flew true and straight, striking the target dead center. A cheer erupted from the Niten Ichi Ryū.

"Come on, Akiko!" shouted Jack, unable to restrain himself.

The official called for silence, and the applause rippled away.

Akiko set herself up for her second and final shot of the match. If she got this, the Niten Ichi Ryū had the first round.

The eyes of the entire crowd were upon her, and her hands began to tremble under the pressure. Jack could see her battling to control her nerves. Gradually, she slowed her breathing, and her hands steadied. Raising the bow above her head, she drew back to make her shot.

"*GAIJIN LOVER!*" came a cry from the Yagyu side.

The shout shattered the silence. For the briefest of moments, Akiko appeared stunned, struggling to control the delicate balance between her mind and body as the insult rebounded within her head.

Jack fumed, knowing Akiko *had* to maintain the flow of her draw, otherwise she would miss.

She loosed the arrow an instant too soon.

The arrow spun awkwardly. Yet it still struck the target. But had it hit the center?

The whole crowd drew in its breath as one. The

official ran over to examine the arrow's placement, its tip barely perceptible at the edge of the center.

"Center strike! Four points Niten Ichi Ryū," announced the official, satisfied with the arrow's mark.

Jack and Saburo both punched the air with their fists. Akiko had done it!

Akiko bowed triumphantly as the official cried, "First around to Niten Ichi Ryū."

CHAPTER 36

THE DEMON AND THE BUTTERFLY

I T WAS NOT even midday, but the Butokuden was already stiflingly hot. The students of both schools lined the edges of the hall, fanning themselves like a cloud of butterflies, while countless other students peered in through the slatted windows.

Masamoto came and found Jack, Akiko, and Saburo getting ready for the next round. He congratulated Akiko on her outstanding *kyujutsu* performance and offered each of them words of encouragement for the forthcoming *taijutsu* match.

"Remember the second virtue of *Bushido*," he said with gusto as he left to take his place in the Butokuden. "Courage!"

"Those are fine words," said Saburo to Jack when Masamoto had gone, "but it's not courage we need, it's a miracle!"

Jack gave Saburo a despairing look and shrugged despondently as he changed into a fresh set of clothes, firmly tying an *obi* around his blue fighting *gi*. When they were all ready, Jack, Akiko, and Saburo entered the Butokuden and formed a line in front of the ceremonial dais.

Masamoto and Kamakura sat within the curving alcove of the hall, looking like two emperors waiting for their gladiators to fight. Kamakura was less buoyant than before, while Masamato exuded an air of quiet confidence following his school's first victory.

"Round two. *Taijutsu*!" announced the Imperial Court official. He glanced pointedly in Raiden's direction and said, "This is *not* a death match. A win will be awarded by points, submission, or knockout only."

Raiden gave a dismissive shrug that implied he had no intention of following the rules.

"During each match, points will be awarded for execution of technique. *Ippon* is a full and winning point given for a demonstration of perfect technique. *Waza-ari* is half a point for a near-perfect technique—two *waza-ari* equals a winning *ippon*. *Yoku* and *koka* are given for lesser techniques and will only count if, at the end of a stick of time, there is no outright winner. The school who wins the most matches takes this round."

The crowd roared like a pack of lions, their shouts reverberating around the Butokuden.

"First match. Akiko versus Moriko. Line up!"

Akiko's face lost much of its color at the mention of her name.

"You'll be fine," encouraged Jack. "Remember what Sensei Kyuzo always says: 'Tomorrow's victory is today's practice.' Well, we've practiced more than enough to win.'

It was true. The diminutive Sensei Kyuzo had been the most demanding of all the sensei. It was almost as if the man had resented having to teach them, and so had punished them with extra-tough training. They had rigorously gone over technique after technique. He had drilled the basics and nothing else.

"What about other techniques, like *ren-geri*, multiple kicks?" Saburo had suggested one day. He was given fifty push-ups for insolence, while Sensei Kyuzo explained, "*Kihon waza* is all you need. Multiple kicks are too open for countering. A good solid block or punch is far more effective. I told you, the basics are for battle."

And it would be a battle. The Yagyu girl, Moriko, hissed and bared her black teeth as she faced Akiko for their bout.

"*Rei!*" said the official. The girls bowed to Masamoto and Kamakura and then to one another. A stick of incense in a brass bowl was lit to mark time, and the official cried, *"Hajime!"*

Moriko launched herself at Akiko at once, firing off a front kick, then a roundhouse kick, and then a back kick. Akiko retreated defensively, attempting to counter the blitz of attacks. She managed to deflect the front kick, and just dodged the roundhouse, but was caught on the hip by the back kick. She went spinning to the floor. Moriko jumped forward to finish her off with a *fumikomi*, a stomping kick.

"YAME!" cried the official, halting Moriko's vicious attack. *"Waza-ari* to Moriko!"

The Yagyu school cheered its approval. Jack was livid. He hated watching Akiko fight. He wanted to rush out and defend her, just as she had once done for him.

"Rei!" said the official, and the girls bowed. *"Hajime!"*

Moriko blitzed Akiko again, but Akiko was ready this time. She sidestepped, trapped Moriko's roundhouse with one arm, and did a straight palm-heel strike to the chest, while sweeping Moriko's standing leg. A simple yet highly effective block and counter, but Moriko grabbed Akiko as she went down, making her perfect technique appear messy.

"YAME!" cried the official, halting the bout. *"Waza-ari* to Akiko!"

The Niten Ichi Ryū went wild. The two girls were even.

"*Rei!*" said the official, and the girls bowed. "*Hajime!*"

This time Moriko kept her distance.

They circled one another, Moriko hissing like a black cat. They each feigned attacks before Moriko made a sudden grab for Akiko's lead arm. Akiko countered, but then they were grappling, each trying to get the upper hand for a throw. Akiko was first, and rolled her body in for an *o-goshi*, a hip throw. Moriko dropped her hips, lowering her center of gravity and preventing Akiko's throw. From behind she yanked viciously on Akiko's hair.

Jack was one of the few to see it. Hair-grabbing was prohibited, and Moriko kept close, hiding the illegal move with her body. Akiko was trapped. Moriko then foot-swept Akiko from behind, dragging her down with her hair.

"*YAME! Waza-ari* to Moriko!" said the official, oblivious to Moriko's cheating. "First match goes to Yagyu Ryū!"

"I can't believe it!" said Jack, incensed, as Akiko knelt down next to him. "How could the referee not see that?"

"Don't worry about my fight. It's over," said Akiko, her face hot and flushed with exertion. "Focus on yours. You *have* to win."

"Second match. Raiden versus Jack. Line up!"

Jack's heart stopped for a beat. He was up against Raiden.

"Good luck, Jack," whispered Yori, who was kneeling behind them with the rest of their class.

"Yes, good luck, Jack," said Emi warmly. She fluttered her eyelashes and lazily waved her paper fan.

Her flirtatious tone was not lost on Akiko, who stared at Emi in mute astonishment.

"Thank you," said Jack, somehow managing to smile back. Now there's a first, he thought. *Emi* noticing him.

Then Kazuki caught his eye, and Jack's amiable feelings evaporated. Kazuki slid a finger across his throat.

His old enemy had been sulking ever since the *hanami*, for Jack was no longer the *gaijin* of the school, but the hero. Kazuki had been sidelined. Now he was relishing the prospect of Jack's forthcoming bout with Raiden. There appeared to be no way on earth he could win, and Kazuki knew no one liked a loser.

Jack walked out into the center of the Butokuden. The heat instantly sapped his strength. There was not a breath of fresh air, and bars of hot sunlight scorched the wooden floor.

The hall appeared larger than ever to Jack, who felt as tiny as an ant opposite the giant that was Raiden. Raiden grinned and tilted his head from side to side, loosening the joints in his neck with a sickening crack.

Jack was about to be torn to pieces.

He glanced at his friends. Their faces reflected his fears like a mirror.

Then he saw Sensei Yamada, Sensei Kyuzo, and Sensei Hosokawa standing in the wings. Sensei Yamada bowed slightly, then indicated with an open hand the size difference between Sensei Kyuzo and Sensei Hosokawa. Jack immediately understood: size had never been an issue for Sensei Kyuzo when fighting. It should not be for him, either.

"*Rei!*" said the official.

Jack and Raiden bowed to Masamoto and Kamakura, then curtly to one another. The official waited for another short stick of incense to be lit before shouting, "*Hajime!*"

Jack had decided on an all-or-nothing approach, and as Raiden lumbered forward, Jack hit him with a front kick, then a roundhouse. But Raiden merely batted his kicks away before throwing a single forearm blow. Jack went flying and ended up sprawled on the floor.

"*YAME!*" cried the official. "*Koka* to Raiden!"

Jack staggered to his feet, dazed but unhurt. Akiko and Saburo gave him encouraging looks, but their support was undermined by Kazuki's gloating face behind, and Nobu miming himself getting hung by a noose.

"*Hajime!*"

Jack was barely ready when Raiden stomped on his

front foot. Jack yelped and tried to get away, but his foot was trapped. Raiden swung a large left hook. Jack ducked, feeling it pass over his head. But as he rose, Raiden launched his right fist into Jack's face.

Jack blocked it with a solid *age-uke*, rising block, but he knew his time was short if he couldn't free himself quickly.

Jack dropped to his knees, and with all his weight, struck the inside of Raiden's thigh, aiming directly at the nerve point Sensei Kyuzo had shown them during training. Raiden howled in pain, releasing Jack's foot, but as he staggered, he managed to catch Jack with a messy but brutal backhanded slap across the cheek.

Jack went flying for a second time.

"*YAME!*" called the official. "*Koka* to Raiden!"

"Come on, Jack. You can beat him," encouraged Akiko, but the groans from the rest of Niten Ichi Ryū were a far more honest reflection of his chances.

On the third attack, Jack lasted a fraction longer before being struck by Raiden's forearm across the neck.

Jack crumpled to the floor.

"*YAME!*" called the official. "*Koka* to Raiden!"

This time Jack stayed down, and the official's count began.

"*One . . . two . . .*"

Raiden's strike had knocked him senseless, and Jack lay there wishing it were all over. His head rung with pain, the cheering was a wash of sound in his ears, and the idea of giving up now was more inviting than ever. He had no chance in this contest. His only hope was to finish the bout alive and in one piece.

"*Three . . .*"

Then he heard a voice above the murmur of the crowd.

"Seven times down, eight times up!"

Jack shook his head, trying to clear it. The hall came back into focus and the voice gained clarity.

"*Four . . .*"

"Seven times down, eight times up!"

It was Yori. He was shouting at Jack. "Seven times down, eight times up!"

"*Five . . .*"

Yori was telling him not to give up. All Jack's lessons suddenly came together as one. He could not accept defeat.

"*Six . . .*"

He had to conquer his own doubt and fear. Sensei Yamada's words rang in his head. "In order to be walked upon, you have to be lying down."

"*Seven . . .*"

"Seven times down, eight times up!"

He could now hear Saburo and Akiko joining in Yori's chant, along with several of the other students.

"*Eight . . .*"

He would not be defeated without a fight.

"*Nine . . .*"

Jack forced himself to his feet. The crowd roared, eager to see the *gaijin* fly again. The count stopped and Jack staggered into line.

"*Hajime!*" said the official without giving Jack any further chance to recover.

Raiden thundered forward.

Jack blocked his first attack.

Raiden lumbered past, turned, and charged again. Jack managed to get a strike into Raiden's side, but Raiden hammer-fisted Jack in the chest and he was projected backward, landing heavily near Akiko.

"*YAME!*" called the official. "*Koka* to Raiden!"

Akiko looked distraught, but Jack got up and tried again.

"*YAME!*" called the official, as once again Jack was driven to the ground like a rag doll. "*Koka* to Raiden!"

Raiden took advantage of Jack's weakened state and executed *ura mawashi-geri*, a hook kick, badly bruising Jack's ribs.

"*YAME!*" called the official, with growing concern in his voice. "*Yoku* to Raiden!"

Jack was glad the floor was springy, although the impact on landing still hurt. He forced himself up again, wobbling slightly, just like the Daruma doll. Jack was now beginning to appreciate all the times Sensei Kyuzo had made him *uke*. The experience had toughened him up against such constant battering, exactly as Akiko had said it would.

"Half a stick of time remaining," announced the official. *"Hajime!"*

Raiden was now breathing heavily from the extended fight. He was obviously used to his opponents giving up after one round. His face had gone bright red and he was sweating like a pig.

He was slowing up, too, noticed Jack, as he easily blocked Raiden's *mawashi-zuki*, roundhouse punch. Then the realization struck him in a blinding flash. Raiden sweating, reddened, and tiring was not a pig. He was a demon—the demon from Jack's vision!

Too tired to even attempt a proper technique, Raiden grabbed Jack and threw him across the *dojo* with pure brute strength. Jack went skidding across the floor on his back, coming to a halt at Sensei Yamada's feet.

"YAME!" called the official. *"Koka* to Raiden!"

The Yagyu School went wild. In less than half a stick of time, the match would be theirs.

Jack stared up at Sensei Yamada, who leaned expectantly over him, as if in prayer.

"Sensei! Raiden's the demon from my vision!" spluttered Jack. "What does that mean?"

Sensei Yamada simply opened and closed his hands

like the wings of a butterfly. The message was clear—
Jack had to be the butterfly.

Jack picked himself up and tidied his blue fighting
gi. Blue! Jack laughed at how blatant his vision had been.
He couldn't defeat Raiden through strength, but he could
win with skill, speed, and stamina.

Jack changed tactics. Raiden clearly had poor technique; he simply relied on his size and weight to do the
work for him. If Jack was as quick and agile as the butterfly, he could avoid the blows. Eventually Raiden
would exhaust himself, just like the demon in his vision.
Jack only hoped he had enough time remaining to tire
the demon out.

"*Hajime!*" announced the official.

The fight resumed.

Keeping out of harm's way was easier said than
done. Jack couldn't simply run around the *dojo*. He had
to remain close enough to make Raiden attack him, force
him to exert himself, but without landing a strike.

Jack drew the fight on, flitting from one spot to
another. He ducked, weaved, and dove, while the heat of
the midday sun cooked the Butokuden and turned it into
a furnace.

Raiden lashed out in frustration, his movements
becoming more sluggish as Jack dodged blow after blow.
Sweat rolled down Raiden's brow and into his eyes.
Wiping the sweat away, he dropped his guard slightly.

This was the chance Jack had been waiting for.

Jack knew there was no way a simple kick or punch could floor Raiden. He would need to get past the boy's apelike arms before being able to land an effective strike. There was only one option open to him, *chō-geri*, the butterfly kick. "Whatever you believe, will be," Sensei Yamada had said, and at this moment Jack believed he could do it.

Without hesitation, Jack launched himself into the air. A season of training converged into a single moment.

As Jack twisted in the air, his arms circling in the form of a butterfly for control, he brought his right leg spinning around to catch Raiden's weakened guard, knocking it clear, then his left leg shot past and slammed into Raiden's jaw. *Chō-geri* connected, and Raiden buckled under its force.

The whole Butokuden went eerily silent.

Jack landed neatly over the groaning body of his opponent just as the incense burned out and its last piece of ash fell into the dish.

"*YAME!*" called the astounded official. "*Ippon* to Jack!"

Against all the odds, Jack had succeeded in performing *chō-geri*. He could not believe it!

The Niten Ichi Ryū erupted in applause, and Jack staggered to his corner, leaving Raiden lying prone on the floor.

"That was remarkable!" yelled Saburo, who had rushed over to congratulate him.

"Where did you learn to kick like that?" called a voice from the crowd.

"What's it called?" demanded another. "The *flying gaijin*?"

Jack was swamped by fellow students, all wanting to be taught his *flying gaijin* kick. Saburo pushed everyone back, reminding them to retain a respectful distance.

Still in a daze from his victory, he knelt down while all the students jostled to be as close to their newfound hero as possible.

The official was desperately calling for silence, and the crowd gradually settled into an excited murmuring.

As everyone took their places, Jack could see Sensei Yamada, an enigmatic smile on his lips, politely deferring to Sensei Kyuzo, who was apparently demanding an explanation for Jack's hidden talent for kicks.

"Final match. Saburo versus Yamato. Line up!" announced the official. All eyes fell upon the two remaining competitors.

The match now level, this final bout was crucial.

If Saburo defeated Yamato, the Niten Ichi Ryū would be the victors of the second round. Saburo was a competent fighter, and there was a strong possibility he could win. Yamato, however, had become an unknown factor.

Yamato squared up to Saburo.

Saburo gave a gracious smile, but Yamato remained impervious, a barren look in his eyes, as if he failed to recognize his former friend.

"Rei!" said the official. The two of them bowed and the incense was lit. *"Hajime!"*

Yamato didn't move.

Saburo hesitated slightly, then struck with a clean front kick followed by a solid reverse punch.

Yamato coolly evaded the kick, blocking Saburo's punch with his forearm. Then in one lightning movement, he spun into Saburo and threw him with a devastating *seoi-nage*, shoulder throw. Saburo sailed through the air and landed hard on the wooden floor of the Butokuden.

"Ippon!" shouted the official over the exultant cheers. "Round two goes to Yagyu Ryū!"

The incense had barely begun to smolder and the match was already over.

CHAPTER 37

THE JADE SWORD

J ACK STARED DEEP into Yamato's eyes, hunting for his first move.

"Most battles are won before the sword is drawn," Sensei Hosokawa had told Jack during one of their *kenjutsu* sessions. "Defeat your enemy's mind, you defeat his sword."

Akiko had won her *bokken* match against Moriko, exacting a sweet revenge with a three-nothing victory. Moriko's sneaky tactics in *taijutsu* had incensed Akiko, who had fought without mercy.

Saburo, on the other hand, having lost so much confidence following his fight with Yamato, was beaten by Raiden two–one. The *Taryu-Jiai* now hung in the balance: either school could win.

Everything came down to Jack and Yamato.

Jack still couldn't believe Yamato was fighting against his father's own school, but the thunderous look in Yamato's eyes made it clear that his fight was with Jack. And Jack alone.

"Best out of three?" teased Jack, throwing down their old gauntlet.

Jack knew how Yamato thought and fought. He had been taught by him, practiced with him, been beaten by him. This time Jack vowed it would be Yamato's turn to lose.

Yamato snorted his disdain, and without replying, brought his *kissaki* in line with Jack's.

"*Hajime!*" announced the official.

Yamato struck with the speed of a cobra. His *bokken* glanced off Jack's weapon and hurtled toward his head.

Jack ducked under the blow, sweeping around to bring his own *bokken* across Yamato's gut. Yamato quickly countered and blocked the strike. Jack immediately pressed forward with another attack, but Yamato anticipated it and neatly sidestepped, bringing his own weapon down onto Jack's leading sword arm.

"*YAME!*" called the official as the crowd applauded. "Point to *Yagyu*!"

"I could see you *thinking* the move before you made it." Yamato laughed. "You haven't changed, Jack."

"But you have," replied Jack. "You've lost face."

Yamato fumed at the insult and launched his attack even before the official started the next round. It was exactly the reaction Jack had hoped for. Yamato still couldn't control his temper. Jack knew he would make fundamental errors of judgment when unsettled by his emotions.

Yamato's blows rained down on Jack, and there it was—Yamato's mistake. He had stepped too close while winding up for a reverse cut. Jack side-slipped and struck him forcefully across the belly.

"*YAME!*" called the official as Yamato crumpled to the floor, the crowd emitting a loud mix of applause and jeering. "Point to Niten Ichi Ryū!"

It was now match point.

The next encounter would decide the *Taryu-Jiai*. No one dared breathe. The Butokuden became quieter than a temple. Masamoto and Kamakura had both frozen in anticipation, like stone gods upon their thrones.

For a brief moment, time seemed to stretch, and Jack and Yamato became locked in an unseen battle, each seeking for the other's first move in their minds. They moved in slow synchronized steps, mirroring each other's stances, raising their *bokken* as one and leveling their *kissaki*.

"*Hajime!*" announced the official.

Their *bokken* clashed. Almost as if they were

dancing, their feet swept past one another, parries met strikes, strikes met parries; then as one they spun on their heels and brought their weapons around for the kill.

Their arms collided, *bokken* striking simultaneously at one another's necks.

"Draw!" shouted the official in astonishment.

Their eyes continued the fight. They were still the same boys who had fought on the little bridge at Hiroko's house in Toba, but neither could deny that they were now equally matched in skill.

Confusion reigned among the students. Could there be a draw in a *Taryu-Jiai*? Of course not! How would the ultimate winner be decided, then? The official called for calm.

Jack and Yamato only stood down when the official stepped in between them. The official then hurried over to Masamoto and Kamakura and began to converse in hushed tones.

The whole crowd craned their necks and listened, hoping to catch a word of what was being said.

After several minutes of intense discussion, the official scurried back to the center of the *dojo*.

"Samurai of the Niten Ichi Ryū! Samurai of the Yagyu Ryū!" he announced with great pomp and ceremony. "By the power invested in me by the Imperial Court, the Rite of the Jade Sword has been invoked."

The crowd exploded and the official was hoarse

from shouting by the time he managed to regain control.

"As deemed by Emperor Kammu, the father of Kyoto, the Rite of the Jade Sword can be invoked upon the occasion of a draw in a *Taryu-Jiai*. It has been agreed that the samurai who retrieves the Jade Sword from the Sound of Feathers waterfall, and presents the sword to the founder of their school, will be deemed the champion. We will commence the rite in four sticks of time outside the Buddha Hall."

The crowd broke up in feverish excitement.

The Rite of the Jade Sword had not been invoked for more than a hundred years. There had not been any need. In living memory, no schools had ever drawn.

CHAPTER 38

THE SOUND OF FEATHERS WATERFALL

THE INCENSE gave a last puff of smoke, then died.

"*Hajime!*" cried the Imperial Palace official.

Jack sprinted for the door, Yamato hard at his side.

The cheers swelled as they broke free from the Buddha Hall and flew down the stone steps two at a time. The crowd, which had amassed in the courtyard, parted like one immense human wave as Jack and Yamato hurtled toward the main gate.

Outside the Niten Ichi Ryū, Jack and Yamato veered left up the street, and the crowd surged out behind, willing them on.

A few students tried to keep up, but Jack and Yamato soon broke away.

At the end of the road, Yamato edged ahead and suddenly dodged down an alleyway. Jack kept close on his tail, the noise of the crowd fading behind them. He didn't want to lose Yamato. Not that he was worried about getting lost. Akiko had told him how to get to the waterfall. Jack just didn't want to get too far behind so early on in the race.

In the run-up to the start of the Rite of the Jade Sword, Akiko and Saburo had bustled Jack into the Hall of Lions in a frantic attempt to prepare him. While Jack changed into a fresh kimono and feverishly gulped down food and water, Akiko explained the history of the Jade Sword.

"The Jade Sword belonged to Emperor Kammu himself, the founding father of Kyoto. It is said that the samurai who wields the Jade Sword can never be defeated. Emperor Kammu therefore commanded that it never leave Kyoto, so that his city would always be protected. He presented the Jade Sword to the Buddhist priest Enchin for safekeeping, who placed it at the very top of the Sound of Feathers waterfall, where it could overlook Kyoto and guard the source of the Kizu River."

"Where is this waterfall?" asked Jack between rushed mouthfuls of rice.

"It is behind the Kiyomizudera temple in the mountains. You reach it by a steep path that leads off from the main bridge."

"You mean the bridge we used to enter Kyoto?"

"Yes. The path will be on your left. It winds up the mountain and will take you directly to the Nio-mon, the Gate of the Deva Kings. This is the main entrance to the temple. You can't get lost," she said emphatically as she tied Jack's *obi* around him.

"It's a pilgrim path and is clearly marked. Once inside the complex, head directly for the Sanju-no-to; it's a three-story pagoda, the same color as the *torii* in Toba. Then cut through the Dragon Temple and the middle gateway to the Hondo. This is the Main Hall. On the other side you will find the Butai, the monk's dancing stage, and to your left the Sound of Feathers waterfall and the Jade Sword shrine."

"That doesn't sound too difficult." If it were simply a matter of running to a shrine and back, thought Jack, he was sure he could beat Yamato.

"Don't be fooled, Jack. Enchin placed the sword there for a reason. The waterfall is extremely dangerous. The rocks are slippery, and the climb is impossibly steep. Many samurai have fallen in their quest to touch the sword, and only a few have ever laid their hands upon it."

Jack suddenly felt his bravado evaporate. Then, before he could ask any more questions, he was hurried into the Buddha Hall to begin, the weight of the Niten Ichi Ryū's honor resting entirely upon his shoulders.

* * *

"Watch where you're going!" shouted an irate merchant as Yamato and Jack careered past the man's market stall, knocking fruit to the ground.

They dodged and weaved through the throng of startled shoppers, Yamato bumping into an old lady in mid-purchase of a set of wind chimes, which rang brightly. Jack evaded the irate woman only to crash into a stall selling bright red parasols, scattering them across the marketplace like giant matchsticks.

They soon reached the outskirts of the city, and Jack was relieved to escape its stifling heat. Yamato got to the bridge first and clattered over it before bearing left up the pilgrim path. In the distance Jack could see the Sanju-no-to, the three-story pagoda poking above the trees.

Akiko had been right: there was no way Jack could have gotten lost. A steady flow of pilgrims were making their way up to the temple. The dusty path was lined with hawkers offering talismans, incense, and little paper fortunes, while more reputable merchants sold water, *sencha*, and noodles to the multitude of exhausted and famished travelers. Jack weaved his way between them, trying to gain on Yamato.

"More haste, less speed!" cried one of the hawkers, waving a paper fortune in Jack's face as he shot by.

Jack kept going, increasing his speed.

Yamato had already entered the forest that marked the lower reaches of the mountain. The path wound its way up the slope, disappearing and reappearing among the swath of trees. Jack welcomed the cool shade as he too reached the forest. His heart hammered in his chest, but he continued to pump his legs, working hard to catch up with Yamato. The route became steadily steeper, and as Jack rounded a bend he saw that Yamato was beginning to slow.

Jack reckoned he could pass Yamato when the path straightened out again, so he gave an extra burst of speed; but as he took the corner he collided full force with a large soft belly. He bounced off and landed unceremoniously in a heap on the stony ground.

"Whoa! Slow down, young samurai," said a rotund monk in saffron robes, rubbing his generous stomach tenderly.

"Sorry," said Jack, hurriedly scrambling to his feet and dusting himself off. "But need to catch up . . . matter of honor."

Jack bowed quickly, then sprinted after Yamato.

"Oh, the youth of today, so eager for enlightenment. Buddha will wait, you know!" the monk called amiably after Jack's rapidly receding figure.

Jack couldn't see Yamato as he dashed around the final bend and passed under the Nio-mon, the Gate of the Deva Kings. Barely glancing at the two huge lion-dogs that guarded the entrance against evil, he ran up the flight of stone steps, past startled pilgrims, and through a second gateway to the Sanju-no-to. The three-story pagoda was painted a deep red color, and stood out clearly against the dull brown of the other buildings.

Yamato was still nowhere in sight as Jack hurried toward the Hondo, the Main Hall, an immense building that dominated the temple complex.

He passed through a small shrine that bore a vivid painting of a coiled jade green dragon on the ceiling; under another gateway guarded by lion-dogs; and entered the outer sanctuary of the Hondo. Weaving his way through the pilgrims prostrating themselves in prayer, he headed straight for the inner sanctum.

Inside, there were a few bemused-looking monks who observed the hot, sweaty, and out of breath *gaijin* with serene interest. The inner sanctum was dark and cool and, unlike the other temples, was decorated with ornate gold-leaf images of the Buddha. But Jack only had time for a fleeting glance as he hunted for an exit.

"Sound of Feathers waterfall?" asked Jack in desperation.

A lithe tanned monk in a half-lotus position pointed to a doorway on his right. Jack briefly bowed his appreciation, ran through, and emerged into the bright sunlight once again.

He found himself standing upon the *butai*—a large wooden platform that jutted out over a deep gorge that was thick with lush vegetation and trees. The sound of water thundered in his ears, and through a fine mist, Jack could see the entirety of Kyoto spread out across the distant valley floor. The city shimmered in all its glory like a mirage, and a faint rainbow fell upon the Imperial Palace at its center.

To Jack's immediate left, the Sound of Feathers waterfall cascaded over a sheer cliff and into a large rock basin, some five stories below. The water churned into a frothy confusion of eddies and whirlpools before easing, then flowing down the gorge into the Kyoto valley.

Jack looked up and saw that Yamato was already scaling the rock face, heading toward the tiny stone shrine perched at the lip of the fall.

Jack judged that the waterfall was about the height of the crow's nest on board the *Alexandria*. Yamato was only a short way above the *butai* and clearly struggling. Even from where Jack stood, he could see Yamato's legs shaking, his hands blindly feeling for the next hold.

Clambering over the rail of the *butai*, Jack spotted a narrow ledge from which he could begin his own ascent. He would have to jump from the safety of the *butai* to the cliff. Way below him, the raging pool of water provided his only safety net. Jack took a deep breath, steeling himself for the jump, and leaped for the rock face.

He landed cleanly upon the ledge, but immediately lost his footing on its slippery surface. He slithered out of control down the cliff face. His hands grabbed for a rocky outcrop, his days as a rigging monkey paying off a hundredfold as they instinctively found handholds and halted his descent.

Jack caught his breath and calmed himself. He would need to be far more careful if he was going to survive this challenge.

Looking up, he could see that Yamato had made little progress. Jack began his climb with renewed vigor—it might still be possible for him to reach the Jade Sword first.

Once Jack got used to the slippery surface of the cliff, he began to increase his pace. Rock climbing, Jack discovered, was not much different from climbing the rigging on board the *Alexandria*, and, suffering no fear of heights, he soon leveled with Yamato.

"Are you all right?" Jack asked, concerned by Yamato's quivering form.

Yamato said nothing. He merely glared at Jack, his face drained of color, and his eyes stony with fear.

"Do you need my help?" said Jack, remembering how terrified he had been the first time he'd climbed to the crow's nest.

"Not from you, *gaijin*! Once more than enough," he hissed, but his voice cracked with fear as he hung grimly to the slippery rock, his knuckles white with the effort.

"Fine. Then fall," replied Jack, climbing past him.

He reached the lip of the waterfall without further

difficulty. He gave a cursory glance at Yamato, who remained fixed to the rock face like a limpet. He crossed several large rounded stepping-stones to the little shrine erected in the middle.

He slipped inside and found the Jade Sword within a shady recess.

It rested upon a ruby red lacquered stand, glistening in the watery light. The Jade Sword was a ceremonial *katana*, its *saya* a scabbard of black lacquered wood into which a golden dragon had been carved. A large jade stone was set in the wood as the eye of the dragon. Jack's blood ran cold. Dokugan Ryu. Dragon Eye.

Jack tried to steady his hands as he lifted the heavy sword from its rack. He gripped the leather hilt, feeling the bubbled texture of the white ray-fish skin beneath, and withdrew a gleaming blade of polished steel so sharp that it cut the eye just to look at it. The faint shadow of a second dragon had been etched onto the metal's surface, and Jack quickly resheathed the shining blade.

He slipped the Jade Sword into his *obi*, carefully tying the *saya* to him, and left the shrine.

Looking down, Jack saw that Yamato still hadn't moved.

He quickly descended and came level with him once more. Yamato didn't even look at him this time. He merely clung to the cliff wall, his whole body shuddering like a leaf in a storm.

"Listen, you've frozen up," said Jack, trying to get his attention.

He had seen this many a time with sailors on board the *Alexandria*. The mind seized up with fear and the body refused to move. A swimming sense of vertigo took hold, and eventually the sailor lost his grip and fell into the ocean, or worse, onto the deck.

Realizing Yamato had little strength remaining, Jack had to get him down fast.

"Let me help you. Take your right foot off. . . ."

"I can't. . . ." said Yamato in a feeble voice.

"Yes you can. Just drop your foot and put it on the little ridge below you."

"No, I can't . . . it's too far. . . ."

"No it's not. Trust me; you can do this."

"What do you care anyway? You stole my father!" said Yamato viciously, the swiftness of his anger breaking his paralysis.

"Stole your father?" said Jack, bewildered.

"Yes, you! Before you came, everything was all right. Father was finally beginning to accept me. I was no longer in Tenno's shadow. Then you stole him—"

"I didn't steal your father. He adopted me! It wasn't as if I had a choice."

"Yes, you did. You could have died with the rest of your crew!" said Yamato with unbridled hate.

"Well, you would have been killed by that ninja if it

hadn't been for me!" retorted Jack.

"That's exactly what I'm talking about. I could have died an honorable death, like my brother. But you went and saved me! I lost face because of you!"

"You Japanese and your sense of pride!" shouted Jack in frustration. "What is it with your 'face'? I saved your life. We were . . . friends. If I'd wanted Masamoto for a father, I could have let you die then. I don't want your father. I want *my* father, but he's dead!"

"Well, maybe I should be dead too!" said Yamato, looking to the submerged rocks below him. "You have the sword. The glory is yours. My father will never recognize me now that I've betrayed him. Whether you want Masamoto to be your father or not, he's yours!"

With that, Yamato jumped.

CHAPTER 39

THE APOLOGY

"No!" SCREAMED JACK, snatching for him, but Yamato had already disappeared into the white swirling curtain of the waterfall.

Jack scrambled down the rock face and leaped back onto the *butai*. He pushed past several pilgrims who had gathered on the wooden deck to see what was happening.

"Can anyone see him?" Jack demanded, peering over the rail and into the churning waters below.

"No. He went under the waterfall. He hasn't come up yet," said one of the pilgrims, eyeing Jack suspiciously.

"He probably hit the rocks," said another.

Several more people emerged from the Hondo and ran over to look.

"Hold on, there he is!" shouted a pilgrim, pointing to the rocky pool.

Yamato surfaced briefly, gasping for air, but was immediately caught in the current and sucked back under.

"Hey, that boy has our Jade Sword!" cried one of the monks emerging from the Hondo's inner sanctum. "Seize him!"

Jack glanced over the edge. He judged that the *butai* was at least as high as the yardarm on the *Alexandria*, but he had seen sailors fall from greater heights into the ocean and survive. Could he make it?

"Stop him! He has the sword!" urged the monk.

Without deliberating any further, Jack leaped from the *butai*.

The air rushed past, and for a brief moment, Jack felt weightless, almost at peace. He caught a glimpse of Kyoto through the mist, before plunging into the freezing waters.

The impact knocked the breath clean out of him, and he swallowed large mouthfuls of water. Kicking hard against the weight of the sword, he broke the surface and retched several times before regaining his composure.

Jack looked around for Yamato, who was nowhere to be seen. Taking several lungfuls of air, Jack dived under the swirling waters.

He swam toward the waterfall but still couldn't see

any sign of Yamato. Rocks loomed out of the murky waters, and eddies pulled at Jack, threatening to hold him under forever.

His lungs reached the bursting point, and he was about to head back to the surface when something smooth brushed against his hand. Blindly, he grabbed for it, dragging the object toward him. He got an arm around the dead weight and kicked with both his legs, driving them both upward.

Jack and Yamato broke the surface as one, only to be carried over the lip of the rock basin and down the gorge with the raging river.

Jack could hear people shouting as he tried to keep himself, Yamato, and the sword afloat in the rapids. The water poured through the gorge, relentlessly bearing Jack and Yamato with it. Jack's energy ebbed away as he desperately swam for the shore.

They were now far beyond the Hondo, the temple disappearing from sight as they rounded a bend in the river. Fortunately the waters calmed, and Jack somehow managed to reach the riverbank. With the last of his strength, he dragged the limp form of Yamato ashore.

Collapsing beside him, Jack lay there for a while, gulping air like a stranded fish in the heat of the sun. As he recovered, he vaguely wondered if he had been too late to save Yamato, but then he heard him splutter loudly, retch, and come to.

"Let me die," Yamato groaned, pulling his wet hair out of his eyes.

"Not when I can save you," panted Jack.

"Why? I've never shown you kindness."

"We're supposed to be brothers. At least that's what your father commanded, isn't it?" said Jack, giving a sardonic smile. "Besides, you taught me how to use the *bokken*."

"So what?"

"You made me realize that I wasn't a helpless *gaijin*," said Jack, letting the offensive word hang in the air between them.

Yamato gave Jack a bewildered look. "When have you ever been helpless?"

"When my father was killed, I couldn't save him. I was defenseless against that kind of skill," Jack admitted. "Dragon Eye laughed in my face when I tried to attack him. You showed me the Way of the Warrior. You gave me a reason to live, and for that I'm grateful."

"I don't understand you, *gai*— Jack," began Yamato, sitting up and holding his head in his hands. "I ignored and despised you, yet when that ninja went to kill me, you attacked without hesitation. With honor and courage. I couldn't have done that. You acted like a brother. A samurai."

"You would have done the same."

"No . . . I wouldn't," said Yamato, swallowing hard

as if his words had become stones in his throat. "The night I saw Kazuki beating you up, I was too afraid to do anything. I knew he was a better fighter than me. He knew it too. I didn't have the guts to take him on. . . ."

Yamato turned away, but Jack could see him wiping the back of his hand across his eyes, shuddering with each tearful breath.

"The Seto twins . . . again I was too scared to help you. I didn't want to be known as a *gaijin* lover. And after that night, I was too ashamed to be your friend. You didn't deserve me. That is the real reason. I'm so sorry. . . ."

Jack leaned forward, a confused expression on his face. "I don't understand. Why are you apologizing?"

"You showed me my true self, Jack, and I didn't like what I saw. My father was right. I'm not worthy to be a samurai, let alone a Masamoto. You're more his son than I can ever be. You didn't steal my father. I lost him by myself."

"Don't be an idiot, Yamato. You haven't *lost* him. He's not dead, like mine," said Jack pointedly. "Masamoto-sama may be angry, but he can have no reason to be ashamed of you. Not with the way you fought today. And if it is a matter of pride between you and me, forget it. Kazuki's not worth getting upset over. He's a pompous pig with the face of a lion-dog's arse!"

Jack grinned at Yamato, and Yamato smiled weakly in return.

"Besides, you've apologized to me now. Doesn't that mean you've regained face?"

"I suppose so, but—"

"No buts, Yamato. Every day I have to apologize to Akiko for some blunder or other! She's taught me every-thing there is to know about Japanese forgiveness. She forgives me each time, and I now forgive you. Friends?" said Jack, offering his hand.

"Thank you, Jack," said Yamato, uneasy in shaking Jack's hand in the English custom. "But I still don't understand why you would forgive me."

"Yamato, you have every right not to like me. I dread to think what it would have been like if my father had adopted some French boy!" exclaimed Jack, grimac-ing at the idea. "I don't blame you for being angry. But it's not me you should be angry with. It's Dokugan Ryu. If he hadn't killed Tenno and my father, we wouldn't be sitting here now, half drowned, a stolen jade sword in our hands!"

The absurdity of the situation suddenly struck home, and both boys began to laugh. The tension between them evaporated, as if it had been washed away by the Sound of Feathers waterfall itself.

After their laughter had died down, they sat there in silence, throwing pebbles into the river, unsure what to say or do next.

"We had better get back," Yamato said eventually.

"The sun will be setting soon, and the Niten Ichi Ryū need to know they have won."

"You should carry it," said Jack, untying the Jade Sword from his *obi* and handing it to Yamato.

"Why me? You were the one to get it."

"Yes, but your father doesn't need to know that, does he?"

CHAPTER 40

STAYING THE PATH

JACK AND YAMATO ran into the Buddha Hall together.

The Yagyu school went wild when they saw their champion carrying the Jade Sword. Kamakura swelled with pride, adjusting his finery in preparation for accepting the sword and victory.

Masamoto sat next to him, cross-legged upon the raised dais. His expression, detached and serious, was fixed. For when Yamato had entered the Buddha Hall bearing the sword, it was as if Masamoto had been replaced with a papier-mâché model of himself, a husk that had had all the life sucked out of it.

The cheering died down to a hushed murmur of

respect as Jack and Yamato approached the dais and bowed.

Akiko and Saburo knelt to the right-hand side, Raiden and Moriko to the other. Akiko gave a forlorn smile, clearly glad to see Jack in one piece but dismayed at their defeat. Yamato stepped forward, the Jade Sword in hand. Kamakura prepared himself to accept the offering.

It had taken Jack a great deal of persuasion to convince Yamato to carry the sword, but he had eventually agreed, accepting it to be the best way to reconcile with his father. Jack didn't care about the honor of winning the *Taryu-Jiai*. Masamoto had shown him great kindness by taking him into his family. Jack didn't want to be the reason for the family breaking apart.

Yamato bowed again and went down on one knee, raising the Jade Sword above his head with both hands. Kamakura reached out to formally accept the offering and seal his triumph of the *Taryu-Jiai*, but before he could lay his hands upon it, Yamato turned and presented the sword to his father.

"Father, I ask for your forgiveness and bestow to you what is rightfully the victory of the Niten Ichi Ryū. I was not the one to retrieve the sword. Jack was."

A moment of perplexed silence fell upon the hall.

Jack's mouth dropped open in astonishment. This is not what they had agreed upon. Yes, Yamato was to give the sword to Masamoto, but he was not to say Jack had retrieved it. That was to be Yamato's glory—the proof Masamoto was looking for that Yamato was good enough to be a samurai warrior, worthy of being a Masamoto.

Akiko looked in wide-eyed wonder at the bowing Yamato, then at Jack, who was shaking his head in silent dispute.

Masamoto gave Yamato a dubious look. "Is this the truth?"

"Yes, Father. But Jack insisted that I be the one to hand it to you."

Ignoring Jack's protests, Masamoto nodded once, the issue decided. He stood up and took the sword from Yamato's outstretched hands.

"The Niten Ichi Ryū are deemed the champions of the *Taryu-Jiai*!" announced the equally baffled Imperial Court official.

The Buddha Hall erupted into a cacophony of cheers from the Niten Ichi Ryū. Raucous heckling exploded from the Yagyu Ryū side. Raiden stamped the ground in frustration, while Moriko bared her black teeth, hissing her disgust. Kamakura's face flushed red with fury and his throat quivered as if he were choking on an oversized frog.

"This is an outrage!" Kamakura eventually cried, shoving the official to the floor. "An outrage!"

Kamakura threw a curt nod in Masamoto's direction, then stormed out of the hall, his samurai hastening close behind. The official picked himself up and called for silence. Once the noise had finally died down, he deferred to Masamoto.

"Students of the Niten Ichi Ryū!" began Masamoto, ceremoniously brandishing the Jade Sword and raising it in a heroic salute. "Today we have witnessed what it means to be a samurai of this school!"

There was an explosion of applause. Masamoto held his other hand up for silence, stepped off the dais, and walked over to Jack.

"At the start of your year, I said every young samurai had to conquer the self, endure punishing practice, and foster a fearless mind. This boy, Jack-kun, is proof of that. Today he fought with valor and courage. He defeated the enemy and won honor for this school!"

There was another explosion of applause even louder than before.

"But *Bushido* is not just about courage and honor. Nor is its purpose fighting and warfare. Though they may be necessary stops on your journey, they are not your destination. The true essence of *Bushido* is rectitude, benevolence, and loyalty."

Masamoto turned to Yamato and placed a hand on his son's shoulder.

"Yamato has demonstrated this very essence. Admitting such truth in the presence of so many takes extraordinary courage. Perhaps greater courage than retrieving the Jade Sword itself."

Masamoto held the gleaming sword aloft, and the school cheered once more.

"Yamato, you have answered my question," he continued, looking down at his son with a warmth Jack had never witnessed before. "I asked you to tell me what it means to be a Masamoto. What you have just demonstrated is exactly what Masamoto spirit is all about. You have honored and respected Jack, your fellow samurai. You have shown integrity. You are truly a Masamoto. I accept your apology a hundredfold and implore you to return to the Niten Ichi Ryū."

Masamoto bent down on one knee to be level with Yamato.

Jack couldn't believe it, and by the shocked look on Akiko's face, neither could she. Despite everything that had happened, Masamoto was formally and publicly accepting Yamato. The moment was not lost on the rest of the students, and a silence descended upon the hall as they all bowed their respects to Masamoto and Yamato.

Father and son bowed to one another.

"*Bushido* is not a journey to be taken lightly," Masamoto declared, getting to his feet. "I told you that the path of the warrior is lifelong, and mastery is simply staying the path. Students of the Niten Ichi Ryū—stay the path!"

The Buddha Hall thundered with fervent applause.

CHAPTER 41

GION MATSURI

THE LITTLE BOY in the stark white robes and black hat of a Shinto priest raised the short *wakizashi* sword above his head and brought it down as hard as he could.

In a single stroke, he cut the rope and the *Gion Matsuri* festival began.

"This is amazing! I've never seen anything like it," enthused Jack.

Immense wooden floats, adorned with tapestries and columns of bulbous white lanterns, passed by in a never-ending procession. Some of the floats were carried upon people's shoulders, while the largest ones, big as river-boats and bearing finely dressed, white-faced *geisha*, were set upon wooden wheels and pulled through the streets.

As the first of these floats approached a street corner, all the men pulling began to chant loudly, *"Yoi! Yoi! Yoi to sei!"* their rhythm pounded out on large *taiko* drums on the float's upper floor. The whole structure began to turn and gradually disappeared around the corner, like some huge bejewelled dragon.

"What's this festival for?" Jack shouted over the noise of the celebration.

"It's a purification ritual," replied Akiko, who stood nearby in a sea green kimono decorated with brightly colored chrysanthemums. "A plague swept through Kyoto seven hundred years ago, and the *Matsuri* prevents its return."

"We had a plague in England too," said Jack. "They called it the Black Death."

The crowd around them surged forward as people jostled for the best position to see the floats passing. Emi and two of her friends joined Jack, Akiko, and Yamato in the throng.

"How is our victorious samurai today?" greeted Emi, fluttering a red paper fan against the heat while maneuvering herself between Jack and Akiko. Akiko frowned at Emi's unexpected intrusion, and bit her lip in obvious irritation.

"Great, thanks!" said Jack. "This is a wonderful festival—"

"Come on!" urged Yamato, seeing Akiko's prickly

reaction. He grabbed Jack's arm. "I know a better place to stand."

"Sorry, I have to go. Perhaps see you later?" said Jack, waving at the disappointed Emi as he was dragged away by Yamato to the back of the crowd, where Saburo, Yori, and Kiku were waiting for them.

"Here, try this!" said Saburo, shoving a small fish-shaped cake into Jack's hand.

"What is it?" asked Jack, eyeing the pastry suspiciously.

"It's *taiyaki.* . . ." replied Saburo through a mouthful of the cake.

"Later. We've got all afternoon to eat," interrupted Yamato. "We need to get ahead of the procession to see it all. Follow me!"

Yamato led them down a back street, and they wound their way through a maze of narrow deserted alleyways before coming out onto the main thoroughfare in front of the Imperial Palace.

Hundreds of people were already gathered, and the street was lined with stalls selling strange sweets, skewers of barbequed chicken, *sencha*, and a vast array of festival delights, from brightly colored paper fans to gruesome papier-mâché masks, all in readiness for the evening celebrations.

"There! What did I tell you, Jack? We can see the whole procession from here," said Yamato eagerly, making his way to the front.

From the moment of their *Taryu-Jiai* victory the previous day, and the reconciliation with his father, Yamato had been a changed person. In fact, he took his new-found friendship with Jack so far that he'd almost become a bodyguard, challenging anyone who referred to Jack as the *gaijin*.

Not many did. Along with Akiko and Saburo, Jack and Yamato were the school's heroes. Although Kazuki and his friends remained hostile to Jack, they were keeping a low profile while everyone celebrated the school's victory over the Yagyu Ryū.

"Look!" said Kiku. "There's Masamoto-san!"

"Where's he going?" asked Jack.

"To meet the Emperor, of course!" said Kiku in reverential awe. "Our Living God."

"You may have won the *Taryu-Jiai*," explained Akiko, "but as the founder of the Niten Ichi Ryū, Masamoto gets the honor of meeting the Emperor."

Masamoto, bearing the Jade Sword and flanked by Sensei Yamada, Sensei Kyuzo, Sensei Hosokawa, and Sensei Yosa, all in full ceremonial regalia, entered through the immense gateway of the Imperial Palace and disappeared behind the tall earthen walls.

Jack wondered what it would be like to meet a "Living God."

The rest of that afternoon was spent watching the

passing parade of floats, *geisha*, and musicians, while Jack was introduced to a variety of bizarre Japanese foods. Saburo got great enjoyment from experimenting with Jack's taste buds—force-feeding him with varying levels of success. Jack enjoyed the *takoyaki*, a dumpling made of batter, ginger, and fried octopus, but he found the *obanyaki*—a thick, round pastry filled with custard—to be sickly sweet. Saburo kept passing Jack various kinds of fried pancake as they wandered the streets.

"They're called *okonomiyaki*. It means 'Cook what you like, when you like,'" explained Akiko, a disgusted look on her face as Jack tucked into his fourth one. "But I wouldn't trust it. You never know what might be in it."

"Don't listen to her," Saburo interjected as Jack warily inspected his fifth pancake. "They haven't used rat meat for years."

"Quick, over here," shouted Yamato, waving them to a stand on the corner of a side street. "This stall's selling some of the best masks I've seen here!"

The stand overflowed with papier-mâché masks, as if it were some multi-headed Hindu god. Almost hidden in its midst was the face of a wizened old man, which Jack thought was one of the masks until it yawned and emerged as the stall's merchant.

"Here, Jack, this one will suit you," said Saburo, handing him an ugly red demon mask with four eyes and metallic gold teeth. "It should be an improvement."

"Well, you'd better take this, considering you fight like one!" retorted Jack, passing Saburo the wrinkled, half-sunken face of an old woman.

"Ha-ha!" replied Saburo humorlessly, taking the mask anyway. "What about this one for you, Yamato?"

"Yes, why not? It's got spirit," said Yamato, examining the gold mask of a madman with spikes of black hair.

"Which one do you like, Akiko?" asked Jack.

"I was thinking of that one," she said, pointing to a red-and-gold butterfly mask.

"Yes, you would look beautiful in that . . ." began Jack, but he stopped when he saw the surprise on Saburo's and Kiku's faces at his unexpected compliment.

"Well . . . it would be better than that . . . lion-dog mask over there," he finished awkwardly, and gave a dismissive wave of the hand.

"Thank you, Jack," she said, smiling graciously and turning to the merchant.

Jack was relieved Akiko had her back to him, for she missed seeing him blush. But Yamato saw, and raised his eyebrows meaningfully.

As dusk fell, the lanterns on the procession floats were lit, transforming Kyoto into a magical nighttime paradise. The lanterns floated through the streets like vast cloud formations lit by tiny suns. Everyone donned their masks, and the streets came alive with music and merriment.

Many of the floats ground to a halt as the men began to drink from large bottles of *saké*, and it wasn't long before the sounds of revelry could be heard from every street corner.

As Jack, Akiko, Yamato, and the others made their way back to the main thoroughfare for the evening fireworks, a group of drunken samurai staggered past, forcing Jack to jump out of their way.

He collided with a man in black who was wearing an ebony devil mask with two sharp red horns and a small white skull carved in the center of its forehead.

"Out of my way!" the black devil hissed.

Jack stared through his own demon mask at the man and froze.

The man irritably shoved Jack out of his way and hurried down the street before disappearing into a narrow side alley.

"Are you all right?" asked Akiko, rushing over to Jack.

"I think . . . I just saw Dragon Eye!"

CHAPTER 42

DOKUGAN RYU

T HEY ALL RAN down the alleyway after the black devil.

"You must be mistaken. Dokugan Ryu wouldn't dare show himself at a festival," said Akiko

"I *definitely* saw him," said Jack. "He only had one eye, and it was green! How many Japanese do you know with one green eye?"

"One," Yamato admitted.

"Exactly. I just pray he didn't recognize me," Jack said through his red demon mask as he ran. "So where does this alley lead?"

Before Yamato could answer, they rounded a corner and found themselves opposite Nijo Castle. They had emerged at one of its side entrances, a small gateway accessed via a narrow bridge across the moat.

"Do you think this ninja of yours went inside the castle?" said Saburo uneasily, his eyes wide with fear behind the old woman mask.

"Must have," Jack said, looking up and down the deserted thoroughfare. "Where is everyone?"

"They'll be gathering for fireworks by the Imperial Palace," said Kiku.

Jack searched the darkness for any sign of Dragon Eye. Nothing moved. That was the problem.

"Where are the guards?" Jack asked. "I thought this is where Emi's father lives. Isn't Takatomi the *daimyo* of Kyoto? Surely he would have guards on all his entrances."

"Yes, but it's *Gion Matsuri*," said Yori. "He'll be at the festival and so will most of his guards."

"Of course! What better time for a ninja to enter a castle?" said Jack.

"But why would one want to?" questioned Kiku.

"Who knows," said Jack, shrugging. "But you can bet it's not to see the fireworks. Come on! Let's find out what he's up to."

"But he's a ninja!" exclaimed Saburo.

"And we're samurai."

Jack pulled off his mask and sprinted across the thoroughfare to the gangway. After a moment's hesitation, the rest of them joined him, with Saburo trailing reluctantly behind.

"Saburo, you'd better stand guard with Yori," suggested Jack, to Saburo's evident relief.

The remaining four cautiously made their way across the narrow wooden bridge to the gate.

"Do you think it'll be open?" queried Akiko. "What if he went over the wall?"

"Only one way to find out," said Jack, pushing on the heavy wooden door.

It swung open without resistance.

Jack peered into the inky blackness. He couldn't see a thing. Taking a deep breath, steeling himself for an ambush, he swiftly slipped inside.

Before he had gone two paces, he tripped and fell facedown on the hard stone floor. He jarred his arm as he tried to break the fall.

"Jack, are you all right?" asked Akiko, alarmed at his muffled grunt of pain.

"Yes, fine," he whispered back. "You can come in. I fell over the guard, that's all. He's dead."

The others found him kneeling over the dead body of a samurai.

"There's another one behind the door," said Jack, grimly nodding toward the shadows.

Kiku let out a stifled yelp as she caught sight of the body of the second samurai, headless.

"It looks like he was killed with his own sword," said Yamato, as Akiko drew Kiku to her.

"Kiku, go back to the others," ordered Akiko in a sharp whisper. "Raise the alarm with Masamoto-san and tell him what's happening,"

Kiko nodded mutely before skirting the decapitated samurai to slip out the door, then ran off toward the Imperial Palace.

"What now?" asked Yamato.

"We find him and we stop him!" said Jack with ominous finality.

Jack began to scan the open courtyard for movement. He pointed to a black shadow barely visible by the battlements. "There he is! Next to that wall, on the far side of the courtyard."

Looking around, Jack spotted the *katana* of the headless samurai on the floor. He snatched up the bloodied sword.

"This is insane!" said Akiko. "You're going to get yourself killed."

"Not if I can help it," said Yamato, hunting the darkness for the other samurai's *katana*.

"Come on! We're going to lose him!" Jack urged, starting in the direction of the disappearing ninja.

"But neither of you have ever used a real sword before!" Akiko whispered.

"It doesn't matter. Once you've mastered the *bokken*, I'm sure it can't be too hard to wield a *katana*. Ah, found it," said Yamato.

He had spotted the second sword discarded on the far side of the guardhouse and went to retrieve it. "I think there's a *wakizashi* for you too, Akiko."

"Perfect! Leave me with the short sword, why don't you?" she muttered.

Jack, though, could no longer wait. He ran off after Dragon Eye, leaving Yamato and Akiko behind.

Jack stopped under the lee of the castle wall from where he could see Dragon Eye ahead, hiding in the shadows. He was making for the five buildings that formed the central complex of the castle. Jack presumed by their highly decorative design that this was Takatomi's palace.

Dragon Eye had not yet seen Jack, for he was too occupied with scouting ahead.

This was Jack's chance.

Jack shifted the *katana* in his hands, adjusting his grip. The sword felt far weightier than his *bokken*, and he knew he'd have to be careful not to let the *kissaki* drop and leave himself exposed.

Jack edged closer. Dragon Eye was still oblivious to his approach.

As he crept to within ten paces of the ninja, all the pent-up anger and pain Jack felt at his father's death welled up like molten rock and exploded within him.

Now was the time!

But Jack hesitated.

He couldn't do it.

"Never hesitate," hissed Dokugan Ryu, his back still turned.

Dragon Eye spun on the spot, and a silver *shuriken* glinted in the darkness.

"Watch out!" screamed Yamato, throwing himself in front of Jack.

The *shuriken* hit Yamato, embedding itself in his chest. He fell to the floor, his blood gushing over the stone courtyard.

Jack saw red, and his fury finally boiled over. Screaming at the top of his lungs, he charged with his sword held high, then brought it down on his sworn enemy with all his might.

Dragon Eye pulled his *ninjatō* from the *saya* strapped to his back, smoothly deflecting Jack's blade at the same time. He then countered, slicing across Jack's midriff.

Jack predicted the move and blocked it. Immediately he pressed forward with his own attack, cutting up at Dragon Eye's face. But the ninja flipped backward to avoid the rising blade. As he flew through the air, Dragon Eye kicked out, and his foot caught Jack's hands, dislodging the *katana*. Dragon Eye landed on his feet just as Jack's sword clattered to the ground, leaving him unarmed and defenseless.

"You've improved, young samurai; for a *gaijin*!" he

said with genuine respect. "One day, you might actually be worth fighting. But you're not my mission today, so go home like a good boy!"

"I don't *have* a home. You killed my father. Remember?" said Jack, outraged. "Was my father a mission too?"

"Your father was nothing. The rutter was my mission!"

Jack stared at the ninja in disbelief. "Who's ordering these missions?"

"You won't give up, will you?" hissed Dragon Eye in irritation. "Let's hope you still live without your sword arm!"

Dragon Eye raised his *ninjatō* and brought it down to sever Jack's right arm.

Out of the night like a shooting star, Akiko's *wakizashi* spun through the air toward Dokugan Ryu. At the last second, the ninja twisted, the arc of his sword shifting and missing Jack's shoulder by a hair's breadth. The *wakizashi* pierced Dragon Eye's side, and though the blade cut deep, he barely made a sound. Staggering slightly, the ninja glanced absently at the weapon protruding from him.

"Who did you learn that from? Masamoto?" he spat in disgust at Akiko as she appeared by Jack's side.

The ninja carefully removed the bloody blade, glaring at them defiantly. He flipped the short sword over in his hand and was about to throw it back at the now defenseless Akiko, when the main gate burst open and Masamoto and his samurai dashed into the courtyard bearing flaming torches.

"Spread out!" ordered Masamoto. "Find them, and *kill* the ninja!"

"Another time, *gaijin*!" hissed Dragon Eye. "The rutter is not forgotten."

The ninja dropped the *wakizashi* and scaled the castle wall like a malevolent four-legged spider, disappearing into the night.

In the distance, fireworks exploded, and bright sparks rained down like a meteor shower in the night sky.

KENDO—THE WAY OF THE SWORD

"**W**E BELIEVE Dokugan Ryu was sent to poison *daimyo* Takatomi," explained Masamoto the following night in the Hō-Oh-No-Ma, the Hall of the Phoenix.

He sat upon his dais, framed by the magnificent flaming phoenix. Sensei Kyuzo and Sensei Yosa were on his left, Sensei Hosokawa and Sensei Yamada to his right.

Jack knelt between Akiko and the bandaged Yamato on the lower floor. Yamato had been extremely fortunate. The *shuriken* had not been poisoned, and while he had suffered a deep chest wound, he would recover.

"But who sent him?" Jack asked.

Masamoto sipped a cup of *sencha*, which he gazed into pensively.

"That we don't know. It may be a sign of things to come," he replied gravely. "*Daimyo* Takatomi has increased his personal guard and ordered new security measures to be installed in his castle. He sends his apologies for not being here tonight. He has been called away to Edo. But he is most appreciative of your efforts in stopping the ninja. He wanted me to give you these as a token of his esteem."

A maid entered bearing three boxes. She placed one in front of each of the young samurai. Jack examined his. It was a small rectangular box made of thickly lacquered wood. The surface was exquisitely decorated in gold and silver leaf, and he could make out a finely engraved *sakura* tree within the design, its blossom picked out in ivory. Attached to the top of the box by a hemp cord was a small ivory toggle carved into the shape of a lion's head. He looked inquiringly over at the others.

They too had received similar gifts, but the boxes bore different designs, and Yamato's had a monkey-shaped toggle, while Akiko's was carved into a miniature eagle.

"They are called *inro*, Jack-kun," explained Masamoto, seeing Jack's puzzled expression. "They're used for carrying things, like medicines, money, pens, and ink. That small ivory lion's head is called a *netsuke*. You slip it through your *obi* and it will secure the *inro* to you."

Jack picked up the beautifully crafted *inro* and ivory *netsuke*. He had always wondered what the Japanese had done without pockets in their *kimono*. The *inro* consisted of a stack of tiny boxes that fitted snugly, one on top of the other. He passed the lion's head *netsuke* through his *obi* and secured the *inro* to his belt.

"Takatomi-sama has also extended his funding of the Niten Ichi Ryū indefinitely," continued Masamoto, "and has bestowed a new training hall upon the school. It is to be called Taka-no-ma, the Hall of the Hawk. For that, I myself am indebted to you. You have once again brought great honor to this school. In recognition of your service, I wish to present you with these gifts."

Three servants entered, each carrying a large lacquered box, which they placed upon the dais.

"Yamato, you have proven yourself to be a true Masamoto. This time with your own blood. I am proud to call you my son. As a mark of my respect for you, please come forward and accept this *daishō*."

Bowing stiffly, Yamato knelt before Masamoto, his injury preventing him from the full respectful bow expected. Masamoto opened the first box and withdrew its contents.

"You may recognize this *daishō*, Yamato. They were Tenno's. It is time you wore them, for you have proven yourself worthy beyond a doubt."

With his two hands outstretched, grimacing against the pain, Yamato accepted the *katana* and the shorter *wakizashi* sword. The two weapons together made up the *daishō*, and were a symbol of the social power and personal honor of a samurai. To be bestowed a *daishō* was an immense privilege.

For a moment, Yamato could only gaze at them, their black lacquered *saya* hinting at the gleaming blades within. Yamato then resumed his place alongside Jack and Akiko. Jack couldn't help but notice that Yamato's eyes shone with pride.

"Akiko-chan, please kneel before Sensei Yosa. For it is she who wishes to present your gift."

Akiko got up and bowed deeply before her sensei.

"Akiko-chan, you have the eye of a hawk and the grace of an eagle," said Sensei Yosa, drawing her box nearer and tenderly removing several items. "You deserve to carry my bow and arrows. Please accept these as a recognition of your fine skills as a *kyudoka*."

Akiko was almost too astonished to show her respect. She took Sensei Yosa's tall bamboo bow and quiver of hawk feather arrows with trembling hands.

"My bow has much to impart to you, Akiko-chan. As you know, a bow holds within it part of the spirit of the person who made it. My bow is now yours, and I hope it will protect you as it has protected me."

"*Arigatō gozaimashita, Sensei,*" breathed Akiko, holding the bow and arrows reverently as she returned to her place.

"Lastly, we come to you, Jack-kun," said Masamoto

magnanimously. "Who would have thought that the drowned wreck of a *gaijin* boy would amount to so much? Your father, if he had survived, would surely be proud of you today."

Jack's eyes were suddenly hot with tears. The unexpected reference to his father was almost too much, and he had to bite down hard on his lip to stop himself from crying.

"You have saved Yamato's life," continued Masamoto. "Twice, if I am not mistaken. You have learned our language and honored our customs. And you have defeated Dokugan Ryu's murderous intent, not once but three times. If my *daimyo* had an army of boys like you, he could conquer any land in a heartbeat. Come forward."

Jack knelt and bowed respectfully in front of Masamoto.

All the sensei returned Jack's bow, Sensei Hosokawa and Sensei Yosa both giving him serious yet approving nods of the head. Sensei Kyuzo offered his typically curt acknowledgement, but Sensei Yamada beamed at Jack.

"You still have a great deal to learn, Jack-kun," continued Masamoto, suddenly serious. "You are but a tiny bud. You have only laid the foundation stone. Taken your first step. You still have a long road to travel on the Way of the Warrior, but as I said in the beginning, we are here to help you make that journey. I therefore present to you my first swords."

By the stunned reactions of the sensei and the inward

drawing of breath from both Akiko and Yamato, Jack judged that this was a considerable and unprecedented honor. Masamoto opened the last lacquered box that lay before him and lifted out two formidable swords.

Unlike the Jade Sword, Masamoto's *daishō* were not overly decorated. The *saya* were pure shafts of black lacquer, the only embellishment an inlay of a small golden phoenix emblazoned near the hilt. This was not a piece of art or a sword for show. It was the weapon of a warrior.

"Jack-kun, the sword is the soul of the samurai," said Masamoto with great import, presenting the *daishō* to him, his amber eyes fixed on Jack.

"With the possession of such a weapon comes great responsibility," instructed Masamoto, not letting go of the swords so that now both he and Jack held them. "It must never fall into the hands of your enemy. And you must always uphold the samurai principles of *Bushido*. Rectitude. Courage. Benevolence. Respect. Honesty. Honor. Loyalty. Do you understand?"

"*Hai, Masamoto-sama. Arigatō gozaimashita,*" replied Jack with complete sincerity.

Jack took the swords from Masamoto and immediately felt his hands sink under the weight of their responsibility. He bowed low and returned to his place between Akiko and Yamato, the *daishō* by his side.

"Now that we have finished here, I ask you all to kindly leave, except for my son. I wish to spend some time with him. We have much to discuss," said Masamoto, a smile brightening the unscarred side of his face.

Everyone bowed and respectfully departed from the Hall of the Phoenix.

Jack and Akiko wandered into the Southern Zen garden to wait for Yamato. They stood together between the two standing stones and stared in silence at the night sky. The moon was bright and gibbous, two days from full, and the stars shone keenly in the heavens.

"See that star, the brightest one in the sky? That's Spica," Jack said after several moments had passed.

"Which one?" inquired Akiko. "They all look the same to me."

"Start from the handle of the Big Dipper, the constellation above us, then follow the arc to Arcturus and speed on to Spica," said Jack, guiding Akiko's eyes with the tip of his finger. "Then the one over to its left we call Regulus, and the one next to that, Bellatrix. The twinkling one over here is Jupiter, but that's not a star, that's a planet."

"How do you know all this?" asked Akiko, turning to Jack.

"My father taught me. He said I would need to know how to navigate by the stars, if I was to ever be a pilot like him."

"And can you?"

"Yes. Enough to guide a ship back to port," said Jack. Then with a sad longing, he added, "Possibly even enough to get home."

"You still want to go home?"

Jack returned Akiko's gaze. The moonlight reflected in her jet-black eyes, sending small shivers down his spine like shooting stars.

Yes, he did still want to go home. He missed England's green fields in spring, and the cozy warmth of his parents' fireplace in winter, where his father would tell him tales of daring sea voyages. He longed for the rowdy chaos of London and the noise of street criers, cattle, and hammering blacksmiths. His stomach ached for beef, pies, and bread thick with butter, while his brain cried out to speak English to someone. But most of all he missed his family. Jess was all he had left now. He needed to find her, make sure she was all right.

Yet, for the very first time, standing next to Akiko under the stars, Jack felt that he could belong in Japan.

"Wherever it is you may be, it is your friends who make your world," his mother had told him when they had moved again between Rotterdam and Limehouse, due to his father's work. He was only seven at the time and resented having to move, but now he understood what she meant. Here in Japan, Jack had found friends. True friends. Saburo, Yori, Kiku, Yamato, and, most important of all, Akiko.

"Akiko-chan!" a voice called.

It was Sensei Yosa.

"May I have a moment of your time? I need to explain the particular characteristics of your bow."

"*Hai*, Sensei," said Akiko, but before going she turned to Jack. "I know you miss your home in England, Jack, but Japan can be your home too."

Then, with a warm gentle smile, she bowed and walked down the garden path.

Jack stared up at the night sky, continuing to name each of the stars in his head in an effort to quell his turbulent emotions. His hand rested absently upon his new swords, and he fingered the hilts.

On an impulse, he withdrew his *katana* and held it up to the moonlight. Admiring the deep graceful curve of its blade, he turned it in the air, gauging its weight, judging its point of balance. It was too soon for it to become an extension of his arm, like his lighter wooden *bokken*, but nonetheless he felt confident enough to attempt a few cuts.

He sliced the moon in half, speared Bellatrix, and cut off a shooting star. Whirling around, he brought his *kissaki* up, ready for another assault, and there was Dokugan Ryu. Standing in the darkness. Motionless. Waiting to attack.

Never hesitate.

This time Jack wouldn't. He lifted the sword above

his head and ran at Dragon Eye to deliver the killing blow.

"Jack!" cried Sensei Yamada from behind.

Dokugan Ryu turned to stone, and Jack spun around.

"What are you doing?" asked the Zen teacher, leaning upon his walking stick in the darkness, a quizzical look in his eyes.

"I was . . ." began Jack, glancing back at the standing stone, "practicing my *kata*."

"On a stone?"

"No, not really," replied Jack. Deflated, he lowered his sword. "I was imagining it was Dokugan Ryu. I was about to kill him. Get my revenge."

"Revenge is self-defeating. It will eat away at you until there is nothing left," observed Sensei Yamada, speaking the truth as if it were as obvious as the moon in the night sky.

"But he killed my father!" Masamoto's sword trembled in Jack's hand as he fought to control his anger.

"Yes. And he will undoubtedly pay for that sin, if not in this life then in his next. But do not believe for one moment that possession of that sword makes you all powerful. You must never forget your *Bushido*. Rectitude, your ability to judge right from wrong, is the keystone to being samurai."

He took Jack by the arm and led him slowly along

the path toward the old pine tree in the corner of the garden, its bough weighing heavily upon its wooden crutch.

"Benevolence, your compassion for others, underpins all of them. There is no place for anger or rage in the Way. In real *budo*, there are no enemies. Real *budo* is a function of love. The Way of a Warrior is not to destroy and kill, but to foster life. To protect it."

He stopped by the old pine tree and faced Jack.

"Jack, as Masamoto-sama said, you've only just begun to learn the Way of the Warrior, but you must also learn the Way of the Sword. *Kendo*."

Sensei Yamada smiled enigmatically, his sharp eyes twinkling like miniature stars, then he disappeared into the veil of darkness beyond the tree, leaving Jack all alone under a Japanese sky.

As Jack glanced up, a shooting star trailed across the heavens.

The little comet flared brightly then died, the path it had burned in the sky fading like the embers of a fire.

In that instant Jack was struck by a moment of *satori*: enlightenment as bright as the star itself. He too was on a journey whose destination was unknown and whose fate was uncertain. But he had set his course and there was no going back.

He had chosen the Way of the Warrior.

The following quotes are used in *Young Samurai: The Way of the Warrior*, and their sources are acknowledged here:

*Page 172: "The way of the warrior is lifelong, and mastery is often simply staying the path." Richard Strozzi Heckler (strozziinstitute.com). (By permission of the author)

*Page 172: "From every tiny bud springs a tree of many branches. Every castle commences with the laying of the first stone. Every journey begins with just one step." Lao Tzu, philosopher and founder of Taosim. (Material in the public domain)

*Page 173: "It's good to have an end to journey toward; but it's the journey that matters, in the end." Excerpt from *The Left Hand of Darkness*, by Ursula K. Le Guin, copyright © 1969,

1997 by Ursula K. Le Guin; published by Ace Books. (By permission of the author's agent)

*Page 176: "Given enough time, anyone may master the physical. Given enough knowledge, anyone may become wise. It is the true warrior who can master both and surpass the result." T'ien T'ai, Buddhist sect. (Material in the public domain)

*Page 188: "In order to be walked on, you have to be lying down." Brian Weir. (Original source unknown; no evidence of publication)

*Page 191: "Courage is not the absence of fear, but rather the judgement that something else is more important than fear." Excerpt from "No Peaceful Warriors!", *Gnosis: A Journal of the Western Inner Traditions*, © 1991 by Ambrose Hollingworth Redmoon (born James Neil Hollingworth).

*Page 264: "The greater the obstacle, the more glory in overcoming it." Molière, French playwright and actor. (Material in the public domain)

*Page 353: "In real *budo*, there are no enemies. Real *budo* is a function of love. The way of a Warrior is not to destroy and kill but to foster life . . . " Morihei Ueshiba, the founder of Aikido. (From *Budo Secrets*, by John Stevens, © 2001 by John Stevens. Reprinted by arrangement with Shambhala Publications, Inc., shambhala.com)

A short guide to pronouncing Japanese words:

Vowels are pronounced in the following way:

"a" as in "at"

"e" as in "bet"

"i" as in "police

"o" as in "dot"

"u" as in "put"

"ai" as in "eye"

"ii" as in "week"

"ō" as in "go"

"ū" as in "blue"

Consonants are pronounced in the same way as English:

"g" is hard, as in "get"

"j" is soft, as in "jelly"

"ch" as in "church"

"z" as in "zoo"

"ts" as in "itself"

Each syllable is pronounced separately:
A-ki-ko
Ya-ma-to
Ma-sa-mo-to
Ka-zu-ki

abunai: danger

arigatō (*gozaimasu*): thank you (very much)

bokken: wooden sword

Bushido: the Way of the Warrior

Butokuden: Hall of the Virtues of War

Butsuden: the Buddha Hall

Chō-no-ma: Hall of Butterflies

daimyo: feudal lord

gaijin: foreigner, barbarian (derogatory term)

gomennasai: sorry

hai: yes

hajime: begin

hashi: chopsticks

Hō-Oh-No-Ma: Hall of the Phoenix

Iie: no

ikinasai: let's go

kami: spirit

kata: a prescribed series of moves in martial arts

katana: long sword

kenjutsu: the Art of the Sword

ki: life force

Kiai: literally "concentrated spirit"—used in martial arts as a shout for focusing energy when executing a technique

kihon waza: basic techniques

kissaki: tip of sword

konnichiwa: good day

kyujutsu: the Art of the Bow

matsuri: festival

ninjatō: ninja sword

niwa: garden

ofuro: bath

ohayō-gozaimasu: good morning

randori: free-sparring

rei: call to bow

saké: rice wine

satori: enlightenment

saya: scabbard

seiza: sit/kneel

sencha: green tea

sensei: teacher

shinobi shozoku: the clothing of a ninja

Shishi-no-ma: Hall of Lions

shoji: Japanese sliding door

shuriken: metal throwing stars

sohei: warrior monks

sumimasen: excuse me; my apologies

tabi: Japanese split-toe socks

taijutsu: the Art of the Body (hand-to-hand combat)

Taka-no-ma: Hall of the Hawk

tantō: knife

tatami: floor matting

torii: gateway

tsuba: hand guard

uchi: strike

wakarimasen: I don't understand

wakizashi: side-arm short sword

wakou: Japanese pirates

yame: stop!

zabuton: cushion

zazen: meditation

Japanese names usually consist of a family name (surname) followed by a given name, unlike in the Western world, where the given name comes before the surname. In feudal Japan, names reflected a person's social status and spiritual beliefs. Also, when addressing someone, *san* is added to that person's surname (or given names in less formal situations) as a sign of courtesy, similar to Mr. or Mrs. in English, and for higher-status people, *sama* is used. In Japan, *sensei* is usually added after a person's name if they are a teacher, although in *Young Samurai*, a traditional English order has been retained. Boys and girls are usually addressed using *kun* and *chan* respectively.

ACKNOWLEDGMENTS

A special thanks must go to the following people who have been instrumental in the formation of *Young Samurai: The Way of the Warrior*: Charlie Viney, my agent, for his early encouragement of the Young Samurai concept and his continued commitment to making my first novel a reality; Lola Bubbosh and Arianne Lewin, my editors at Hyperion, who grasped the spirit of *Bushido* with great enthusiasm; Sarah Hughes, my editor at Puffin, for her ruthless eye and samurai-like abilities to hone my manuscript into a battle-hardened book; Pippa Le Quesne for her expert guidance and incisive suggestions while editing the initial drafts; Tessa Girvan at ILA for taking on the world; the Sasakawa Foundation and the Society of Authors for awarding me the Great Britain Sasakawa Award 2007 and enabling me to travel to Japan to carry out essential research for the book; Sensei Akemi Solloway for organizing such a wonderful and supremely informative cultural trip to Japan, *arigatō gozaimashita*; Steve Cowley and all the sensei at his Martial Arts Academy for helping me achieve my black belt in *Taijutsu*; Hiroko Takagi for her Japanese translation; Katherine Hemingway for her Japanese insights; Matt Bould for his attention to detail; my mum and dad for their unwavering support and belief in me; and my wife, Sarah, for being my first reader!

DEMCO